THE GORDIAN KNOT

BY TIM GUDITUS

Dedication

To the shadowy figures who walk the tightrope between right and wrong, to those who chase justice in the darkest corners of the world, and to the readers who dare to step into their world.

This book is a testament to your resilience, your grit, and your relentless pursuit of something… more.

It is also dedicated to the memory of those lost—the lives extinguished in the violent dance of betrayal and revenge. Their stories, though untold, linger in the shadows of these pages.

To those who have felt the sting of betrayal, who have known the chilling touch of fear, who have walked the unforgiving path in search of justice—this is for you. May you find solace in the knowledge that even in the depths of darkness, a flicker of hope—however faint—can endure.

For some, that hope may come in the form of redemption. For others, it may be the simple act of survival. Whatever its form, may it sustain you through the longest night.

This is a dedication to the complexities of the human spirit—the capacity for both immense evil and unwavering courage. It is a tribute to the moral ambiguities that make life so compelling, so terrifying, and so undeniably human.

May this book capture even a fraction of the intensity, the fear, and the relentless pursuit of survival that defines those who dwell in the shadows.

Preface

This story, born from the murky depths of countless late nights and fueled by an unhealthy amount of caffeine, is a testament to the enduring fascination with the morally gray.

Sharon, our protagonist, isn't a hero in the traditional sense. He's a survivor—a ghost drifting through the world, leaving behind a trail of violence and shattered lives. He's not someone you'd want to meet in a dark alley, but he's someone whose story demanded to be told.

I've always been drawn to characters who exist on the fringes of society—the ones who operate outside the confines of law and morality, who are forced to make impossible choices, who compromise their values in the desperate struggle to survive. In crafting this narrative, I immersed myself in the labyrinthine world of international espionage, the brutal realities of contract killing, and the relentless pursuit of justice. My goal was to capture the raw emotions, the gritty details, and the palpable tension that come with living on the edge.

This is a world where betrayal is inevitable, where the lines between right and wrong blur into an indistinguishable haze. But more than just a thriller, this book is a character study—an exploration of the human condition in its most extreme forms. I wanted to lay bare Sharon's internal battles, to expose the war between his instincts and the fragments of his conscience that refuse to be silenced.

I invite you to embark on this perilous journey—to feel the visceral thrill of the chase, the crushing weight of betrayal, and the intoxicating allure of revenge. But be warned: once you step into Sharon's world, you may never see the darkness the same way again.

This journey is not for the faint of heart.

Acknowledgments

First and foremost, I extend my deepest gratitude to my Juliet, whose unwavering support and patience throughout the long and often grueling process of writing this book were invaluable. Her insightful feedback and constant encouragement kept me going when the words wouldn't flow. A special thanks to my editor, for their sharp eye and insightful suggestions, which significantly improved the final manuscript. Finally, to my readers – your feedback has been indispensable, and I appreciate your time and keen observations. Any remaining errors are, of course, entirely my own.

Table of Contents

Introduction

The world of international espionage is a dangerous game—a high-stakes chess match where human lives are mere pawns. Sharon Cohen, our protagonist, is a master player, a ghost moving through the shadows of deception and violence. But even ghosts can be hunted.

His story begins in the vibrant chaos of Marrakech, where a meticulously planned assassination goes terribly wrong. Betrayed by those he trusted, he barely escapes with his life, fleeing to Manila in search of refuge and anonymity. But in a world where past sins never stay buried, the hunt is relentless. His transformation isn't just physical—it's a journey through the darkest recesses of his soul.

Ceta, a beauty queen unknowingly caught in the crossfire, becomes the catalyst for a brutal reckoning. Her tragic fate serves as a reminder that even in a world built on lies, some connections are too profound to ignore. From the winding alleys of Morocco to the neon-lit streets of Manila and the towering skyline of New York, Sharon's existence is a deadly puzzle—each piece revealing a past steeped in conspiracy, betrayal, and blood.

Opposing him is NYPD Detective Tom Pickens, a relentless investigator determined to peel back the layers of deception and uncover the truth. As he hunts Sharon, he exposes a vast network of enemies and hidden forces pulling the strings behind the chaos. Pickens serves as the moral counterbalance to Sharon's rogue existence, forcing a confrontation not just between law and lawlessness, but between the remnants of Sharon's conscience and the ruthless survival instincts that have kept him alive.

This isn't just a story about a hitman on the run—it's a visceral descent into the heart of darkness, a relentless pursuit of justice that challenges the very nature of good and evil. With tension hanging thick in the air, every twist and turn will leave you gasping for breath. In this world, betrayal is inevitable, revenge is costly, and survival comes at a steep price.

Get ready for a wild ride.

Ambush in Marrakech

The midday Marrakech sun bore down on Sharon, turning the already labyrinthine souk into a shimmering, disorienting maze. The air hung thick and heavy, a cloying blend of exotic spices, sweat, and the underlying musk of a thousand unwashed bodies. He had been in Morocco for three days, lying low, waiting for the contact. The contact who was now, he realized with a sickening lurch in his gut, a double-cross.

The first sign wasn't a gunshot but a subtle shift in the crowd. A jostle here, a murmured conversation there—seemingly innocuous, yet orchestrated with chilling precision. Then came the pressure, a relentless tide of bodies pushing him toward a narrow alleyway, a dead end. He smelled the metallic tang of blood before he saw it—crimson blooming on the dusty cobblestones.

The attack was swift and brutal. No fancy footwork, no theatrical flourishes. Just efficient, deadly violence. Three men, their faces obscured by keffiyehs, moved with the practiced grace of predators. Sharon reacted instinctively, his years of training kicking in. He rolled, a blur of motion, his body a weapon honed to a razor's edge. A silenced pistol barked, its report muffled by the din of the souk, but the sting of a bullet grazing his shoulder was unmistakable.

He fought with the savage fury of a cornered animal, each blow calculated, each movement a desperate bid for survival. The alleyway became a claustrophobic killing ground, the scent of spices replaced by the acrid tang of gunpowder and sweat. He tasted blood—his own and theirs. The narrow confines left little room to maneuver, turning the fight into a brutal, close-quarters brawl. One attacker went down, a crimson stain spreading across his white djellaba. Another lunged, a wickedly curved knife flashing in the sunlight.

Sharon parried the blow, his own knife meeting the attacker's with a sickening crunch of steel on bone. He disarmed the man, using his momentum to send him crashing into the third assailant. Taking advantage of the brief distraction, Sharon broke free, scrambling out of the alleyway and back into the chaotic crush of the souk. He could hear the shouts behind him, the pounding of feet in pursuit. He wasn't just fighting for survival; he was fighting for escape—a desperate race against the relentless pursuit of his enemies.

His heart hammered against his ribs, a frantic drumbeat against the cacophony of the marketplace. The sensory overload was nearly unbearable. The vibrant colors of the souk—the deep reds of carpets, the rich blues of ceramics, the dazzling gold of jewelry—swam in a dizzying blur. The pungent aromas of saffron, cumin, and cinnamon were overpowered by the metallic tang of blood and the sharp scent of fear. The sounds—the haggling merchants, the bleating of goats, the rhythmic clang of a blacksmith's hammer—blurred into a deafening roar.

He weaved through the throngs of people, a ghost moving among the living, his senses honed to a razor's edge. He recognized the faces of his pursuers now—fleeting glimpses through the shifting gaps in the bustling crowd. He knew them, or rather, he knew the organization they belonged to—the Abergil mob, a shadowy network operating in the murky underbelly of Moroccan power. He had underestimated them, underestimated the depth of their reach, their ruthlessness.

He'd been betrayed. The contact—supposed to be his safe passage out of Morocco—had been nothing more than a lure, a carefully laid trap leading him straight into an ambush. A cold dread washed over him, colder than the chill of the desert night. He was alone, exposed, hunted. His carefully constructed plan to disappear, the elaborate scheme he had put into motion, had shattered into dust.

Sharon's escape was a ballet of desperation, a chaotic dance between survival instinct and sheer luck. He darted into alleyways, scaled walls, and used the labyrinthine nature of the souk to his advantage. Moving like a shadow, he weaved through the crowds, using them as both cover and obstacle. He could feel their eyes on him, the relentless, suffocating presence of pursuit. This was more than just a contract gone wrong. This was personal—a carefully orchestrated takedown.

He had to get out. He had to disappear. Manila was his only hope, a city he'd heard whispered about in darkened bars—a place of contrasts, where the opulence of the wealthy collided with the desperate poverty of the masses. It was a city of shadows, a place where he could vanish into the anonymity of millions.

He reached a dusty backstreet, where the stench of rotting garbage mingled with the faint sweetness of jasmine flowers. Slipping into a crumbling riad, its once-grand entrance now lost to neglect, he found her—a wizened old woman seated on a low stool, her face etched with the lines of hardship and secrets. She was his contact, a woman with connections he had cultivated over the years, someone who could arrange passage on a cargo ship bound for the Philippines.

He bribed her, paid her handsomely—more than her services were worth. She didn't question his sudden flight, her gaze betraying only a knowing wisdom. He understood. In Marrakech, everyone had their secrets, and hers were far less dangerous than his own.

The escape wasn't glamorous, but it was effective. He left behind the intoxicating scents and chaotic beauty of the souk, trading the familiar dangers of Morocco for the unpredictable terrors of Manila. His journey was far from over. He was a hunted man, and the hunt had just begun. The taste of betrayal lingered, bitter on his tongue, like the dust of Marrakech. But survival was all that mattered now. The only thing he was focused on. And Manila was his next, uncertain step toward it.

Flight from the Shadows

The salt spray stung Sharon's face as he clung to the rusty railing of the cargo ship, the rhythmic churn of the engine a dull throb beneath the relentless roar of the ocean. The air was thick with the acrid scent of diesel and fish, a stark contrast to the intoxicating perfumes of Marrakech's souks. Below him, the churning waves mirrored the turmoil within him.

Betrayal. The word clawed at his insides, a raw, festering wound that matched the throbbing pain in his side. He'd taken a bullet—just a graze, but enough to remind him of his precarious existence. The contact, a man he had trusted implicitly, had sold him out. The price on his head, it seemed, was higher than he'd ever anticipated.

He had escaped Marrakech through sheer luck and a hefty bribe—paid to a woman who understood the language of survival better than most. She had slipped him through the back alleys, past the watchful eyes of the men now hunting him, and guided him to the docks. The ship, a rust-bucket named *The Wandering Star*, was his only ticket out. He had paid a king's ransom, but money, he'd learned, was a fickle friend in his line of work. It could buy passage, but not safety. Not peace of mind. There was no peace for Sharon—only the constant, gnawing anxiety of the next betrayal, the next bullet.

Manila. The name echoed in his mind, a distant promise of anonymity, of a chance to rebuild, to disappear. Facial reconstruction surgery was his only hope. He couldn't outrun his past, not with the Mossad's relentless pursuit already in motion, but he could change his face, erase his identity. He had to become someone else—a ghost among the millions teeming through the streets of Manila.

The voyage blurred into monotonous days and sleepless nights. The cramped, stifling quarters of the cargo hold reeked of sweat, mildew, and the ever-present stench of fear. Disease thrived in the damp air. He shared the space with a motley crew of smugglers, thieves, and desperate souls, each burdened with their own secrets. He kept to himself, his face hidden in the shadows, his mind consumed by the gnawing fear that every creak of the ship, every splash of the waves, might signal his capture. Each sunrise brought a renewed sense of dread, a constant reminder of how exposed he truly was.

Food was scarce, the rations meager and barely palatable. He survived on scraps, his body weakened by hunger and the lingering effects of his injury. Sleep offered little reprieve—nightmares of Marrakech, of betrayal, haunted his dreams. He saw the faces of his pursuers, their eyes cold, unyielding. He relived the gunfire, the searing pain of the bullet, over and over.

He spent his days watching the others. Most were migrants, fleeing poverty and despair, clinging to fragile hopes of a better life in the Philippines. Their whispered stories, exchanged in hushed tones in the darkness of the hold, painted a grim portrait of hardship and desperation. Yet their dreams still burned bright. Sharon, on the other hand, had no dreams. He had only a desperate need to survive—to erase himself, to become nothing more than a shadow.

The journey felt endless. Days bled into weeks, the vast expanse of ocean a relentless reminder of his isolation. He was adrift—not just at sea, but in life itself. A castaway with no past, no future. Yet through it all, a fierce will to live burned within him. A primal instinct to survive. The need for anonymity was stronger than his fear.

Finally, after what felt like an eternity, the ship approached Manila Bay. A hazy smudge of land broke the horizon, filling him with a strange mix of relief and apprehension. Relief that his journey was nearing its end. Apprehension at what came next.

The surgery. The safe house. A new identity.

Daunting tasks.

But he had no choice.

He had to disappear. His life depended on it.

The disembarkation was chaotic and hurried, a frenzied ballet of bodies and luggage. He moved through the throng, senses heightened, eyes scanning every face for a flicker of recognition. There was no contact, no prearranged meeting—he was entirely alone. He slipped through the crowd, a shadow among shadows, his heart hammering in his chest. Manila was a city of millions; his anonymity was almost assured. The city itself seemed to conspire in his favor, offering its restless energy as a shield for his reinvention.

The first few days were spent securing a safe house—a cramped, dingy room at the Salem Hotel, nestled in a forgotten corner of the city, far from the neon excess and polished façades of Manila's wealthier districts. It was squalid, but it was secure, and that was all that mattered. He paid in cash, ensuring no paper trail. He had learned long ago that such things had a way of coming back to haunt you. His only tether to the outside world was a burner phone—a fragile link to the underworld contacts he desperately needed.

Arranging the surgery was more complicated. He moved cautiously, communicating through cryptic messages, encrypted channels, leveraging what remained of his network. He needed someone discreet, someone who wouldn't ask questions. The price was staggering, but money was the least of his concerns. What mattered was severing the link between his past and his future. The face he wore was a liability. A death sentence. It had to go.

The surgery was agony. A brutal, invasive procedure that pushed him to the limits of his endurance. He felt the scalpel slice through flesh, the searing pain dulled only slightly by a haze of anesthetics. When he awoke, the mirror offered him a stranger's face—familiar yet foreign, his features warped by swelling and stitched seams. His reflection no longer bore the mark of the hunted man. A new identity had been born, his old self buried beneath reconstructed skin.

But the scars remained. They would fade, in time, but they would never truly disappear. They were etched not just on his flesh but deep within him, reminders of a life steeped in blood and betrayal. He stared at his new reflection, unblinking, absorbing the weight of what had been done. Relief washed over him, but it was fleeting.

Because freedom was an illusion. A temporary reprieve from the shadows closing in around him. The weight of his past clung to him, suffocating, inescapable. Manila, for all its anonymity, held dangers of its own—hidden threats lurking beneath the surface. He was still Sharon. The hitman. The hunted. A new face didn't change that.

His escape from Marrakech had only been the beginning. The chase was far from over. The flight from the shadows had only just begun.

Manilas Underbelly

The air hung thick and heavy, a humid blanket clinging to Sharon's skin as he stepped off the ferry. Manila. The city assaulted his senses—a cacophony of car horns, the insistent chatter of a thousand conversations, the pungent aroma of exhaust fumes mingling with the sweeter scent of street food. It was a sensory overload, a stark contrast to the relative quietude—the deadly quietude—of the Moroccan desert. He pulled his collar higher, trying to disappear into the teeming crowds, a ghost in a city of ghosts.

He had chosen Manila for its anonymity, its chaotic energy the perfect cover for someone trying to erase their past. The city's underbelly, a sprawling labyrinth of shadowed alleys and hidden deals, promised both refuge and the tools for his transformation. He needed to disappear, to become someone else entirely. The bullet wound in his side, a constant reminder of his past life, throbbed with each jarring step on the uneven pavement.

His contact, a shadowy figure named Silas, known for his connections to the city's underworld, had arranged everything. The plastic surgeon, Dr. Reyes—a man who dealt in discretion as much as scalpel work—was waiting. The location was cryptic: a nondescript building tucked away in a back alley, its entrance shrouded in the perpetual twilight of the city's overgrowth. Finding it had been a test of both navigation and nerves, a journey through a maze of twisting streets and bustling markets where the scent of durian battled with the stench of open sewers. He had paid Silas handsomely, but in this city, even money couldn't guarantee trust.

Dr. Reyes' clinic was stark, almost sterile—a bizarre contrast to the chaos outside. The doctor himself was a quiet, meticulous man, his eyes betraying a weariness that spoke of years spent navigating the city's murky depths. He spoke little, but his hands worked with an almost artistic precision, reshaping Sharon's face, erasing the features that linked him to his past. The process was excruciating, a prolonged dance with pain, but Sharon endured, driven by the raw need for survival. Days bled into nights. The constant hum of the clinic's machinery became the soundtrack of his transformation.

During the weeks of recovery, he lived in a small, cramped room above a bustling noodle shop, the rhythmic clatter of spoons and chopsticks a constant reminder of his vulnerability. He watched the city from his window, observing its pulse, its rhythm, the intricate dance of life and death. He saw the smiles, the laughter, the joy—but he also saw the desperation, the poverty, the undercurrent of violence simmering beneath the surface. Manila was a city of contrasts, beautiful and terrifying in equal measure. He was a stranger in a strange land, both a hunter and the hunted.

His escape from Marrakech had been a desperate flight, a gamble. But Manila was different. It was a city that demanded respect, a place where survival was a constant negotiation. He learned to blend in, adopting the rhythms of the street, attuning himself to the subtle cues of the city's unspoken codes. He learned to discern the safe from the unsafe, the friend from the foe. What had first seemed threatening gradually began to reveal its secrets—its hidden pathways, its unspoken rules. He learned to use the darkness to his advantage.

One humid evening, while walking along the Pasig River, he saw her. Carma Ceta. She was everything Sharon wasn't—vibrant, alive, a beacon of light in the city's shadows. He had seen her photo before, a fleeting image from his past, connected to a mission, a job gone wrong. A beautiful woman. A beauty queen. A link to the life he was trying to escape. He had been warned about her—a woman with dangerous connections of her own. But he hadn't been prepared for this.

She saw him. Her eyes widened in recognition, a flicker of understanding passing between them. Her surprise quickly gave way to something else—a mixture of fear and determination. Cold dread tightened around his heart.

He knew then that his anonymity was shattered, that his carefully constructed sanctuary had been compromised. The surgery had erased his face, but it couldn't erase the ghosts that followed him. He had thought he had left the past behind, but it had followed him across oceans and continents, clawing at his heels, whispering insidious promises in his ear.

The next few days were a blur of clandestine meetings, shadowed alleys, and whispered conversations. Ceta, initially wary, slowly revealed a connection to his past—one far more tangled, far more dangerous than he had imagined. She held information that could lead back to him, exposing his identity to those who hunted him. Her beauty was a mask, concealing a cold intelligence and a will of steel.

The situation escalated with terrifying speed. Ceta's knowledge was a ticking time bomb, and Sharon knew, with chilling certainty, that silencing her was his only option. The decision tore at him, but it was a choice born of necessity—a brutal act of self-preservation. He killed her quickly, efficiently, leaving no trace but the faintest whisper of his presence in the suffocating humidity of Manila's night.

The act, though necessary, left a mark on his soul—a chilling echo of his violent past. He left Manila, his new face still unfamiliar, reflected in the grimy windows of the departing bus. He carried with him not just the physical scars of his surgeries but the burden of his choices, the weight of the city's stifling air, and the ghosts of those he had left behind. Manila, with its allure and danger, remained etched into his memory—a landscape of betrayal, violence, and the relentless pursuit of survival.

But his escape was only temporary. His past, it seemed, had an unnerving ability to find him, no matter how far he ran. The game was far from over. The shadows of his old life stretched long and ominous across his path. The hunt was still on. He was still running.

Ceta A Dangerous Encounter

The humid Manila air clung to him like a second skin, seeping through the thin cotton of his new shirt. He had chosen anonymity—bland, unremarkable clothing meant to help him blend into the chaotic tapestry of the city. But Manila refused to let him disappear. It was relentless, an assault on the senses—a vibrant, tangled mess of color, sound, and smell that clawed at his carefully constructed façade of calm. He walked with purpose, his eyes scanning the crowds, his senses sharp despite the surgeries that had altered his appearance. He was still a target. He was still hunted.

His refuge was a small, rundown apartment in a less-touristy part of the city—a place where shadows stretched long and deep, mirroring the darkness within him. It wasn't luxurious, but it offered something he craved: privacy. Since his harrowing escape from Morocco, solitude had become a necessity. He needed time to heal—physically, mentally. The surgeries had been brutal, invasive, leaving behind more than just scars. His reflection no longer felt like his own. He looked in the mirror and saw a stranger staring back—a ghost of the man he once was, a carefully constructed illusion that still felt like it might shatter at any moment.

He avoided the tourist traps, the glittering casinos and five-star hotels, places where his old life might catch up to him. Instead, he sought solace in the city's less polished corners—where the pulse of

Manila beat raw and unfiltered. It was here, in a dimly lit bar tucked away on a forgotten side street, that he met Ceta.

She was unlike anything he had expected—breathtaking, magnetic. Her beauty was undeniable, but it was her confidence that unsettled him. She wasn't just a beauty queen. There was something sharp, something knowing beneath the surface. Her laugh was melodic, intoxicating, her eyes full of intelligence and quiet defiance. He had sought anonymity, yet she seemed drawn to him, sensing the weight he carried, the darkness he tried to conceal.

At first, their conversations were polite, careful—small talk over half-empty glasses. But she intrigued him. She spoke of her ambitions, her frustrations with the superficiality of pageants, her desire to study law and make a difference. She was sharp, witty, and disarmingly perceptive. He listened more than he spoke, offering only vague answers about himself, maintaining the careful detachment he had perfected over the years. He was a ghost, a shadow, and intended to keep it that way. But with Ceta, the walls he had built around himself began to crumble, one brick at a time.

There was an undeniable spark between them—dangerous, reckless, entirely inappropriate given his circumstances. He knew he should keep his distance, should push her away, but the pull was too strong. He sought her company when he shouldn't have. Their meetings became more frequent, their conversations more intimate. He walked her home, navigating the labyrinthine streets of Manila, their fingers brushing in fleeting touches that sent electricity crackling through the humid air. A dangerous game of cat and mouse.

He found himself confiding in her more than he intended. He spoke in riddles, in metaphors, but the weight of his words carried the truth—of things he had done, people he had hurt, lives he had left in ruin. He saw the way her eyes sometimes flickered with something—understanding, suspicion, maybe both. She never pressed him for details, but her intuition was razor-sharp. And that terrified him.

He began to wonder if he had made a mistake. If letting his guard down, even for a moment, had been the gravest miscalculation of all. The thought filled him with dread. Any exposure would be catastrophic. He had spent months meticulously constructing this new identity, this new life. He couldn't risk it. Not for her. Not for anyone.

One night, as they sat on her balcony overlooking the sprawling city, she brought up his past. It wasn't an accusation, not quite. More of a quiet probing—a subtle test to see if his carefully constructed façade would crack under scrutiny. He felt the shift immediately. A tightening in his chest. The way his muscles tensed, coiled, ready. His heart pounded, an erratic drumbeat against his ribs. He could feel the sweat gathering at his temples, the weight of her gaze pressing down on him. His lies, once effortless, had become suffocating. The walls he had built were starting to buckle. He was naked. Exposed.

The silence between them thickened, heavy with unsaid truths. The city stretched out below, its glittering lights an illusion of beauty, masking the raw, unforgiving reality beneath. And then he saw it—the moment of realization flickering across her face. A shift in her eyes, from cautious curiosity to stunned disbelief. She knew.

There was no question now. No space left for doubt.

He had to act.

There was no other choice. He couldn't allow her to expose him. He couldn't risk the fragile life he had so meticulously constructed—the identity built on deception, on running, on disappearing. The consequences would be catastrophic. Not just for him. For her.

The night unraveled with swift, brutal finality. No second chances. No hesitation. Just the quiet, suffocating stillness that followed. Manila, a city of vibrant beauty and hidden dangers, had claimed another victim. This time, it was someone he had come to care for.

Ceta lay there, the life drained from her beautiful eyes, her voice forever silenced. And he walked away, swallowed by the unforgiving night, leaving only devastation in his wake. The game was far from over. The hunt continued.

His past, like a relentless predator, was always just a step behind.

The Price of Silence

The humid Manila air hung heavy, thick and cloying, clinging to the sweat beading on his forehead. The surgery had been a success—a masterful reconstruction that erased years of lived experience from his face. But it couldn't erase the memories etched into his soul, the ghosts lurking in the quiet corners of his mind. He had chosen this city, this chaos, hoping to lose himself in the anonymity of the teeming masses, to become a ghost among ghosts. But even here, in this sprawling metropolis, the past had a way of finding him.

He sat at a small, dimly lit café, nursing a lukewarm coffee, his eyes flicking over the crowded street. The café, a temporary refuge from the relentless humidity and noise, offered a brief moment of calm—an illusion of safety. He was supposed to be invisible, a phantom. Yet, the feeling of being watched persisted, an unsettling sensation that clung to him like the damp air. His instincts, honed by years of survival, screamed at him now. Danger.

Then he heard it.

A casual conversation, just fragments of words piercing through the low murmur of the café. Two men, their faces shadowed by dim lighting, speaking in hushed tones. A hit. A job executed with brutal efficiency, surgical precision. Their words were like hammer blows against his skull. And then—his code name.

A jolt of ice shot through his veins.

It was a name he hadn't used in years, a name buried beneath layers of false identities and careful deception. A name that tied him irrevocably to the Abergil mob. A name that Ceta, unknowingly, knew.

Panic constricted his chest. He had been meticulous, ruthless in burying his past. Yet here it was, clawing its way to the surface, a monstrous truth that could destroy everything. He felt cold sweat slick his palms, his heartbeat hammering like a war drum. He had to move. Had to disappear before they connected the dots. But it was already too late. The seed of doubt had been planted, the fear rooted deep.

He watched Ceta from a distance, her beauty untouched by the city's grime, her laughter ringing out against the harsh urban sprawl. She had been a distraction, a fleeting moment of light in a life suffocated by shadows. He had grown fond of her—too fond. It was a mistake, a reckless indulgence. And now, that mistake had become a death sentence.

That night, he found her near the bay, the city lights shimmering on the water, the scent of salt heavy in the air. She stood beneath the moonlit sky, framed in silver, breathtaking in her innocence. A vision of something he could never have.

A vision of something he had to destroy.

For a moment, he searched for an alternative, a way out. But there was none. The realization hit with crushing weight, cold and inescapable. She knew too much. And he knew what had to be done.

It happened quickly. Precisely. A lifetime of training reduced it to instinct—a silent shadow striking with lethal finality. It wasn't a fight. It was an execution. Cold. Swift. Merciless.

Her body lay still, her eyes vacant, her warmth gone. He watched as flames consumed the car, the fire reflecting in the dark water like a funeral pyre. The heat licked at his skin, but the cold inside him was far worse.

Ceta was gone. And with her, the last fragile illusion of something more.

The price of silence had been paid.

And he would keep paying it.

The silence that followed was deafening. The city's sounds, once a comforting cacophony, were now a cruel mockery of his solitude. The salty air filled his lungs, but it brought no solace—only the bitter taste of regret, guilt, and fear. He left her there, beneath the moonlight and the whispering sea breeze, a tragic casualty of his choices. A price paid for his survival. He was a creature of darkness, a predator among men.

The act, though necessary, carved a deep, gaping wound in his soul—a void that no amount of surgery or self-deception could ever fill. It mirrored the emptiness within him, an abyss formed by years of violence and betrayal. He was a ghost, a shadow. But even shadows cast long, inescapable darkness.

This wasn't just another job for the Abergil mob or any criminal organization. This was something else. This was the killing of a woman he had come to care for. However fleeting, however dangerous—it had been real. And now, it was gone.

He walked away, leaving behind more than just a corpse. He left behind the fragile remnants of his humanity. The city lights blurred into an indistinct haze as he drifted through the urban sprawl. The adrenaline that had sharpened his focus was wearing off, replaced by a chilling emptiness. He felt untethered, a lone wolf abandoned even by his own conscience. He had crossed a line—one he never thought he would. But there was no turning back. His past hunted him still, relentless as the humid Manila air.

He couldn't stay. Not now. The mark of his actions was seared into the city's underbelly. He had killed someone he cared for—someone who had unknowingly stumbled too close to the darkness that followed him. Manila, once a place of refuge, had become a cage. And he had no choice but to flee.

The next few days passed in a blur of frantic preparation. A new name. A new passport. A flight to New York—a city of ghosts, a battlefield of secrets. He had called it home once, but now, it was just another place to hide. As the plane cut through the night, his mind remained in Manila, in the echoes of Ceta's laughter, in the warmth of her touch. Innocence—such a cruel illusion. It had no place in his world. And yet, it haunted him.

The price of silence had been paid. But the debt was far from settled.

The moment he landed in New York, his burner phone rang. A voice on the other end, clipped and precise. "It's there. Everything you asked for."

If *he* read this book, he would know exactly who I was talking about. No doubt.

Sharon took a cab through the city's neon-drenched streets, slipping into the anonymity of the crowd. Under the cloak of darkness, he scaled the fence of the Jewish cemetery. He moved swiftly, weaving through the graves until he found it—the stone, the marker. He knelt, his fingers tracing the cold granite before slipping beneath the grass at its base.

There it was.

A box.

Inside—a plastic bag. A handgun. Cash. A fresh passport.

His face, now a masterpiece of subtle surgical deception, was unrecognizable to the algorithms that hunted him. Facial recognition would no longer betray him. He was free. At least, as free as a man like him could ever be.

But freedom was a fragile illusion.

New York was no safer than Manila. The city that had once been his haven was now a hunting ground. A game of cat and mouse had begun, and he was both the predator and the prey.

Standing by the hotel window, he looked out at the city skyline—a mosaic of light and shadow, a mirror of his fractured existence. He was a hitman. A killer. A man running from his past. But beneath the layers of deceit, guilt, and fear, a sliver of something else remained. Something human.

He had to be careful. He had to move wisely.

Because the game was far from over.

And the true cost of silence had yet to be tallied.

Surgical Transformation

The sterile scent of antiseptic stung Sharon's nostrils—a stark contrast to the humid, spice-laden air of Manila. He lay on the cold steel table, his body a canvas of incisions, the rhythmic whir of the surgical drill a relentless counterpoint to the frantic beat of his heart. Dr. Ramirez, a wiry man with eyes that held both professional detachment and a flicker of something akin to pity, moved with the practiced precision of a seasoned craftsman, reshaping Sharon's face— his identity. The pain was a dull roar, a constant companion to the chilling realization of his own mortality. Each cut, each stitch, felt like a severing of his past, a desperate attempt to outrun the long shadow cast by his former life.

This wasn't just about changing his appearance. It was about shedding skin, discarding the persona of a killer, a ghost hunted by the Abergil mob and the relentless eyes of the Mossad. The surgery was a brutal, agonizing rebirth. Each incision felt like a wound not just on his flesh, but on his soul. He could feel the delicate work being done— the slow, painstaking process of reshaping his bones, his muscles, his very existence. Each tug, each scrape, was a reminder of the price he was paying for freedom—a freedom that felt more like a fleeting illusion than a tangible reality.

Hours blurred into an eternity of pain and numbness. He felt the pull of his skin, the scrape of bone against metal, the precise, methodical work of the surgeon. He was a sculptor's clay, molded and reshaped into something new, something unrecognizable. The anesthetic's embrace was both a blessing and a curse—dulling the sharp edge of pain but leaving him adrift in a sea of disorientation, his mind a battlefield of memories and fears. He saw flashes of Marrakech—the blinding sun, the glint of steel, the taste of blood. He saw Ceta's face, hauntingly beautiful, eternally frozen in a silent scream. The weight of her death pressed down on him, a suffocating blanket of guilt that even the potent anesthesia couldn't completely erase.

The surgical team moved around him in a silent, efficient ballet of white-coated figures. Their movements were precise, their actions calculated. They were transforming him, stripping away his past and molding him into someone else. Yet, even beneath the scalpel, beneath the layers of skin and muscle, his essence remained. He was still Sharon—the killer, the betrayer, the survivor. The transformation was physical, cosmetic, but it wouldn't erase the indelible mark of his past. He knew that. He felt it in the tremors that ran through his body, even under the influence of the powerful drugs.

When the surgery finally ended, a profound exhaustion washed over him, heavier than the bandages encasing his face. He was wrapped head to toe, cocooned in sterile white, a prisoner of his own transformation. He was no longer the man he had been. Or was he? The question hung in the air, unanswered, a haunting echo in the silence of the recovery room.

Days bled into weeks. The healing was slow, agonizing. The pain was constant, a dull throbbing that mirrored the turmoil in his mind. When he finally looked in the mirror, his reflection was that of a stranger. His face—once ruggedly handsome—was now a blank canvas, smoother, younger, different. Yet the eyes, those intense, penetrating eyes, remained the same. They were the windows to his soul—a soul that had witnessed too much, a soul that carried the burden of his actions.

He spent his days in a hazy purgatory, a prisoner of his own making, caught between lingering pain and the constant fear that his past would catch up to him. His life had been reduced to the four walls of his room, the rhythmic beeping of machines the soundtrack to his existence. The city outside—the city he had chosen as his refuge, teeming with life and danger—felt like a universe away. He was alone, suspended in time, waiting to see if this new face, this new life, was a shield or a trap.

Finally, the day arrived when he could leave. Dr. Ramirez, his face etched with fatigue, gave him a cursory examination before releasing him. "You've endured a great deal," the doctor said, his voice barely a whisper. Sharon merely nodded, his throat raw from weeks of silence. The doctor's words, though simple, resonated with a truth that cut deeper than any surgical blade.

He left the clinic, his body still weak, his face still tender, his mind still reeling from the ordeal. The air of Manila hit him—heavy, humid, a sensory overload that nearly made him stumble. He navigated the crowded streets, a phantom drifting through a world he no longer recognized. He was a ghost, an apparition, both familiar and alien in his own skin. His new face was a mask, a shield, but it couldn't entirely hide the haunted look in his eyes.

His escape from Manila was a desperate scramble through the city's underbelly—a frantic dash through crowded markets and labyrinthine alleys. He felt the weight of his new identity, a cloak of invisibility, but it was fragile, a garment that could easily tear. Fear was a constant companion, a relentless shadow that clung to him, whispering of the precariousness of his existence.

He secured a flight to New York—a city that held both bitter memories and a chilling sense of familiarity. The journey was a blur of sleepless nights and uneasy dreams. When he arrived, his heart pounded a relentless rhythm against his ribs, his body humming with nervous energy. The familiar skyline, once a source of comfort, now loomed menacingly, like a predator watching from above. New York held the dissonance of homecoming and exile. He was back, but he was a stranger. A fugitive. An outcast living on borrowed time.

The airport was a cacophony of noise and movement, but Sharon remained focused, his senses razor-sharp, attuned to any hint of danger. The familiar unease prickled at him—the instinctive awareness of being watched, measured. He wasn't alone. The eyes of the Abergil mob, the Mossad, and Detective Pickens were still on him, waiting for him to falter. And he knew, as he stepped into the city's relentless pulse, that his escape was far from over. The surgery had been just the beginning—a desperate bid for survival. Now came the harder part.

Surviving the shadows of New York.

Return to the States

The plane descended, and the glittering cityscape of New York unfolded beneath him like a malevolent jewel. A chill, deeper than the November air, settled over Sharon. This was home—or what was left of it. A home he had abandoned, a life he had shed like a snake's skin, yet the city still held him captive, its steel and concrete a cage of his own making. The surgery had blurred his features, but it couldn't erase the memories etched into the very marrow of his bones. The scent of exhaust fumes, the insistent blare of sirens, the cacophony of a million voices—they were a brutal symphony of a life he thought he had escaped.

He emerged from JFK, the harsh fluorescent lights a stark contrast to the dim-lit alleys of Manila. He had chosen a quieter terminal, preferring relative anonymity over the risk of being noticed, yet his senses remained on high alert. Every shadow seemed to hold a threat, every stranger a potential enemy. He pulled his worn leather jacket tighter, the familiar weight a small comfort against the chilling realization of his vulnerability. His new face was a mask, but the fear— the ever-present dread—was unmistakable. It lived in the sharp angles of his posture, in the wary glint of his eyes, in the tension coiled beneath his skin.

The taxi ride to Miriam's apartment in Brooklyn was a blur of speeding cars and neon reflections. The city pulsed with nervous energy, a chaotic rhythm that both mirrored and amplified his own inner turmoil. Miriam. The thought of seeing her, of facing her after all this time, sent a knot of apprehension tightening in his stomach. He hadn't spoken to her since he had run—a decision born of necessity, a sacrifice made to keep her from the darkness that consumed him. And yet, returning to her now felt both reckless and inevitable.

The building was as he remembered: a slightly rundown brick structure clinging to the edge of a gentrifying neighborhood. He paid the cabbie, his fingers trembling slightly as he fumbled for the cash. Taking a deep breath, he stepped forward, the cold air stinging his lungs as he pushed open the heavy metal door. The dimly lit hallway smelled of old paint and stale cigarette smoke. Each creaky step up the stairwell echoed in the silence, his heartbeat hammering in his ears. The apartment number was familiar, yet somehow foreign, like a half-remembered dream.

Miriam opened the door before he could even reach for the bell. Surprise flickered across her face, quickly followed by apprehension. She hadn't changed much—her fiery red hair, still unruly, framed a face marked by the lines of their shared past. But her eyes, once bright with life, now held a haunting weariness. Time had settled heavily on her.

"Sharon?" she whispered, her voice barely more than a breath. Her gaze lingered on his altered features, recognition flickering before confusion clouded her expression. The years apart had carved a gulf between them.

He nodded, the word he wanted to say lodged in his throat. The familiarity was there, undeniable, yet it felt as though he were staring at a ghost—a pale imitation of the woman he had once known.

The apartment was small, sparsely furnished, but clean. The air was thick with the scent of old books and something else, something faintly metallic. The tension between them was palpable, heavy as the city fog. For a long moment, they stood in silence, unspoken accusations and regrets simmering between them.

"Come in," Miriam finally said, her voice unsteady. She stepped aside, and he crossed the threshold, his steps muted by the worn carpet. He was a ghost himself, a phantom returned from the dead.

Miriam poured him a glass of whiskey, her movements stiff, her gaze locked on him. He took a long gulp, the fiery liquid searing his throat, momentarily easing the tightness in his chest. He had come here for a reason. He had to tell her. But the words caught in his throat, weighted with too many secrets.

"I'm in trouble," he finally said, his voice rough, stripped of its usual confidence. The words hung between them, thick with unspoken meaning.

Miriam's eyes widened, her expression a mixture of fear and resolve.

Outside, the city roared on, indifferent to the storm brewing behind these four walls.

The next few days blurred into a haze of hurried conversations, stolen glances, and an ever-present sense of unease. Detective Tom Pickens was still on his trail, his relentless investigation a shadow looming over their every move. Miriam, despite her fear, refused to abandon him. Her loyalty was a beacon in the encroaching darkness. She had resources—contacts, an underground network of informants that reached into the city's underbelly. She was his unlikely ally, his only lifeline in a sea of treacherous currents.

But the illusion of safety was fleeting. The city, with its relentless rhythm and unseen threats, closed in on them. A failed attempt to acquire explosives, a meeting with a contact who turned out to be a double agent, a near miss with Pickens himself—each incident chipped away at their fragile peace. The city was not just a setting; it was an entity, a force unto itself, testing their resilience, their courage, their very sanity.

One night, a frantic knock shattered the uneasy quiet of the apartment. Miriam hesitated only a second before opening the door. A pale, trembling figure stood in the dim light—a contact from her network. His breath came in ragged gasps as he delivered a cryptic warning: the Abergil mob was closing in. The urgency in his voice sent an icy current through Sharon's veins. They needed to leave. Now.

The escape was chaos—a desperate flight through the city's labyrinthine streets. They wove through alleys and side roads, evading pursuing vehicles in a reckless game of cat and mouse. The neon lights of the city reflected in their eyes like fractured promises, while sirens wailed in the distance, a relentless reminder of how precarious their existence had become. The city, once a familiar refuge, had transformed into a hostile battlefield.

Their sanctuary became a decaying warehouse by the waterfront, where the air was thick with salt and damp rot. They collapsed inside, bruised, breathless, but alive. For now. The silence pressed against them, heavy with the knowledge that this momentary reprieve wouldn't last. The shadows of New York, both literal and unseen, were still closing in.

This wasn't the end. It wasn't even close. The chase, the fight, the inevitable reckoning—it was all still ahead of them. The city, their sanctuary and their prison, watched in silence, waiting for the next move.

Family Ties Twisted Bonds

The warehouse reeked of mildew and despair, a fitting stage for their reunion. Miriam arrived, not with the warmth of familial embrace, but with the cold detachment of someone who had learned to survive in a world where trust was currency and betrayal was inevitable. The reckless spark of her youth had been extinguished, replaced with a chilling composure that sent a shiver down Sharon's spine. The years hadn't softened her sharp features; instead, they had carved lines of weariness and honed a calculated shrewdness in her gaze. She was a reflection of their past, a living testament to the brutal choices that had shaped them both.

"You look… different," she murmured, her voice barely breaking the silence. It wasn't a remark on his surgically altered features but an unspoken acknowledgment of the deeper transformation—the one that had hardened him into someone unrecognizable.

"So do you," Sharon countered, his voice rough with exhaustion. He had been swallowed whole by the abyss of his criminal life. Now, standing before her, he felt like a specter of his former self, an echo trapped between past and present. He studied her carefully, searching for any sign of weakness, any crack in her carefully constructed façade. There was none.

She lit a cigarette, the brief flare of the lighter casting shadows across her face. Her hands were steady, but he caught the subtle tremor—betraying the illusion of control. "You always were a terrible liar, Sharon," she said, exhaling smoke laced with bitterness, the taste of old wounds lingering between them.

She knew. Of course, she knew. The surgery had masked his face, but not his soul. She had stayed away from his life, made a choice to sever ties, yet here she was, stepping back into his world. And he couldn't figure out why.

"Why are you here, Miriam?" His voice was low, stripped of warmth. The question hung between them, heavier than the years they had spent apart. It was more than curiosity—it was a demand. An unspoken challenge.

"Let's just say I need your help," she answered, her gaze unwavering. "And let's just say I have information that could be… useful to you."

She spoke of their past, of the ghost that had loomed over them both—her father. A brutal legacy, one neither of them had ever truly escaped. A hidden account. Money—enough to disappear forever. But it wasn't just stashed away; it was tangled in a web of danger, sitting at the heart of a deadly game involving the Israeli underworld. And worse—Sharon had unknowingly crossed the very players who were now hunting for it.

The mention of her father sent an icy wave through him. The man had been both a phantom and a storm, his presence looming even in his absence. Ruthless. Unforgiving. His ambition had scarred them both, dictating the course of their lives in ways neither of them had fully reckoned with. Now, even from beyond the grave, he was pulling them into one final act of violence.

Sharon's instincts screamed at him—this could be a trap. Was she using their shared history as bait? Was he just a pawn in a game she refused to name?

Miriam seemed to sense his hesitation. She leaned in, her voice lowering. "A faction within the Abergil family knows about the money. They want it. And they want to erase any loose ends. That means us, Sharon."

The words struck like a gut punch, confirming his worst fears. He was being hunted—not just by the Mossad, not just by Pickens, but by ghosts of his own bloodline's sins. His return to New York had never been an escape. It was a descent into something far worse.

And now, the only way out was through.

The following days blurred into a whirlwind of clandestine meetings, whispered exchanges, and the suffocating weight of impending doom. The city felt like a noose tightening around them, its towering steel and glass structures indifferent to the desperate game unfolding in its shadows.

Miriam, despite her unsettling composure, proved invaluable. Her network ran deeper than Sharon had imagined, threading through the underbelly of the city with a precision that spoke of years spent mastering its secrets. She moved with the ease of someone who belonged in this world, who had long accepted its brutality. And as the layers of her past began to unravel, Sharon realized with growing unease that he had never truly known her.

They operated together, an uneasy alliance bound by necessity rather than trust. The line between ally and adversary blurred with every move, every risk, every choice that pushed them further into the labyrinth of betrayal and revenge. And yet, against his better judgment, he began to trust her. He saw the flickers of vulnerability beneath her hardened exterior, the fear she tried so desperately to conceal. Was this redemption? An attempt to rewrite the past? Or was it something far more dangerous?

Doubts gnawed at him. Miriam's motivations remained obscured, her true allegiances locked behind unreadable expressions. Was she truly seeking reconciliation, or was this a masterful manipulation, a carefully orchestrated deception?

Then, one evening, as they planned their next move, a detail caught his eye—so small it might have gone unnoticed. A thin, nearly imperceptible scratch on her wrist. But Sharon recognized it instantly. A distinct mark left by a specialized blade, one used by only one person—the Serpent.

Cold dread coiled in his gut. The Serpent was more than just an assassin. He was the most feared executioner within the Abergil crime family. A ghost whispered about in criminal circles, a figure of myth and terror.

And Miriam knew him. Intimately.

The weight of her deception crashed down on him like a final, brutal blow. This wasn't just about hidden money, family legacies, or revenge. This was about survival. About power. And about the brutal, unrelenting games played in the darkest corners of New York.

He had been played. Manipulated. Dragged into a vortex of betrayal far deeper than he had ever imagined.

The city, once his sanctuary, had become a battlefield. And the enemy wasn't just out there in the streets. She was standing right in front of him.

The fight was no longer just his own. It was a war between them now, a deadly game with no rules, no mercy. The city held its breath, waiting for the night to decide which of them would survive.

The final act had begun. And there would be no encore.

Detective Pickens A Relentless Pursuit

The stale air in Pickens's office hung heavy with the scent of old coffee and disillusionment. He stared at the blurry photograph, the grainy image barely capturing the fleeting glimpse of Sharon's face—a ghost of a man, lost in the labyrinthine streets of Manila. The open case file on his desk was a testament to weeks of relentless work, a frustrating puzzle with far too many missing pieces. The murder in Manila had been messy, brutal—the kind of job that screamed professional yet carried the hallmarks of frantic desperation. It was a signature he hadn't seen in years, a specter from a past he had long thought buried. And now, the name Sharon, a name he'd once known intimately, had resurfaced—a poisonous weed pushing its way through the cracks in the concrete jungle of his life.

Pickens ran a hand through his thinning hair, the weariness etched deep into his eyes, mirroring the countless sleepless nights spent chasing shadows. He knew Sharon. He knew the chilling efficiency, the almost preternatural ability to vanish without a trace. Their history was tangled and venomous, rooted in the unforgiving streets of New York, leaving scars on both of them—deep, festering wounds that refused to heal. Pickens had seen Sharon operate firsthand, had witnessed the cold, calculating precision that made him one of the most elusive assassins the city had ever known. That same precision marked the Manila murder, yet something about it felt off—a trail of breadcrumbs meticulously designed to mislead.

Their rivalry stretched back to a time when Pickens was just a rookie cop, fresh out of the academy, his idealism barely clinging to the tattered edges of his worn-out uniform. Back then, Sharon had been a ruthless young thug, slipping through his fingers more times than he cared to count. He had chased him through smoky back alleys, across rooftops bathed in the harsh glare of streetlights, each near-miss fueling his determination, deepening the animosity carved into his soul. Pickens had let him get away before. He wouldn't this time. This wasn't just another case—it was personal.

The case file was thick with inconsistencies. The Manila police report was cursory, offering little assistance. The only concrete lead was the blurry photo—a testament to the difficulty of chasing ghosts in the digital age. Pickens had cross-referenced the victim's background: a beauty queen with questionable connections, a woman who, on the surface, had no reason to be the target of such calculated violence. The murder scene was clean, almost surgically precise—a stark contrast to the chaotic nature of Sharon's usual modus operandi. Something didn't add up.

He leaned back in his chair, the cheap vinyl creaking under his weight, as he reviewed the intelligence gathered from his informants. Whispers in dimly lit bars, hushed conversations in smoky backrooms, scraps of information that seemed insignificant at first glance but gradually began to form a fragmented narrative. He had learned of Sharon's recent surgeries, the painstaking efforts to alter his appearance, to erase his identity. It was a desperate gamble, a testament to his fear and paranoia. The trail had led to the Philippines—a distant island paradise, a world away from the gritty reality of New York's underbelly.

Yet, the intelligence confirmed Sharon's return to New York, though his exact location remained elusive. Pickens's network of informants—a ragtag collection of ex-cons, low-level thugs, and disgruntled associates—painted a fractured portrait of a man living on the edge, always looking over his shoulder, haunted by his past. Their reports, often embellished with exaggerations and personal biases, still provided valuable insights into Sharon's movements, his methods, and the people he surrounded himself with.

Pickens knew his nemesis. He knew Sharon's methods—precise, ruthless, leaving little to chance. He could anticipate his strategies, the way he'd use the city's labyrinthine streets and shadows to his advantage. Their game was a deadly dance, a cat-and-mouse chase played out against the backdrop of the city that never sleeps. And this time, Pickens was determined to end it.

The thought of Miriam lingered in his mind. Her sudden appearance in the case, her mysterious role in the unfolding drama, added another layer of complexity to an already tangled web. Their shared history—shrouded in secrecy and mutual distrust—created fertile ground for manipulation and deception. Pickens suspected that Sharon wouldn't have involved Miriam unless it was absolutely necessary, unless there was something far more at stake than just survival.

Pickens tapped his fingers on the desk, the rhythmic beat echoing the relentless tempo of his pursuit. He had to find Sharon—not just to bring him to justice, but to understand the deeper game at play. This was more than a simple assassination; it was a conspiracy, one that reached far beyond New York City. The international connections, the whispers of a powerful cabal, all pointed to something much larger, something far more sinister—an invisible force poised to engulf the city in its deadly embrace.

He had a hunch, an instinct he couldn't ignore. This wasn't just about money or revenge. There was something deeper, something more insidious at play. Something Sharon was desperately trying to protect—or perhaps destroy. The Manila murder was merely a single move in a far more dangerous game.

The city's shadows held their secrets tightly, shielding Sharon in their impenetrable darkness. But Pickens, hardened by years of experience and driven by unrelenting determination, was ready to tear through that darkness, to drag Sharon into the light and force him to face justice. This was a fight to the death, a duel between two men bound by a shared past—a past that had shaped their destinies and forged an unbreakable bond of hatred.

Pickens wasn't just chasing a killer; he was hunting a ghost, a phantom, a man he had to bring down, no matter the cost. The game was on. And this time, Pickens was ready to play.

The city held its breath, oblivious to the storm gathering in its concrete jungle, a storm that would soon unleash its fury on all involved. The chase was far from over. The stakes had never been higher. The shadows of New York might guard their secrets, but Detective Pickens was determined to unearth them all.

The Web of Deception

The flickering neon signs of Times Square cast a lurid glow on the rain-slicked streets as Sharon navigated the labyrinthine alleys. He felt the city's pulse—a chaotic rhythm of sirens, shouting, and the relentless hum of traffic—a fitting backdrop to his own frantic existence. He'd been back in New York for less than a week, the ghost of Manila clinging to him like a second skin, and already the city, his city, felt like a cage. The familiar scent of exhaust fumes and hot dogs did little to ease the knot of anxiety tightening in his chest.

Miriam had been the catalyst, the unexpected wrench thrown into the finely tuned machinery of his escape. He'd found her living in a cramped Brooklyn apartment, a stark contrast to the opulent life they'd once shared. Miriam—once the spoiled darling of her father's considerable wealth—now looked gaunt and haunted, her eyes reflecting the same fear he'd carried for years. She had a story, a desperate plea cloaked in cryptic pronouncements and veiled threats. It involved the Israeli mob, the Abergil family—the very organization he'd once served with brutal efficiency. She claimed they were after her, that she possessed information capable of shattering their empire. Information Sharon knew nothing about. Information she refused to divulge, except to whisper that it was connected to their father's mysterious death—a death ruled a suicide years ago but that Miriam vehemently believed was murder.

The details she did offer were enough to set Sharon's teeth on edge. Names, dates, locations—fragments of a puzzle he instinctively knew was far larger and far more dangerous than anything he had ever encountered. It spoke of a network of corruption stretching from the shadowy backrooms of New York's diamond district to the sun-drenched beaches of the Mediterranean, a web woven from greed, betrayal, and enough violence to stain a thousand streets crimson. The Abergil family wasn't just a petty crime syndicate; they operated with the precision and ruthlessness of a well-oiled machine, their influence extending into the highest echelons of power.

At first, he'd dismissed Miriam's claims as the ramblings of a desperate woman clinging to a semblance of her former life. But he'd seen the fear in her eyes, the genuine terror that resonated with his own ingrained sense of self-preservation. He'd seen the bruises—the evidence of a brutal beating—a warning. His loyalty, that twisted, familial bond, had overwhelmed his inherent caution. He was in too deep.

The Abergil family's reach extended far beyond the predictable. They weren't just involved in gambling and loan sharking; they were deeply entrenched in international arms dealing, laundering money on a scale that made governments tremble. Their influence bled into high-profile political scandals, safeguarded by layers of corruption that made uncovering the truth feel impossible.

Detective Tom Pickens, the man who haunted his dreams, was another piece of the puzzle. A ghost from Sharon's past. A relentless investigator with a personal vendetta, fueled by years of frustration and a shared history neither man could escape. Miriam's information, as scant as it was, painted Pickens as a pawn in a far larger game—a pawn the Abergil family was willing to sacrifice if it suited their long-term plans.

The nights blurred into a whirlwind of clandestine meetings in dimly lit bars, hurried exchanges in crowded streets, and the ever-present threat of betrayal. Sharon found himself juggling his own survival with the need to protect Miriam—a mission that threatened to consume him entirely. He moved like a phantom through the city's underbelly, a master of disguise, using every skill he had to stay one step ahead of the Abergil family's relentless pursuit. All the while, the shadow of Pickens loomed closer.

Each meeting peeled back another layer of deception. Informants—shadowy figures speaking in hushed tones, their faces obscured by darkness—fed him pieces of the truth. These were the city's whispers, the ones who knew its secrets. They hinted at betrayals, double-crosses, and hidden agendas, a tangled web so complex that even Sharon struggled to unravel it.

One meeting, arranged in a secluded corner of a dilapidated warehouse, unearthed a cache of documents—bank statements, coded messages, and photographs that exposed the true extent of the Abergil family's operations. The scale of their criminality was staggering. Their influence spanned continents, entangling politics, international trade, and high finance. The evidence pointed to a network so vast and insidious that it had the power to destabilize entire governments.

Another meeting, this time in a lavish penthouse overlooking Central Park, introduced him to an unassuming yet dangerous figure—a high-powered lawyer whose polished demeanor concealed a ruthless pragmatism. This man was more than just legal counsel; he was the family's fixer, the one who ensured their crimes remained buried beneath layers of legal maneuvering and bribery. The encounter left Sharon uneasy. He sensed an intelligence, a cunning so precise that one wrong move could turn the tables on him in an instant.

The stakes had never been higher. He was no longer just fighting for survival; he was fighting for the possibility of a life beyond the shadows. The weight of Miriam's fate, the relentless pursuit of the Abergil family, and the unwavering determination of Detective Pickens pressed down on him, threatening to crush him under their collective force. He began questioning everything, everyone. Was Miriam truly innocent, or was she a pawn in a larger game, a piece maneuvered by unseen hands? And Pickens—was he hunting Sharon, or was he, too, being manipulated by forces beyond his control?

Sleep became a luxury he could no longer afford. His existence narrowed to a constant state of vigilance, his senses honed to detect the slightest sign of danger. He moved from safe house to safe house, each one carefully chosen, each one a temporary refuge against the ever-present threat. His days blurred into a cycle of fleeting encounters, hurried phone calls, and the overwhelming sensation of being watched. The city itself seemed to turn against him, its shadows shifting into faceless pursuers, its sounds carrying whispers of his impending demise.

Then, one evening, a meeting with a former Abergil associate—a man whose loyalty was as fickle as the city's weather—revealed a buried truth. The Abergil family wasn't just operating within the realm of organized crime. They had forged an alliance with a branch of the Mossad, Israel's intelligence agency.

The revelation sent a chill down Sharon's spine. This wasn't just about crime; it was about espionage. The relentless pursuit wasn't merely a vendetta—it was an international power play. The implications were terrifying. He wasn't just up against a ruthless crime syndicate; he was entangled in a conspiracy that extended far beyond New York, reaching into the corridors of global power.

With each discovery, the danger escalated. He was no longer just a fugitive—he was a threat. A liability. The shadows of New York concealed their secrets well, but Sharon was starting to unearth them, and with every revelation, he inched closer to a truth that could change everything. The fight was far from over, and the stakes were higher than he had ever imagined.

International Manhunt

The humid New York air hung heavy, a suffocating blanket clinging to Sharon's skin. He had chosen the city for its anonymity, its swirling chaos a perfect camouflage. But the illusion of safety was crumbling faster than a cheap sugar cookie. The Moroccan betrayal, the brutal efficiency of the ambush, still echoed in his nightmares. The surgery in Manila had changed his face, but it hadn't erased the target on his back. Now, the Mossad was hunting him.

The first sign was subtle—a flicker of movement in his peripheral vision, a shadow that lingered too long. Then came the whispers, the hushed conversations in dimly lit bars, the unsettling feeling of being watched, analyzed, judged. He felt their gaze even in solitude, a chilling reminder of their relentless pursuit. He knew the Mossad. He had dealt with their kind before, back when he ran with the Abergil crew. Their reputation preceded them: meticulous, patient, utterly merciless. They wouldn't stop until he was dead. Or worse.

His apartment, a cramped space in a forgotten corner of Brooklyn, felt like a cage. Each creak of the floorboards, each rustle of wind outside, sent shivers down his spine. Sleep came in short, fitful bursts, his mind racing through the events that had led him to this moment. The betrayal in Marrakech. The frantic escape. The chance encounter with Ceta—the beautiful woman he had been forced to kill, another innocent life sacrificed in his brutal game. Guilt gnawed at him, but fear was the stronger motivator. Fear of capture. Fear of the Mossad's methods. Fear of what they would do to him if they found him.

He moved through the city like a phantom, every step calculated, every sense hyper-alert. The streets of New York, once familiar, now felt like a labyrinth of potential ambushes. He changed his routes, his routines, his haunts. Paranoia became second nature. He switched apartments frequently, relying on the network of contacts he had cultivated over the years—contacts he had never trusted until now. The whispers followed him like a persistent shadow, always just out of reach, yet undeniably close.

Detective Pickens added another layer of complexity to his predicament. The NYPD detective was relentless, a man who knew Sharon's past intimately. They had clashed before, their history tangled in a web of close calls and near misses. Pickens wasn't driven by personal vendetta—at least not entirely. He was a man of principle, a relentless seeker of justice, and that made him more dangerous than any mobster or intelligence operative. Pickens wouldn't stop. He couldn't be bribed, threatened, or distracted.

One evening, holed up in a dilapidated East Village bar, Sharon overheard two men talking about him. He couldn't catch every word, but the fragments he did hear chilled him: "...the surgeon in Manila... Abergil's... Mossad's already alerted..." His fears were confirmed. The Mossad was closing in. Their intelligence network was far-reaching, surgical in its precision. His carefully constructed facade was unraveling. He had to act.

His plan was reckless. Almost suicidal.

He had always been a master of improvisation, adept at twisting situations to his advantage. Now, he would leverage the conflict between the Mossad and the Abergil crew, playing them against each other. It was a dangerous game, a high-stakes gamble, but he had no choice. He knew the Mossad was efficient, but they weren't without weaknesses. Their resources were vast, but their actions were bound by regulations. Abergil's, on the other hand, had no such limits.

He started reaching out to old contacts, men from his days with Abergil's. Dangerous men, but men who understood the rules of the game. He offered them lucrative jobs, knowing they wouldn't refuse— even if it meant going against the Mossad. It was a calculated risk, but the alternative was worse: capture, torture, or a bullet in the dark.

Then, he began laying traps. Small, deliberate moves, just enough to throw off his pursuers. He left breadcrumbs—false leads, conflicting information—enough to overload the Mossad's intelligence channels. Enough to let them know that he was still a step ahead.

For now.

The game of cat and mouse intensified. Sharon would leave a package in a specific location, knowing it would be found. Sometimes, it contained nothing but a photograph or a scrap of paper with cryptic information—just enough to bait his pursuers, to keep them guessing. Each action was a calculated step, designed to manipulate them, to push them into reckless decisions. He used his deep knowledge of both sides—the Mossad's meticulous strategy and Abergil's brutal efficiency—to sew chaos in their ranks. Their own resources became his weapons, turning their pursuit into a tangled mess of confusion and infighting. He didn't have the patience to be cautious, nor the luxury of silence.

Days bled into nights, a blur of clandestine meetings, risky maneuvers, and near-misses. Sharon found himself forging uneasy alliances with people he once considered enemies. In the shadowy world of espionage and organized crime, loyalty was a fleeting illusion. One moment, an ally could be a lifeline; the next, they could be a traitor, selling him out for a better deal. Trust was a gamble he could no longer afford. He had to outthink, outmaneuver, and outlast them all.

He was no longer just running. He was fighting back.

Every move was a test of his cunning, every encounter a high-stakes gamble. But the toll was undeniable. The relentless pressure, the sleepless nights, the ever-present fear—it was grinding him down. He ran on adrenaline, on sheer willpower, knowing that his survival depended on staying ahead.

But for how long?

How long before the Mossad, or Pickens, or Abergil's finally caught up?

The question loomed over him, an unspoken threat that shadowed his every step. The game was far from over.

The international manhunt had only just begun.

A Game of Cat and Mouse

The city that never sleeps offered little refuge. For Sharon, it was a labyrinth of shadows, each alley a possible escape, each street corner a potential death trap. He moved like a ghost, his new face a mask over the hunted man beneath. But the Mossad, relentless as wolves, were closing in. He could feel them, an ever-present chill at his back, a reminder that freedom was fleeting.

His first instinct was to disappear. Manhattan's underbelly welcomed those who knew how to blend in. He frequented dimly lit bars where secrets were traded over cheap whiskey, where no one asked questions as long as you paid in cash. Burner phones, false identities, a different hotel every night—each stop a temporary sanctuary before moving again. He needed time. Time to anticipate the Mossad's next move. But time was a luxury he no longer had.

Meanwhile, Detective Tom Pickens was methodically assembling the puzzle of Sharon's movements. The trail was fractured, spanning continents, but Pickens thrived on impossible cases. From the surgically cleaned crime scene in Morocco to the hastily erased Manila hotel records, he followed the faintest traces—a silenced gunshot, a discarded passport, the ghost of a name scribbled on a ledger. He had before-and-after photos of Sharon, an unsettling testament to his ability to vanish and reinvent himself. The only thing missing was the man himself.

The first real encounter came in a dimly lit jazz club in Greenwich Village. Sharon, under yet another alias, nursed a drink, his senses attuned to the crowd. Then—movement. A familiar presence cutting through the smoky air. Pickens. He wasn't looking directly at Sharon, but he didn't need to. He was absorbing everything. Calculating. Closing in.

Sharon slipped out the back before Pickens could make a move, vanishing into the night like a wisp of smoke. He knew the city's hidden arteries—the alleys, the rooftops, the forgotten tunnels beneath its streets. He moved like a phantom. But Pickens had his own map of New York, built on informants, leverage, and the quiet power of his badge. He wasn't just chasing a ghost. He was hunting a predator.

The chase intensified, weaving through the city's living, breathing chaos. They crossed paths in Chinatown, where Sharon used a staged fight—a sudden outburst of flailing limbs and flying merchandise— to slip away in the confusion. Later, under a moonless sky in Central Park, he lurked in the shadows, watching Pickens stalk him in return. Every encounter was a calculated risk, a battle of nerves played out in silence.

The pressure was suffocating. Sharon's body screamed for rest, but adrenaline kept him moving. Exhaustion nipped at his heels like a second pursuer, just as relentless as the first.

For Pickens, the near-misses were fuel. Each lost opportunity only sharpened his resolve. Sharon was a living enigma, a puzzle with pieces scattered across the world. But no one ran forever without leaving a trail. And Pickens was patient.

The chase wasn't just physical; it was a war of minds. A cryptic message left on a burner phone. A coded phrase overheard in a bar. A fleeting glimpse of a familiar tattoo, barely visible beneath a cuffed sleeve. Each clue deepened the mystery of Sharon, drawing Pickens closer, step by step.

And the hunt was far from over.

The chase swept through the bustling streets of Brooklyn, the quiet elegance of the Upper East Side, and the gritty industrial corridors of Queens. Each location became a stage for their deadly ballet—every confrontation a heart-stopping exchange that left both men bloodied but unbowed. The city itself was no mere backdrop; it was a participant in their relentless game, its diverse landscape offering both refuge and relentless obstacles.

Sharon moved like a phantom, slipping through the city's veins with the ease of a shadow. He relied on instinct, street smarts, and an intimate knowledge of New York's hidden passageways, leaving behind only the faintest trace of his presence. Pickens, in contrast, wielded the full force of the city's resources. He tapped into informants, monitored phone lines, followed digital trails—his investigation a vast web, tightening with every passing moment.

Their encounters were a dance of shadows and whispers, a contest of calculated risks and lethal surprises. Sharon's edge lay in his agility, his cunning, and his ruthlessness. Pickens countered with experience, resources, and an unshakable determination. It was a collision of two worlds—the lawless underbelly and the unyielding machinery of justice—played out in the restless heart of a city that never slept.

The stakes were high, the consequences deadly. The game of cat and mouse, waged in the concrete jungle of New York, was far from over. The city, a silent witness to the unfolding drama, pulsed with the tension of the hunt. And as the chase continued, one question remained unanswered: who would prevail, the hunter or the hunted? The answer lay hidden in the shadows, waiting to be revealed.

Miriams Betrayal

The flickering neon signs of Times Square cast a lurid glow on the rain-slicked streets, mirroring the turmoil churning in Sharon's gut. He had agreed to meet Miriam at a secluded bar in Greenwich Village—a dive he had once frequented, back when his life had some semblance of control. He wasn't sure what he was hoping for. Answers? A thread of familial connection in the chaos? Or simply the reassurance of knowing what his sister was up to, what she knew. Whatever the case, this meeting was a risk—a calculated gamble he couldn't afford to lose. The Mossad's pursuit was relentless, a suffocating pressure that never eased. And Miriam, with her unpredictability, was a wild card.

The bar was dimly lit, the air thick with the acrid scent of stale beer and regret. Miriam was already there, hunched in a booth, her usual flamboyant style replaced by something muted, almost mournful. She looked older, wearier—her once-vibrant energy reduced to a fragile flicker.

"Sharon," she whispered, her voice raspy, as if she hadn't spoken in days.

He slid into the booth opposite her, the worn leather creaking beneath his weight. There was no time for pleasantries.

"What's going on, Miriam?" His voice was low, edged with urgency. "What do you know?"

She hesitated, her gaze fixed on the empty glass before her. "I know more than you think," she murmured, barely audible over the low hum of conversation. "I know about the Mossad. About their pursuit." She took a breath, steadying herself. "They're not just after you, Sharon. They're after us both."

The words hit like a cold blade to the spine.

His fingers curled into fists beneath the table. "What do you mean, 'us both'?"

Miriam swallowed hard. "I... I worked with them." The confession came out as a breath, barely there. "I've been feeding them information."

Silence.

The revelation slammed into him, a physical blow that stole his breath. He stared at her, struggling to reconcile the sister he'd trusted with the woman sitting before him now. Miriam—the one person who had always been on his side—had betrayed him.

The weight of it was suffocating. His trust, already fragile after the chaos in Manila and the relentless hunt in New York, shattered into a thousand jagged pieces.

"Why?" His voice was raw, thick with disbelief and something dangerously close to grief.

She looked away. "It started small," she admitted, her voice cracking. "They offered me protection. Money. I was desperate,

Sharon. You know how things were. How we were." She exhaled shakily. "I was afraid."

Fear. The word echoed through him like a haunting refrain.

He understood all too well. The years of struggle after their parents' deaths, the impossible choices, the ever-present threat of survival. He had always believed he was protecting her. But now, he realized, she had been making her own choices—ones with catastrophic consequences.

"Protection from what?" he pressed, his voice tight.

She hesitated, her expression clouded with something close to dread.

"From Abergil." The name was barely a whisper.

A cold dread crept into his bones. "They wanted me," he said, the realization sinking in like lead. "And you helped them."

Tears welled in her eyes. "I thought I could control it," she whispered. "That I could protect us both. If I gave them just enough information, I could buy us time." Her voice broke. "I was so stupid."

Sharon didn't respond immediately, letting the weight of her words settle like a stone in his chest. He had spent so long running from the Mossad that he had overlooked the danger lurking closest to him. He had been so consumed with hunting shadows that he hadn't realized one had been standing right beside him all along.

His voice, when he finally spoke, was devoid of emotion. A chilling calm. "What did you tell them?"

Miriam hesitated before launching into a painful confession. She detailed her meetings with her contact—a shadowy figure known only as "Agent Ezra"—a man who had earned her trust through veiled threats and quiet manipulations. She explained how, piece by piece, she had fed them information—his movements, his associates, his plans. Each whisper, each slip of information, a thread in the web they were weaving around him.

And now, that web was closing in.

Each detail was excruciating, every word a fresh wound tearing through his already battered soul. The betrayal wasn't just about information—it was about the violation of trust, the unraveling of a bond he had once thought unbreakable. Miriam, his sister, his only family, had become something else entirely.

An enemy.

A cold wave of anger surged through him, raw and all-consuming. He had faced death more times than he could count, endured violence and betrayal, but this—this was different. This was personal. This was blood.

When she finished her confession, silence settled between them, thick and suffocating. The only sound was the rhythmic clinking of glasses from the bar, a distant murmur of normalcy in a world that had just shifted beneath his feet. Sharon studied her face, etched with remorse and fear. He searched for the sister he once knew, the woman who had stood beside him through every storm. Instead, all he saw was a stranger—trapped, desperate, tangled in the web of her own making.

"So, what now?" Miriam's voice trembled. The question wasn't just about their next move. It was a plea, a fragile attempt to salvage something from the wreckage.

Sharon didn't answer immediately. His gaze drifted across the bar, the people around him reduced to shadows, ghosts of a life he no longer belonged to. He was alone now—truly alone. The Mossad was closing in, and Miriam's betrayal had only tightened the noose. The weight of it pressed down on him, suffocating, absolute.

"Now," he said finally, his voice low, dangerous, unyielding, "we survive."

The words were not just a statement but a promise. A threat. A vow.

The game wasn't over—it was only escalating. The hunt was intensifying, and with the twin burdens of betrayal and relentless pursuit on his shoulders, Sharon was preparing for the ultimate fight. Not just for survival. Not just to outrun those hunting him.

But for something deeper. For redemption. For a chance to reclaim even the smallest shred of what had been lost.

Outside, the city pulsed with the same relentless energy burning within him. A city as unforgiving as the world he inhabited. A city that never stopped moving, never stopped hunting.

And neither would he.

Explosive Confrontation

The air in the cramped, windowless apartment was thick with the metallic tang of gunpowder and the acrid scent of burnt plastic. Sharon, his face still raw from the recent surgery, worked with a chilling precision, his movements sharp, deliberate. He wasn't a bomb-maker by trade—not exactly—but years spent on the fringes of the underworld had made him an expert in improvisation and destruction.

Tonight, he was an architect of chaos.

His workbench, a battered kitchen table, was strewn with the makings of his deadly creation: a repurposed fire extinguisher, meticulously emptied and cleaned; a circuit board, painstakingly wired and rewired; a lump of C4 plastic explosive, its pale, putty-like consistency a stark contrast to the darkness of the room. Procuring the materials had taken weeks, each transaction a calculated risk, each contact from his Manila days a potential liability. But this wasn't just about survival anymore. This was about erasure. Oblivion.

Or at least, that's what he told himself.

He hummed under his breath, a low, almost imperceptible tune, the rhythm a counterpoint to the frantic beat of his heart. His hands moved with a surgeon's precision, measuring, cutting, sealing. He wasn't just assembling a bomb—he was crafting a masterpiece of destruction, an instrument fine-tuned for revenge. There was no room for error. One miscalculation, one misplaced wire, and he'd become nothing more than another piece of shrapnel.

The ticking clock on the wall mocked him, each second a reminder of the deadline closing in. Precision. Efficiency. No room for hesitation. No space for sentimentality. The lives of his enemies—the Mossad agents hunting him, the Abergil mobsters who had betrayed him, even Detective Pickens, relentless in his pursuit—were now reduced to mere variables in his equation. He wasn't just reacting. He was shaping the battlefield.

The detonator clicked into place. He sealed the compartment. The metallic clink echoed in the silence. Wrapping the device in duct tape, he transformed it into something unremarkable, something that wouldn't raise suspicion. Deception was an art, as crucial as the explosion itself. He'd spent a lifetime learning how to disappear. But this time, his disappearance wouldn't be silent. It would be spectacular—a final, fiery exclamation point in the chaos of his existence.

Stepping back, he surveyed his work. Beautiful. A testament to his cunning, his ruthlessness. A weapon designed not just to kill, but to dismantle—to burn everything to the ground.

The phone rang.

A sharp, jarring sound. His pulse spiked.

He hesitated, his hand hovering over the receiver. The number was unfamiliar. Another threat? A warning? Or had the Mossad finally caught up?

A shiver ran down his spine.

He couldn't afford to be caught off guard. Slowly, he answered. His voice, when it came, was cold. Controlled.

Betraying nothing.

The voice on the other end was smooth, almost hypnotic—a stark contrast to the storm brewing inside him. A woman's voice, laced with subtle menace.

"Sharon," she purred. "We have a problem. A rather large problem."

His hand instinctively went to the gun at his hip. He had been expecting the Mossad, but this was different. This was something else.

"What kind of problem?" he asked, his voice flat, controlled.

"Detective Pickens," she hissed. "He's closing in. He's onto your bomb. He's onto everything."

A cold dread settled over him. Pickens—the relentless, infuriating detective—was closing the gap. Sharon had spent weeks weaving his web of deception, crafting his perfect escape. And now, thread by thread, it was unraveling. He had underestimated Pickens's tenacity, his refusal to let go. Now, time was slipping through his fingers like sand in a broken hourglass.

"He doesn't know it's you yet," the woman continued, her voice smooth, urgent. "But he's getting close. We need to move. Now."

Sharon's mind worked fast. He had to act—quickly, ruthlessly. He couldn't let Pickens win. Not now. Not after everything.

"Where?" he asked, his voice tight.

"The docks," she said. "There's a boat waiting. Leave the bomb. It's not worth the risk anymore."

The idea of abandoning his creation, his masterpiece of destruction, sent a surge of fury through him. He had poured everything into that device—his rage, his vengeance, his need for control. But she was right. He couldn't risk capture. This wasn't the end. It was a setback. A shift in strategy. He had survived worse.

He exhaled sharply and hung up.

The bomb sat before him, heavy in his hands, a physical manifestation of his vendetta. His fingers tightened around it. This was power. This was destruction. And, for now, he had to let it go.

Shrugging into his worn leather jacket, he stepped out into the night. The rain fell steadily, washing away the traces of his work, erasing evidence but not consequence. The city, oblivious, churned around him. It had no idea of the war raging in its shadows, no clue that a ghost was moving through its streets, altering the course of fates with every step.

He disappeared into the dark.

The hunt wasn't over.

The game continued.

Pickens Closes In

The rain, a relentless curtain of grey, mirrored the mood in Detective Tom Pickens' mind like a mad pitbull waiting to be fed. He stared at the photograph— a grainy image of a man's back, the distinctive swagger gnawing at something deep inside him. It was from the security footage of the Chelsea bombing, the one that had nearly leveled an entire block and sent shockwaves through the city. The bomber, a phantom, had vanished into thin air, leaving behind only destruction and a chilling sense of impunity.

But Pickens felt a prickling certainty—he knew that gait, that way of holding himself. It echoed a memory, a phantom limb of a case long closed, a case that had haunted him for years.

He ran a hand through his already disheveled hair, his stubble scratching against his palm. The case files lay scattered across his desk, a chaotic tapestry of witness statements, crime scene photos, and cryptic intelligence reports. Each piece of the puzzle, painstakingly gathered, pointed toward a single, terrifying conclusion: the bombings, the assassinations, the seemingly unrelated acts of violence—they were all connected, all orchestrated by the same individual.

And that individual, he was growing increasingly convinced, was Sharon. The same Sharon who had vanished, leaving a trail of bodies and unanswered questions in his wake.

His phone buzzed, yanking him from his thoughts. It was Miller, his perpetually stressed-out informant. The man's voice was a low rasp on the other end of the line.

"Pickens, I got something. Remember that Moroccan connection we discussed? The one who disappeared after the Abergil hit?"

Pickens stiffened. He'd almost forgotten that lead, buried beneath the avalanche of recent bombings. "What about him?"

"He had a sister. Lives in New York. I think she's got some information—might know more about the whole Abergil thing than she lets on."

The pieces were falling into place with terrifying speed. Sharon, the notorious hitman, had seemingly vanished after his escape from Morocco, only to resurface in New York, leaving a trail of destruction in his wake. His ex-girlfriend, Miriam, now residing in the city, provided a crucial link.

Pickens felt a surge of adrenaline—a mixture of excitement and apprehension. This could be the break he needed, the key to unlocking the mystery surrounding Sharon's sudden reappearance and his reign of terror.

The address Miller provided was in a rundown section of Brooklyn, a warren of crumbling brownstones and dimly lit streets. Pickens arrived under the cover of darkness, the city's nocturnal symphony a discordant chorus of sirens and distant shouts. The building was dilapidated, its paint peeling—a testament to years of neglect. The air hung heavy with the smell of decay and desperation, a fitting backdrop to the grim business he was about to undertake.

He found Miriam's apartment on the third floor, the door slightly ajar. He hesitated, the weight of the situation pressing down on him. This wasn't just another suspect—this was Sharon's ex-girlfriend, a potential key to understanding the man he was hunting.

He pushed the door open, his gun drawn, his senses on high alert.

The apartment was small, sparsely furnished, the air thick with the scent of stale cigarettes and unwashed clothes.

Miriam sat at a small table, her face etched with worry, a half-empty glass of whiskey in front of her. She looked up as Pickens entered, her eyes widening in surprise—then narrowing in suspicion.

"Detective Pickens," she said, her voice low and husky. "What is the meaning of this?"

Pickens didn't waste time on pleasantries. "We know you're connected to Sharon. We know he's in the city. We have evidence linking him to the recent bombings."

Miriam's face remained impassive. "I don't know what you're talking about."

But her eyes betrayed her. The fear was palpable, laced with a hint of something else—perhaps guilt or regret.

Pickens pressed on, laying out the evidence he'd accumulated—the fragmented pieces of the puzzle slowly forming a coherent picture. He showed Miriam the photograph of the bomber's back, the one from the Chelsea attack. He spoke of the Moroccan connection, of Sharon's escape, his surgery, his return. He laid bare the trail of violence and destruction that had followed Sharon's shadowy path across continents. The story unfolded—a grim narrative of betrayal, vengeance, and the relentless pursuit of justice.

As the hours passed, Miriam's facade of denial crumbled. The weight of her silence, the burden of her knowledge, became too much to bear. She confessed—not willingly, but under the steady pressure of Pickens' relentless questioning and the crushing weight of guilt.

Her confession painted a more complex portrait of Sharon than Pickens had imagined. She spoke of a past riddled with violence and trauma, of a man driven to extremes by betrayal and an insatiable thirst for revenge. She revealed details of Sharon's connections, his network of accomplices, the hidden agendas that shaped his actions. She spoke of the Abergil mob, the simmering conflict that fueled Sharon's bloody enterprise, and the web of deceit and conspiracy that stretched far beyond New York.

With each revelation, Pickens felt the net tightening around Sharon. He pieced together the fragments of Miriam's confession, cross-referencing them with the evidence he had already gathered. Sharon's movements were mapped out. His next target was in sight. His ultimate goal was within reach.

The information Miriam provided led Pickens to a derelict warehouse on the docks, a place shrouded in darkness and the scent of salt and decay. He arrived with a SWAT team, the night alive with the hum of helicopter blades and the nervous anticipation of the impending confrontation. The warehouse loomed before them, a monolithic structure of shadows and secrets. This was it—the final showdown, the climax of a relentless pursuit.

Inside, the air hung thick with the acrid scent of gunpowder and sweat. Sharon was there, surrounded by his arsenal, ready for a fight to the death. The confrontation was brutal—a violent ballet of gunfire and close-quarters combat. The warehouse became a battlefield, the cacophony of gunshots and shattering glass amplifying the ferocity of the fight.

Pickens fought with the desperation of a man who had hunted a ghost for too long, fueled by years of frustration and a deep-seated need for justice. He wasn't just fighting to apprehend Sharon—he was fighting to put an end to the carnage, to bring closure to the bloody saga that had haunted him for so long. The battle was relentless, a test of endurance, skill, and sheer willpower.

In the end, justice prevailed—but not without a heavy cost.

The warehouse fell silent, the only sound the ragged breathing of the survivors. Sharon was finally brought to justice. The city, at last, breathed a collective sigh of relief. But it would forever bear the scars of his reign of terror, a chilling reminder of the consequences of unchecked violence.

Outside, the rain continued to fall, washing away the blood—but not the memories.

The night, however, belonged to Pickens—a quiet victory in the heart of unrelenting chaos. The hunt was over, but the scars remained, etched deep within both the city and the soul of the detective.

Executing Contracts

The humid Manila air hung heavy, thick with the scent of exhaust fumes and frying street food. Sharon, his face still raw from the recent surgery, felt the familiar chill of fear despite the oppressive heat. He had escaped Morocco, shed his old skin in the Philippines, but the shadow of the Abergil mob, the gnawing hunger of revenge, and the relentless pursuit of Detective Pickens clung to him like a shroud.

He needed money. Lots of it. And the only way to get it was to do what he did best: execute contracts.

His contact, a wiry man named Kai, spoke in clipped, almost inaudible whispers as he led Sharon to a dimly lit backroom of a karaoke bar, where the off-key strains of a Filipino pop song drifted through cigarette smoke and the cloying sweetness of cheap perfume. Kai slid a photograph across a sticky table.

The picture showed a portly man in a silk suit, his face etched with the arrogance of wealth and ill-gotten power.

"Mr. Hernandez," Kai murmured. "He owes some people a lot of money. They want him… persuaded… to pay."

The unspoken threat lingered in the air. Hernandez wasn't just a debtor—he was a stepping stone, a necessary evil on Sharon's path to securing the funds he needed to disappear completely. The price was high, but it was enough. Enough to buy his way into anonymity, to vanish beyond the reach of Mossad, Pickens, and the ghosts of his past.

A Dance with Death

The following weeks blurred into a whirlwind of violence and fleeting moments of respite. Sharon's new face was a mask, shielding his true identity, but it couldn't hide the cold precision in his eyes or the lethal grace of his movements. Each contract was a dance with death, a meticulously choreographed ballet of brutality.

He moved like a phantom, a whisper in the night, leaving behind only a trail of shattered lives and unanswered questions.

One target, a corrupt politician, was found slumped over his mahogany desk, a single, perfectly placed bullet hole in his temple. Another, a drug lord, had his opulent penthouse transformed into a grotesque crime scene, the air thick with the metallic tang of blood. Sharon worked swiftly, efficiently, leaving no trace of his presence— except for the chilling evidence of his deadly expertise.

The work was brutal, soul-crushing. But it paid handsomely.

With each kill, he felt himself slipping deeper into the abyss, the moral compass that once guided him now shattered beyond repair. He justified his actions as necessary, a means to an end, a path to redemption. But the line between right and wrong had long since blurred into nothingness.

The Hunter Draws Near

Meanwhile, in New York, Detective Pickens was assembling the scattered fragments of Sharon's bloody trail. He had traced the Manila connection, recognizing the unmistakable signature of Sharon's modus operandi—the precise placement of the bullet, the meticulous crime scene cleanups, the almost artistic flair of execution.

Sharon wasn't just a hired gun. He was a ghost. A phantom haunting the underbelly of the criminal world.

Pickens' investigation intensified, each revelation adding to his growing sense of dread. He uncovered the link between the victims, the common thread tying them to the Abergil mob and its far-reaching tendrils. He delved into Sharon's past, unearthing old files, interrogating informants, piecing together a dark tapestry of betrayal, vengeance, and relentless violence.

He saw the pattern. The rhythm of Sharon's actions.

And he knew he was getting closer.

But Sharon was always one step ahead.

The constant threat of discovery gnawed at Sharon's nerves. He was a master of deception, but the feeling of being watched, of unseen eyes tracking his every move, refused to fade. The long arm of the law—and the even longer reach of Mossad—were closing in. He could feel it. The weight of his past, the burden of his sins, pressed down on him, a relentless force threatening to crush him beneath its immense pressure.

In the midst of this chaos, Sharon found a strange solace in the solitude of his Manila apartment. He often stared at his reflection, barely recognizing the man who stared back. The surgery had changed his face, but it hadn't erased the darkness in his eyes—the haunted look of a man who had taken too many lives, endured too many betrayals.

One night, as he meticulously cleaned his weapons—a ritual that both calmed and unsettled him—his phone vibrated. A cryptic message from Kai.

A new contract. A different kind of target.

This one was personal.

Kai sent him a photograph. The gaunt, menacing face staring back at him sent a chill down Sharon's spine. A face synonymous with treachery and despair. The man who had orchestrated his betrayal in Marrakech.

This wasn't about money. This was vengeance.

The location: a secluded villa overlooking the South China Sea. The target: well-guarded, well-connected, and utterly ruthless. This wasn't just another job—it was a suicide mission. But the chance to settle the score, to finally confront his betrayer, was too tempting to ignore.

The Hunt for Retribution

Sharon's preparation was meticulous. He studied the villa's layout, memorized security patterns, calculated every angle, every possible contingency. He checked and rechecked his weapons, ensuring perfection. A strange calm settled over him—a cold detachment that was both unsettling and empowering.

The night of the operation arrived, draped in a storm's fury. The wind howled like a banshee, waves crashed against the shore in a deafening roar. Lightning split the sky, illuminating the villa in macabre brilliance.

Sharon moved through the night like a shadow, silent and swift. A ghost. A wraith. A harbinger of death.

The confrontation was swift, brutal, decisive.

His target fought, but Sharon was faster, deadlier. Every move was precise, honed to a razor's edge. He showed no mercy, gave no quarter. His enemy's final breath was barely a whisper against the storm.

As he slipped from the villa, his mission accomplished, he expected satisfaction. Instead, he felt nothing.

Vengeance had lifted its weight from his shoulders, only to leave behind a gaping void.

The Final Reckoning

Back in his apartment, amidst the chaos of his thoughts, Sharon's phone buzzed again.

Urgent.

Pickens was closing in.

The detective had uncovered enough evidence to link him to the recent murders. The net was tightening. The escape Sharon had so meticulously planned was unraveling before his eyes.

His blood-soaked path was leading him toward a final, devastating confrontation.

And this time, there would be no easy escape.

The Price of Revenge

The humid Manila night pressed down—a suffocating blanket woven from sweat and the stench of decay. Sharon, his newly sculpted face still tender, felt the phantom itch of his old scars. The surgery had been brutal, a testament to the lengths he'd gone to erase himself, to outrun the Abergil mob and the relentless pursuit of Detective Pickens. But the phantom pain was nothing compared to the burning rage that consumed him. Revenge. It gnawed at his insides, hollowing him out, leaving only desperation in its wake.

His first target was Ezra, the mole who had betrayed him in Morocco. He had tracked Ezra to a seedy casino in Makati—a den of iniquity glittering with false promises and cheap thrills. Once, Ezra had been like a brother. Now, he was nothing more than a bloated carcass, oblivious to the doom creeping toward him. From the shadows, Sharon watched, a predator studying its prey. Ezra, lost in a poker game, exuded complacency. The irony wasn't lost on Sharon— the betrayer was about to be betrayed.

The killing was swift, precise. A silenced pistol. A single shot to the temple. Ezra crumpled onto the table, cards scattering across the green felt like autumn leaves in the wind. The other players froze, their shock melting into a cacophony of screams and curses. But Sharon was already gone, swallowed by the labyrinthine streets before the police sirens even began their mournful wail. The taste of blood—metallic, bitter—clung to him, a grim reminder of what he had become.

His next target was David, the enforcer who had led the hit squad in the Marrakech souk. David had been harder to find. He had vanished into the teeming anonymity of Manila's underbelly, a ghost drifting through the city's neon-lit shadows. Sharon had to resort to unorthodox methods, calling in favors from the criminal underworld. The information came at a price—a debt owed to a ruthless gang leader, a bargain that would come back to haunt him. But it led him to David, deep inside a secluded cockfighting arena, his hands slick with sweat and blood, reveling in the violent spectacle.

This time, Sharon chose a different approach. He didn't want a quick, silent execution. He wanted David to suffer—to understand the agony he had inflicted. Sharon waited until the fight ended, the air thick with the stench of blood and feathers, then approached as David counted his winnings. A single, deliberate stab to the throat. A slow, precise cut. Blood gushed in warm torrents as David gurgled, choking on his own life. The look in his eyes—terror, disbelief—was a gruesome masterpiece, a portrait of vengeance painted in red.

The killings weren't just about revenge; they were about survival. Every body he left behind was a loose end tied up, a threat neutralized. Each death bought him time, delaying the inevitable confrontation with the Abergil mob and the ever-tightening grip of Detective Pickens. But with every life he took, Sharon felt himself slipping further into the abyss. The darkness was seductive, a siren song luring him into the depths. He was losing himself, becoming the very monster he had once fought to escape.

His next target was Rebecca—the mastermind, the architect of his downfall. She was a shadow moving through the corridors of power, always a step ahead. Finding her required patience, cunning, and deception. Weeks of relentless surveillance, meticulous digging, and ruthless manipulation led him to her weaknesses—her love for opulence, her insatiable hunger for excess.

Sharon infiltrated one of her high-society gatherings, posing as a wealthy businessman. The event was an orgy of wealth and decadence, a spectacle of power draped in silk and diamonds. He watched from a distance, studying her. Rebecca was a viper in human skin, her smile a mask concealing the poison beneath. The opportunity came in a moment of chaos—a flicker of distraction, a ripple in the crowd. In a single, practiced motion, he slipped a small, meticulously crafted explosive device into her handbag.

The explosion was a sudden, brutal punctuation mark to a night of opulence. The blast ripped through the room, scattering debris and bodies like discarded toys. Rebecca's screams were lost in the ensuing pandemonium.

From a safe distance, Sharon watched the chaos unfold, his heart pounding like a war drum. He had chosen a method that was both efficient and theatrical—a fitting end for the woman who had orchestrated his near demise. The night dissolved into a symphony of sirens and the desperate cries of the injured. Then, like a ghost, he vanished into the darkness, leaving behind a trail of destruction.

Revenge was a bitter medicine. It did not bring back what he had lost, did not restore the peace he yearned for or the trust he had once held sacred. It only left him emptier, more alone, more hunted than ever. Satisfaction was fleeting—a brief, hollow catharsis before the grim reality of his existence crashed down upon him. He was still running, still pursued, still drowning in a sea of blood and betrayal. The price of vengeance was steep, measured in lives and the slow erosion of his own soul.

His escape from Manila was fraught with peril. The police were closing in, his bloody trail too conspicuous to be fully concealed. The Abergil mob was still hunting him, their reach stretching across continents. The streets, once his refuge, had become a treacherous maze where every shadow harbored danger. Desperation forced his hand; he secured passage on a cargo ship, a risky gamble. The ship's cramped, stifling hold became his prison, a steel tomb rattling over the waves. The voyage was agonizing—a slow, silent journey into the unknown.

He arrived in New York, a city of shadows and secrets. It both beckoned and repelled him, its familiar streets a bittersweet reminder of the life he had abandoned. He reached out to Miriam, his sister—a woman he had always felt conflicted about. Their bond was a tangled knot of loyalty and resentment. Miriam knew of his past, but she had always kept her distance—perhaps out of fear, perhaps out of self-preservation. Now, he needed her help, a lifeline in the raging storm.

Their reunion was tense, a fragile truce in a world where trust was a dying currency. Miriam provided him with a safe house, a temporary refuge from both the authorities and the vengeful specter of the Abergil mob. Yet even within her walls, Sharon felt the weight of unseen eyes. The Mossad. He could feel them lurking, watching, waiting. The past, relentless and insidious, refused to let him go. His refuge was nothing more than a pause before the next inevitable storm.

The price of revenge had been exacted in blood and suffering. Sharon was a ghost in his own life, forever looking over his shoulder, forever running. The trail of destruction he had left behind would never fade, a grim testament to the choices that had led him here. His descent into darkness was complete; the abyss had claimed him, leaving only a broken, bitter shell of the man he once was. But the game was far from over. The final confrontation loomed—a reckoning that would determine not just his fate, but the fate of everyone ensnared in his violent wake. The cycle of bloodshed was unbroken, a relentless storm threatening to consume him whole.

Pickens Investigation Deepens

The stale air in Pickens' office felt heavy, thick with the weight of unsolved cases and the lingering scent of cheap coffee. He stared at the Manila police report, the grainy photograph of Ceta's lifeless body mocking him with its unsettling stillness. The initial report had been vague—just another homicide, a case the local authorities seemed content to bury. But Pickens had a gut feeling, that nagging suspicion that this was no ordinary street killing, and it drove him to dig deeper.

He had spent weeks poring over Interpol files, chasing shadows, following tenuous leads that often led to dead ends. The details were scant, frustratingly so—a beautiful woman found in a cheap Manila hotel, a single gunshot wound to the head, no witnesses, no obvious motive. But Pickens refused to let it go. Something about the case resonated with the fragmented information he already possessed concerning Sharon's movements.

He traced the path of Sharon's supposed escape from Morocco, focusing on the points of contact and the potential intersections of their paths. Each new piece of evidence felt like a tiny stone added to a vast, intricate mosaic—one that was slowly coming into focus, revealing a disturbing picture of a man who seemed to be a phantom, yet a phantom with a considerable blood trail.

The first breakthrough came from an unexpected source—a customs manifest listing a shipment of high-grade surgical instruments to a Manila clinic specializing in reconstructive surgery. The timing coincided almost exactly with Sharon's supposed presence in the city. The clinic was discreet, catering to a wealthy clientele who valued privacy above all else. When Pickens secured a warrant to search their records, he found the name Elias Vance—a fabricated identity that matched Sharon's description. The trail was scorching hot.

Next, he delved into the records of the Abergil Israeli mob, sifting through mountains of intelligence reports, financial transactions, and coded communications. Abergil's records detailed a brutal hit team of specialists—a meticulously trained group of assassins. Among their operatives, one name stood out: "Serpent"—a master strategist and marksman, rumored to be their deadliest asset.

Pickens recalled a cryptic reference in an old case file about a failed assassination attempt on a minor politician in Tel Aviv. The only witness, an aging security guard, had described the assassin as having strikingly cold eyes and the precise, deliberate movements of a dancer. This detail resonated with descriptions given by Sharon's former associates—individuals Pickens had painstakingly tracked down. The connection was tentative but powerful. Serpent and Sharon—were they one and the same? The circumstantial evidence was mounting.

He turned his focus to Sharon's known associates—the small circle of individuals who could have helped him escape, secure a new identity, and undergo surgery. Each interview was a tense dance, a delicate balancing act between intimidation and persuasion. Pickens used every tool at his disposal, from old-fashioned legwork to sophisticated forensic analysis. Every contact yielded a piece of the puzzle, another fragment of the truth.

One associate mentioned a rendezvous in a seedy Manila bar, a haunt for low-level operatives and informants. Pickens located the place—a dimly lit, smoke-filled den of iniquity—and spent a night there, mingling with the clientele, gathering whispers and rumors. He learned that Sharon, or Elias Vance, as he was known there, was more than just a skilled killer—he was a master manipulator, able to charm and intimidate with equal ease.

That information led Pickens to another hotel, one where Sharon had allegedly stayed—not the one where Ceta had been found. This revelation unlocked another breakthrough.

The second hotel room offered a different perspective. It was sparsely furnished, yet its meticulous cleanliness betrayed a fastidious nature—a stark contrast to the chaotic life the man led. But it was what was missing that intrigued Pickens the most.

There were no personal effects. No photographs. No mementos. Nothing to suggest a permanent residence. The room felt sterile, almost clinical, as if it were a temporary staging area for a larger operation.

Then, Pickens found something that made his blood run cold.

Buried in the trash—carefully wiped down and nearly impossible to detect—were remnants of what appeared to be bomb components. Small traces of chemicals and wiring. The precision suggested careful planning, not recklessness. And worse, it bore chilling similarities to another case—the bombing of a high-profile business magnate's offices earlier this year.

The realization settled like a weight in his chest.

Sharon wasn't just a ghost—he was a ghost with a plan.

Pickens delved deeper into the financial records of the businesses Sharon had frequented—small, insignificant transactions that, when pieced together, revealed a pattern of suspicious activity. He uncovered a complex web of shell corporations, offshore accounts, and coded messages, all pointing to a conspiracy that stretched far beyond Sharon's crimes.

A series of wire transfers traced back to accounts linked to the Abergil mob, funneled through seemingly legitimate businesses with direct ties to influential politicians. The scale of the operation was staggering. This wasn't just about Sharon. He was a pawn in a far greater, far more dangerous game.

The pieces were beginning to fit together, though the full picture remained elusive. Pickens saw a trail of deception—a labyrinthine scheme of carefully orchestrated assassinations and bombings. Someone, possibly a shadowy organization, had been pulling the strings, using Sharon as an expendable tool. The woman in Manila, Ceta, was likely a casualty of Sharon's paranoia—just another loose end to be eliminated. This wasn't a simple revenge plot. This was a well-oiled machine of organized crime, spanning continents—from the shadowy alleyways of Manila to the bustling streets of New York, its tendrils wrapped around political corruption and international syndicates.

The investigation had transformed, evolving from a straightforward murder case into something vast, dangerous, and deeply unsettling.

It became a brutal mental marathon. Sleep was a luxury Pickens couldn't afford. Days bled into nights, fueled by cheap coffee and the relentless pursuit of justice. He'd lost count of the hours spent poring over documents, analyzing data, and chasing leads—most of them leading to dead ends. The pressure was immense. The stakes, impossibly high.

Each new discovery only deepened the mystery, unraveling more layers of deception, revealing a complexity that was both fascinating and terrifying. He was walking a tightrope—on one side, capturing a deadly criminal; on the other, stepping straight into the crosshairs of a powerful, ruthless organization. This wasn't just about Sharon anymore. This was about dismantling a network of corruption that reached the highest levels of power.

But Pickens knew he was getting close.

He could feel it in his bones, in the tightening net around Sharon.

The evidence was overwhelming—each thread leading back to him. Sharon was Serpent. He was tied to Ceta's murder, to the bombing attempt, to a string of crimes spanning multiple continents. The shell corporations, the offshore accounts, the carefully crafted lies—it all pointed to the same man.

Pickens had built a case that was as airtight as it was dangerous.

And now, he was ready to bring Sharon in—even if it meant risking his own life.

The final confrontation was looming—a brutal, inevitable clash of wills that would determine not just justice, but survival. The game was far from over. And as the truth finally came into focus, one thing became clear:

It was far more terrifying than Pickens had ever imagined.

A Desperate Alliance

The flickering neon sign of the Manila dive bar cast a lurid glow on the rain-slicked streets. Inside, the air hung thick with the smell of stale beer and desperation. Sharon, his face still raw from recent surgery, nursed a lukewarm San Miguel, his gaze constantly scanning the room. He was a ghost, a phantom flitting through the city's underbelly—always looking over his shoulder, forever on the run. The Mossad was relentless, their shadow stretching across continents, their reach extending further than he had ever imagined.

His new face was a mask, a carefully crafted illusion, but the fear—the ever-present, gnawing dread—was etched in his eyes. The Manila killing, Ceta's lifeless face, burned into his memory. He hadn't intended to kill her, but the risk she posed was too great. She had seen too much. He had no choice.

A shadow fell across his table. He didn't flinch, his hand instinctively reaching for the small, easily concealed pistol tucked into his waistband. He looked up, his eyes narrowing as he assessed the newcomer.

It was a woman, older than he had expected, her face etched with the harsh lines of a life lived on the edge. But her eyes held a surprising spark of intelligence, a glint of cunning that mirrored his own.

"Serpent," she said, her voice a low, husky whisper, the name dripping with a familiarity that sent a chill down his spine.

He knew then—his name had been leaked. Some betrayal he hadn't foreseen. The game was changing.

"You know who I am," he replied, his voice a gravelly rasp, his own name—Sharon—a forgotten relic of a past life.

"Everyone knows who Serpent is," she said, a wry smile playing on her lips. "Or rather, everyone who's still alive knows."

She introduced herself as Isabella—a name that sounded as sharp and dangerous as a shattered bottle. She was a fixer, she explained, a woman who dealt in secrets and shadows, arranging disappearances, orchestrating transactions, and smoothing out the rough edges of the underworld. She had heard about him—about his skills, his ruthlessness, his uncanny ability to vanish without a trace. And she needed his help.

"And what makes you think I'd help you?" Sharon asked, his suspicion unwavering.

Isabella chuckled, a dry, brittle sound. "Mutual interest, my dear Serpent. We both have enemies in high places—enemies who wouldn't hesitate to eliminate us if given the chance. Working together, we can protect each other, make each other stronger."

She laid out her proposition. A rival organization—the Triad— was encroaching on her territory, threatening her lucrative operations. She needed someone to send a message. A message that would be both brutal and unforgettable. Someone like Serpent.

Sharon remained silent for a long moment, weighing his options. He was a fugitive, hunted by the Mossad and the Manila police, his every move shadowed by danger. An alliance, however tenuous, offered a temporary respite—a chance to consolidate his position, to gain leverage. But trust was a dangerous commodity in this world, and Isabella, despite her air of competence, was still a stranger.

"What's in it for me?" he finally asked, his voice betraying none of the turmoil raging within him.

"Information," Isabella replied. "Information about the people who betrayed you in Morocco. Information that could lead you to your revenge."

That struck a chord—a deep resonance that transcended even his immediate need for survival. The betrayal in Morocco, the ambush that had nearly cost him his life, burned with raw intensity, fueling his every action. He craved vengeance, a hunger that consumed him, clouding his judgment, driving him to recklessness.

"Tell me about your target," Sharon said, a flicker of grim determination in his eyes.

Isabella described her enemy—a ruthless Triad leader known only as *The Dragon*. She provided details of his movements, his security, his weaknesses. Her plan was meticulous, demonstrating a level of expertise that matched—or perhaps even exceeded—Sharon's own.

Over the next few weeks, Sharon and Isabella worked together, an uneasy partnership forged in the crucible of mutual need. Their alliance was built on pragmatic self-interest, not friendship or loyalty.

They were two predators sharing a kill, their bond as fragile as ice on a frozen lake.

Sharon eliminated The Dragon with his usual brutal efficiency. The Triad suffered a devastating blow—their operations disrupted, their power weakened.

Yet even as he worked alongside Isabella, Sharon remained wary. He observed her every move, listened to her every word, always aware of the possibility of betrayal. This was a temporary truce, a fleeting respite before the inevitable storm. Isabella, in turn, watched him just as closely, assessing his strengths, calculating the risks. The air between them crackled with unspoken tension—a silent acknowledgment of the precarious nature of their partnership.

The information Isabella provided about the Morocco betrayal was scant but significant. It pointed to an inside man—a mole within the Abergil organization. The path to revenge was long and arduous, but now Sharon had a new direction, a new target.

As they celebrated their victory, sipping expensive whiskey in a hidden bar far from the city's clamor, a quiet understanding passed between them. They would continue working together—for now. But both knew the alliance was built on shifting sands, liable to collapse at any moment. Each kept a watchful eye on the other, ready to strike if the need arose.

The world of assassins was treacherous, full of shifting alliances and inevitable betrayals. Survival demanded constant vigilance, ruthless pragmatism, and a healthy dose of paranoia. The taste of victory was sweet, but its aftertaste was bitter—a lingering reminder that trust was a luxury neither could afford.

The path ahead remained uncertain, fraught with danger. The game, however, was far from over. The shadows still lengthened, and new enemies lurked within them, their motives hidden in the darkness.

Ticking Clock

The humid Manila air hung heavy, a suffocating blanket clinging to Sharon's skin. Sweat beaded on his forehead—not entirely from the oppressive heat. The ticking clock of his bomb plot was his own personal guillotine, each second a blade dropping closer to his neck.

Three days.

Three days until the meticulously crafted device—a masterpiece of destruction disguised as an innocuous package—was set to detonate in the heart of the New York diamond district. Three days to execute a plan so intricate, so audacious, it made even Sharon pause and question his own sanity.

He stared at the crude map spread across the stained Formica tabletop in his dingy hotel room. The hastily scribbled ink lines mapped out delivery routes, security checkpoints, and escape paths. He had studied it countless times, memorized every detail, every potential pitfall. Yet the closer the deadline loomed, the more the lines blurred, the more the plan seemed to unravel in his mind.

Doubt, a rare and unwelcome visitor, crept in.

It was a luxury he couldn't afford, a poison that could paralyze him, turning him into a sitting duck. He had spent years operating in the shadows, moving with the precision of a phantom. But this operation was different. This wasn't a simple assassination—this was an act of war. The target wasn't a single individual; it was an entire system, a vast and powerful network of organized crime that had wronged him in ways he could never forgive.

He ran a hand through his still-healing hair, wincing slightly at the tug. The facial reconstruction had left him with a phantom ache, a constant reminder of the brutality of his escape from Morocco—the betrayal that had almost cost him his life. He thought of Ceta, her beautiful face now forever erased, a casualty of his own ruthless pragmatism. The memory sat like a cold, heavy stone in his gut, a constant reminder of the price of survival.

His phone buzzed, shattering the silence.

It was his contact, a shadowy figure known only as *Viper.* Even over the encrypted line, his voice was a raspy whisper.

"Everything is in place, Sharon," Viper murmured, his tone laced with the cold precision of a professional. "The package is ready. The delivery team is ready. You just need to—" He paused, the silence stretching, amplifying the tension. "You just need to pull the trigger."

"And if something goes wrong?" Sharon's voice was a low growl, barely audible over the hum of the air conditioner.

"There's always a risk. That's the nature of the game. But we've covered all our bases. Your escape route is clear. There's very little room for error. The timing is everything." Viper's voice remained chillingly calm, a stark contrast to the volatile situation. "Three days, remember? The clock is ticking."

Sharon slammed the phone down, the sharp sound echoing in the cramped room. He needed a drink—something to clear his head, to push back the rising tide of anxiety. He had to focus. Panic was a luxury he couldn't afford.

He poured two shots of cheap whiskey and downed them in quick succession, the burn a fleeting comfort against the icy grip of fear. He had to regain his composure before making another crucial decision.

He took a slow breath and began mentally listing everything again—the risks and rewards, the pros and cons, the escape routes and contingency plans. He revisited each step of the operation, meticulously reviewing the details he had spent weeks perfecting.

The choreography of chaos had to be flawless.

If he wanted to walk away from this mission alive, there was no room for error.

The escape plan was as crucial as the bomb itself. Sharon wasn't just up against the organization—ruthless, meticulous, and well-connected—he had Mossad on his trail. Planting the bomb was only half the battle. Surviving was the real challenge.

He dissected every possible failure, every complication. What if the delivery team was compromised? What if the bomb was discovered before detonation? What if the escape route collapsed? The possibilities spiraled into a vortex of paranoia, but Sharon forced himself to stay calm. He had contingency plans for every scenario, backups for his backups. Improvisation was second nature, but even he couldn't account for every variable.

Years in the shadows had given him an intricate understanding of the criminal underworld—the shifting alliances, the betrayals, the silent power struggles. His network spanned continents, built on favors, leverage, and whispered promises. But trust was a currency easily devalued, and even the most loyal contacts could be turned. This mission demanded absolute precision. One mistake meant death.

As night settled over Manila, Sharon stood by the window, staring at the chaotic sprawl of the city. Neon lights flickered like dying stars, each one a life moving obliviously forward, unaware of the catastrophe he was orchestrating half a world away. The air smelled of gasoline and street food, an intoxicating mix of life and decay.

Time was slipping away.

The weight of the detonation pressed down on him, every second a reminder of the consequences of failure. Sweat gathered at his temples—not just from the heat, but from the knowledge that the abyss was closer than ever. His life balanced on the edge of a knife, the final outcome still unwritten.

He picked up his phone. Dialed a number he hadn't called in years.

"Miriam." His voice was barely a whisper. "I need your help."

His estranged sister. The woman he had once trusted, then lost in a web of betrayals and unspoken wounds. He had sworn to keep her out of his world, but now, she was his only hope.

The conversation was brief, cloaked in coded words and hurried assurances. He explained what he could, leaving the most dangerous details unsaid. He was taking a risk, handing her a secret that could destroy them both. But she listened, and when she spoke again, her voice was tight with fear and something else—grim determination.

She agreed to help.

For the first time in weeks, a sliver of hope cut through the suffocating dread. It was fragile, as fragile as the bond between them, but it was something. With Miriam on his side, the fight felt less lonely. The game was far from over, the path ahead riddled with danger, but resolve hardened in his chest. The final countdown had begun.

The next two days blurred into motion.

Sharon moved like a ghost through the city, coordinating with Viper's team, verifying every detail, ensuring no loose ends. He checked and rechecked, each contingency plan honed to perfection. There was no room for error. Sleep became a distant memory, replaced by adrenaline and cheap coffee.

Failure meant death—not just for him, but for Miriam.

And then there was Ceta. Her face haunted him, a silent accusation carved into his mind. She had been a casualty of his choices, of his ruthless pragmatism. Her absence burned. But he couldn't let that pain slow him down.

The organization had stolen everything from him. Now, he would return the favor.

His war wasn't just about vengeance. It was about survival. About finally breaking free from the past that had bound him for too long.

But he knew one thing: justice—real justice—might cost him more than he was willing to pay.

The clock kept ticking. Each second a hammer blow. Each breath a step closer to the final reckoning.

Unveiling the Mastermind

The air hung thick and suffocating in the dimly lit warehouse, the only illumination coming from a single bare bulb dangling precariously from the ceiling. Sweat beaded on Sharon's forehead, mingling with the grime clinging to his newly acquired face. The scent of decay—a peculiar blend of rotting wood and stale seawater—filled his nostrils. A familiar knot of tension coiled in his stomach, sharpened by the knowledge that tonight, everything would change.

For weeks, he had been piecing together fragments of a vast, insidious conspiracy, a game orchestrated by shadowy figures pulling strings across continents. He had eliminated Ceta, a necessary evil, and navigated the treacherous waters of his relationship with Miriam, a woman as unpredictable as she was dangerous. He had played cat and mouse with Detective Pickens, whose relentless pursuit was as much a personal vendetta as it was a quest for justice. And through it all, one chilling question had echoed in his mind: Who was pulling the strings?

The answer, he now realized, stood before him.

A low, guttural cough broke the silence. From the shadows, a figure emerged, silhouetted against the flickering bulb. He was tall and imposing, his face etched with the lines of a life spent in darkness. But his eyes held a chilling brilliance, a spark of cold intelligence that sent a shiver down Sharon's spine. This was it—the culmination of months of running, killing, and deceiving. This was the man behind the web of betrayal that had ensnared him.

"Shalom, Sharon," the man said, his voice a low rumble that seemed to vibrate through the floorboards. The Hebrew word, a greeting in his native tongue, felt like a violation of his assumed identity. The man knew him—knew his real name, knew more than he should.

Sharon's hand instinctively went to the Beretta tucked into his waistband. He had anticipated confrontation, expected violence, but the man's calm, almost chilling composure unsettled him more than any gunfight ever could.

"You know who I am," Sharon said, his voice tight, controlled. A surge of adrenaline coursed through his veins—a potent cocktail of fear and fury.

The man smiled, a slow, deliberate movement that did not reach his eyes. "I know everything about you, Sharon. Your past, your present, your future. I know why you're here."

He gestured toward a rickety wooden crate in the corner of the warehouse, its contents obscured by a heavy burlap sack. A tightening gripped Sharon's chest. He knew what was inside.

"Inside that crate," the man continued, "is the evidence that will bring down everything you ever knew. The Abergil mob, the Mossad, Detective Pickens—they're all pawns in a much larger game."

He paused, letting the weight of his words settle in the thick air. "A game I orchestrated."

The revelation hit like a gut punch, leaving Sharon reeling. He had suspected a mastermind, a puppet master pulling the strings from behind the scenes. But he had never imagined the true identity of the puppeteer.

The man was Avraham Ben-Zion—a name whispered only in the darkest corners of the Israeli underworld. A man whose power extended far beyond the reach of the law. A man Sharon had believed to be dead.

Avraham chuckled, a dry, rasping sound that echoed through the cavernous space. "You see, Sharon, you were a valuable asset. Disposable, of course, but valuable nonetheless. I used you to eliminate my rivals, to sow chaos within the Abergil mob. And Detective Pickens? He's just a distraction, a convenient scapegoat."

The words dripped with ruthless calculation. Avraham had manipulated events, orchestrated betrayals, and used Sharon as a pawn in his grand scheme. The realization struck with the force of a physical blow.

"Why?" Sharon finally asked, his voice barely a whisper. The question hung in the air, heavy with years of unspoken betrayal. The bloodshed, the loss of innocence, the endless flight—all for this man's game.

Avraham leaned back, his silhouette growing taller, more menacing in the dim light. "Because," he said, his voice laced with cold satisfaction, "power is a game, Sharon. And I am a master player."

He laid out the details of his grand plan: a scheme to destabilize the Israeli mob, seize control of their vast empire, use Sharon's deadly skills to eliminate key figures, and plant evidence that would frame the Mossad. A masterpiece of calculated manipulation and controlled chaos.

Sharon felt a wave of nausea wash over him. The sheer complexity of the conspiracy was staggering—its reach unfathomable, its consequences potentially catastrophic. He had been nothing more than a pawn in this intricate game, a weapon wielded and discarded at the whim of a ruthless mastermind.

The revelation shook him to his core. The rage that had driven him for so long, the burning need for vengeance, seemed to dissipate, leaving behind a hollow ache of betrayal. He had chased ghosts, killed for a cause that was nothing more than a meticulously constructed illusion. The man he had been hunting was never the mastermind— never the true villain. He had spent months tracking a puppet while the puppeteer had remained hidden in plain sight.

He considered his options. Striking back, unleashing his fury on Avraham, would be futile—a hollow act of vengeance in a game he had already lost. He had been outmaneuvered, outplayed, reduced to nothing more than a discarded chess piece in Avraham's deadly gambit. The weight of that realization pressed down on him, suffocating. Was there even a way out?

His entire life—his identity—seemed to unravel before him. He was not just a hitman, not just a fugitive. He was a victim. A pawn. And the game had only just begun.

Betrayal and Redemption

The warehouse floor was cold, the concrete leaching its chill into his bones despite the stifling air. He had chosen this place—a forgotten corner of Brooklyn, smelling faintly of fish and decay—for its anonymity, its capacity for oblivion. But anonymity was a fragile shield, easily shattered.

Avraham's betrayal had cut deeper than any bullet, leaving behind a wound that festered with self-doubt and a gnawing sense of failure. Sharon had been so close, so very close to escaping the web of deceit Avraham had spun around him. But the old man's ruthlessness had proved to be his undoing. He had spent months as a ghost, reshaping his identity, slipping through the cracks. And yet, Avraham's reach had been longer than he had ever imagined.

Miriam. The thought of his sister—a flicker of warmth in the desolate landscape of his existence—pierced through the haze of despair. He hadn't contacted her since his escape from Morocco, fearing the inevitable trail he would leave behind. She was innocent, caught in the crossfire of his bloody profession. And she was in danger.

Detective Pickens—the relentless, incorruptible bulldog—was closing in. More than the Mossad agents, it was Pickens who gnawed at Sharon's conscience. Pickens represented justice, a concept Sharon had long since abandoned, a ghost of the life he had left behind in the wreckage of his past.

He pulled a crumpled photograph from his pocket—a faded image of Miriam laughing, her eyes bright with a carefree joy that felt like a lifetime ago. He clutched it tightly, the paper creasing beneath the pressure of his trembling fingers. The guilt was suffocating, a weight pressing down on his chest. He had become a monster, a creature of violence and shadows, forever stained by the blood of his victims.

Yet, a tiny ember of hope still flickered within him.

He wouldn't let Avraham win. He wouldn't let Miriam be hurt. He had to find a way to redeem himself, even if it meant facing the consequences of his actions.

Ceta.

The beauty queen whose life had been tragically intertwined with his own. Her image haunted him—her beauty, her innocence, the way she had looked at him with a trust he had never deserved. Killing her had been a cold, calculated act of necessity, a means of survival. But it wasn't the act itself that tormented him—it was the betrayal. The violation of a bond, however fleeting, that had been built on something real.

The moral compass he had long since shattered now pointed in an impossible direction. He had to betray Avraham. But doing so would demand deception, manipulation, and a willingness to embrace the very darkness he sought to escape. It was a dangerous game, one that would test the limits of his morality.

But he had no choice.

Miriam's life was at stake.

And Avraham's conspiracy stretched far beyond anything he had imagined—from the dusty streets of Casablanca to the gleaming skyscrapers of New York City.

This wasn't about revenge anymore. It was about survival. And redemption.

He began to plan meticulously. He needed leverage, information—something to crack Avraham's seemingly impenetrable organization. He had spent years studying the old man, understanding his methods, his ruthlessness, his unwavering loyalty. If Avraham had a weakness, Sharon would find it. And when he did, he would exploit it.

For the next few days, he moved through the city like a phantom, reactivating old contacts, pulling strings, gathering intel. His newly acquired face was a mask, allowing him to slip through the cracks unseen. But the past still clung to him. The guilt. The memories. The weight of everything he had done.

With each new piece of information, the picture became clearer. The conspiracy ran deeper than Avraham. It extended beyond crime syndicates and intelligence agencies. This was something larger, something older. A shadowy organization manipulating events from the background, pulling the strings of governments and corporations alike.

Avraham had been right about one thing.

This was a game.

And Sharon was no longer content to be a pawn.

He discovered that Avraham wasn't the mastermind behind the conspiracy, but merely a powerful pawn in a larger game—a game involving international arms dealers, corrupt politicians, and shadowy intelligence agencies. The stakes were astronomical, and the consequences potentially catastrophic. The more he learned, the clearer it became that the danger he faced was immense. He was no longer just fighting for his own survival or even for Miriam's; he was fighting to prevent a global catastrophe.

The information he gathered pointed toward a clandestine meeting of the key players in the conspiracy, scheduled at a secluded mansion on Long Island. This was his chance—his only chance—to expose the truth and dismantle the entire network. Infiltrating the meeting, however, would be incredibly dangerous; it was a suicide mission with slim odds of success. He weighed his options: the risk to his life, the certainty of further violence, and the moral compromises he would be forced to make. He was a man on the edge—a fugitive caught in a deadly game of cat and mouse with forces far greater than himself.

He knew he couldn't do it alone. He needed an ally—someone he could trust, someone who could provide support and backup. Reluctantly, he reached out to Detective Pickens. It was a risky move, a dangerous gamble, but it was his only option. He knew Pickens despised him and regarded him as a ruthless killer, yet he also knew that Pickens was a man of integrity, driven by a fierce sense of justice.

He sent Pickens an anonymous tip—a carefully crafted message containing enough information to draw him into the investigation while protecting his own identity from Avraham and the rest of the conspiracy. It was a long shot, a desperate attempt to turn an enemy into an ally.

Then came the waiting. Days stretched into a torturous eternity, each moment fraught with anticipation and fear. He knew Pickens would investigate, but whether he would believe him or accept his help remained to be seen. The weight of uncertainty pressed down on him, compounding the burden of his past. He was walking a tightrope, each step fraught with danger, every move potentially his last.

The response arrived sooner than expected—a cryptic message and a coded rendezvous point. Pickens was in; he had swallowed the bait. Yet, the agreement was not based on trust but on a pact forged in mutual self-interest—a dangerous dance where both men pursued their own agendas. It was a treacherous alliance built on the shifting sands of betrayal and redemption.

The next few days became a blur of frantic preparation. He studied maps, planned escape routes, and gathered every resource he could muster for the inevitable confrontation. He knew the mansion would be heavily guarded by a network of skilled mercenaries and advanced surveillance technology. Still, he possessed a significant advantage—access to information that Pickens did not. He planned to use his deep understanding of Avraham's network and the intricate workings of the conspiracy to turn their own strategies against them.

When the night of the meeting arrived, it came like a storm—dark and ominous, with an atmosphere heavy with tension. Disguised and armed, he arrived at the mansion, ready for anything. Moving through the shadows like a ghost, he carried with him the memories of a violent past—a past of bloodshed and darkness that he was finally determined to leave behind.

As he infiltrated the mansion, the tension reached a fever pitch. He was a ghost among them, about to unleash the truth that could shatter their world and, in doing so, perhaps finally achieve his own redemption. The game was far from over; it was only just beginning.

A Race Against Time

The mansion loomed, a gothic behemoth against the bruised twilight sky. Inside, the air crackled with unspoken tension, the scent of expensive perfume a thin veil over the stench of fear and betrayal. Sharon, his face still raw from recent surgery, felt the familiar tremor of adrenaline—a cocktail of fear and exhilaration that had become his constant companion. He moved like a wraith, his steps fluid and silent, a ghost navigating the opulent labyrinth. Pickens, his shadow, trailed close behind, his hand never far from the cold steel of his service revolver.

Their target: Avraham, the patriarch of the Israeli mob, the architect of Sharon's betrayal, the puppet master pulling the strings of an intricate conspiracy. Avraham, who believed he had buried Sharon beneath a mountain of lies and bloodshed. He was wrong.

The first casualty of their infiltration was silence. The grand rooms, once echoing with the laughter and clinking glasses of the city's elite, were eerily quiet. The staff—either dismissed or strategically hidden—left a vacuum in their wake, adding to the oppressive atmosphere. Every creak of the floorboards, every whisper of wind through the tall windows, sounded like a gunshot in the suffocating quiet.

Sharon and Pickens moved with practiced ease, their steps synchronized—a deadly ballet of stealth and precision. Pickens, despite his inherent distrust of Sharon, acknowledged the hitman's expertise. This wasn't a police raid; it was a surgical strike.

They bypassed the security cameras not with brute force, but with Sharon's intimate knowledge of the mansion's layout—a remnant of his past life. A past he was desperately trying to outrun but could never escape. He knew the blind spots, the hidden passages, the weak points in the system—the places where secrets were kept, where the truth lay buried.

Reaching Avraham's study, they found him hunched over a large desk, his face illuminated by the soft glow of a lamp, poring over documents. He looked frail, his once-sharp features softened by age, but his eyes still held a spark of cold intelligence—a chilling reminder of his ruthlessness. He wasn't alone. Two heavily armed guards flanked him, their hands resting casually on their weapons, oblivious to the danger lurking in the shadows.

Pickens moved first, his gun drawn, but Sharon held up a hand, silencing him. This wasn't a simple arrest. Avraham was too dangerous, too well-connected, too powerful for a quick cuff and perp walk. They needed to expose the conspiracy, not just neutralize Avraham. This was chess, not checkers. And Sharon was playing for the highest stakes.

He struck with lethal grace, his movements a blur. One guard was down before he even registered the attack, his neck twisted at an unnatural angle. The other, reacting instinctively, lunged for his weapon—only to meet Sharon's fist, a crushing blow that sent him sprawling.

Avraham, momentarily stunned by the sudden violence, watched in horrified fascination as Sharon approached, his eyes blazing with a cold fury that mirrored his own. The documents on the desk—glimpsed in the brief chaos—revealed a complex network of international arms deals, money laundering, and political corruption. A conspiracy that reached far beyond the petty vendettas of the Israeli mob.

"You think you've escaped me, Sharon?" Avraham rasped, his voice a mix of disbelief and impotent rage. "You're a pawn. A disposable tool. You were always just a pawn."

"I was," Sharon replied, his voice low and deadly. "But the game has changed, Avraham. The pawns are now the players."

The ensuing struggle was brutal—a clash of wills as much as a physical confrontation. Avraham, despite his age, fought with the tenacity of a cornered animal. He knew he wasn't just battling a hitman; he was fighting to keep a lifetime of secrets from unraveling.

But Sharon, fueled by years of betrayal and a desperate need for redemption, was relentless.

Pickens, despite his initial reservations, proved to be an effective force in the fight. His police training complemented Sharon's raw power, turning the tide in their favor. He disarmed the remaining guard, adding to the chaos. The study, once a sanctuary of power, had become a battlefield.

As the fight raged, the truth behind the conspiracy began to surface. A frantic call from the outside confirmed the imminent delivery of an arms shipment—enough to ignite a regional war. The documents on Avraham's desk revealed a web of connections, a tapestry of corruption stretching from the underworld's darkest corners to the highest levels of government. This wasn't just about the Israeli mob; it was a global threat.

The climax came with a violent crash as a heavy bookcase toppled, burying Avraham beneath its weight. He was subdued, but not defeated. His eyes still burned with rage and defiance. His fall wasn't the end—it was the beginning of a larger, more intricate battle for justice.

As sirens wailed in the distance, signaling the arrival of backup, Sharon and Pickens stood amidst the wreckage, their faces etched with exhaustion and grim satisfaction. They had won this battle, but the war was far from over. The conspiracy had been exposed, but its tentacles stretched far and wide.

The race against time had been won, but a new, more complex struggle had just begun. They had stopped one threat, but many more loomed in the shadows. They had merely scratched the surface, and the depths were far more terrifying than they could have imagined.

The unraveling of the conspiracy was only the beginning. Rebuilding—restoring even a semblance of order—was their next daunting task. And the shadow of betrayal still hung over them both, a chilling reminder of the darkness they had encountered and the uncertain path ahead.

The taste of victory was bittersweet. The fight was far from over.

Confrontation at the Docks

The salt-laced air hung heavy, thick with the stench of fish guts and diesel. The Manila docks, a labyrinth of shadows and shifting crates, offered little solace. Sharon, his newly sculpted face still tender, felt the familiar prickle of unease.

He had agreed to meet Pickens here—a location as treacherous as it was anonymous. It was a gamble, a desperate roll of the dice in a game where the stakes were life and death.

Pickens arrived precisely at midnight, silhouetted against the weak glow of a distant streetlamp. He was a study in controlled aggression, his usual rumpled suit replaced by something more practical—dark jeans, a leather jacket, and a grim set to his jaw. His eyes, however, held the same unwavering intensity Sharon had come to know and fear.

"You look… different," Pickens said, his voice a low rumble barely carrying over the sounds of the bustling port. He didn't need to elaborate; the subtle shift in Sharon's features, the ghost of his old self peeking through the surgeon's handiwork, spoke volumes.

Sharon shrugged, a careless gesture that belied the churning anxiety within. "And you look like you haven't slept in a week. I'm surprised you haven't fallen into a coma from lack of caffeine."

The air crackled with unspoken accusations. Trust between them had never existed; now, it was little more than a distant, fading memory. Their uneasy alliance, forged in the crucible of mutual necessity, was fraying at the edges.

"Miriam," Pickens said, the name a venomous dart. "She's in deeper than we thought. The Abergil family aren't the only players in this game. There's a larger conspiracy at work—something far more sinister than we imagined."

Sharon remained silent, his gaze fixed on the churning black water. Miriam. The name was a raw wound, a reminder of his fractured past. He had tried to shield her from his world of shadows and violence, but he had failed. The conspiracy had reached her, ensnaring her in its deadly web.

"I need your help," Pickens continued, his voice laced with weary desperation. "This goes beyond the Abergil family. We're talking international arms dealers, corrupt officials, and a network of informants so deep it reaches the highest levels of power."

Sharon chuckled, a harsh, bitter sound. "And you think I'm your knight in shining armor, here to save the world?"

Pickens didn't flinch. "I know you're not a hero, Sharon. But you're the only one who can get us to the truth. You're connected to this mess in ways I can only begin to understand. We both know it."

Before Sharon could respond, a figure emerged from the shadows—a hulking brute, his face obscured by a balaclava. He moved with the lethal grace of a predator, his hand clutching a wicked-looking knife. The attack was swift and brutal.

The confrontation escalated from words to violence in a heartbeat.

The docks became a battleground. Steel clashed against steel, punctuated by grunts and pained cries. Sharon, despite his weakened state, fought with the ferocity of a cornered animal. Years of brutal training took over. His movements were precise, deadly—each strike calculated to inflict maximum damage.

Pickens, equally adept at hand-to-hand combat, fought alongside him. Their combined skills became a whirlwind of controlled fury. The metallic tang of blood filled the air, mixing with the harsh, guttural sounds of their struggle. Pickens's experience showed in the way he moved—pragmatic, precise, his focus unwavering. His past encounters with Sharon's world had given him a crucial edge, an understanding of his methods and movements.

The attacker, though strong, was no match for them. With a swift, precise move, Pickens disarmed him, sending the knife clattering onto the concrete. A moment later, he delivered a crippling blow, bringing the assailant down with a thunderous crash.

As the attacker slumped to the ground, another figure emerged from the darkness—a specter of death. This one was armed with a silenced pistol.

Before Sharon could react, the gun spat a deadly burst.

The shot found its mark. Pickens staggered, a crimson stain blossoming on his chest.

Sharon roared, fury erupting like a volcano. He lunged at the attacker, his movements blurring into a deadly dance.

The fight was brutal, desperate—a chaotic ballet of violence. Fueled by adrenaline and rage, Sharon fought with raw, primal intensity. He wrestled the gun away, the cold steel a familiar comfort in his hands.

Their struggle spilled onto a nearby container, scattering crates and cargo. The sounds of their battle—grunts, gasps, the scrape of boots against metal—mingled with the distant cries of gulls. The night air vibrated with tension.

Sharon, finally gaining the upper hand, disarmed the attacker and delivered a devastating blow. The body crumpled, lifeless. Chest heaving, Sharon stood over the fallen figure, his breath coming in ragged gasps.

Then he turned—Pickens lay slumped against rusted metal, his blood staining the dock.

Sharon dropped to his knees, heart hammering. He checked for a pulse—a faint, fragile beat remained. Pressing down on the wound, he fought to stem the bleeding.

"Damn it, Pickens," he hissed, frustration laced with something dangerously close to concern. "We're not finished yet."

A siren wailed in the distance, its mournful cry slicing through the night. Backup was coming.

But this wasn't over.

They had won this battle, but the conspiracy still lurked—a shadowy menace, waiting to strike again. The fight was far from finished. The stakes remained high, the future uncertain.

And Sharon knew, with chilling certainty, that the darkness had only begun to show its true face.

The consequences of this night—the ripples stretching far beyond the bloodied docks of Manila—were still waiting to unravel.

The war had only just begun.

The Bomb Explodes

The air vibrated with a low hum that built to a deafening roar. The warehouse, once a cavernous space echoing with the metallic clang of machinery and the hushed whispers of conspirators, became a maelstrom of fire and debris. The bomb—a meticulously crafted device Sharon had built himself—detonated with a force that ripped through the concrete structure, shattering windows a block away and sending a shockwave that knocked people off their feet. Dust and smoke billowed into the sky, a dark, angry cloud against the bruised purple of the Manila twilight.

From a rooftop overlooking the chaos, Sharon watched with a strange mix of exhilaration and dread. The exhilaration was the cold, calculated thrill of a successful operation—the satisfaction of a job well done. The dread, however, stemmed from the gnawing uncertainty of the consequences. He had targeted this particular warehouse, a known hub for arms trafficking linked to a shadowy organization he had been dismantling piece by piece for months. But he hadn't anticipated the scale of the destruction—the sheer, horrifying force unleashed in that single moment. Bodies lay scattered among the wreckage, little more than silhouettes in the swirling dust. The air crackled with the energy of a thousand shattered lives.

He had timed the explosion to coincide with a meeting of high-ranking members of the organization—men whose names were whispered in hushed tones in the darkest corners of the underworld. He had hoped to cripple their network, to send a message that would reverberate through their ranks. But the collateral damage... the innocent bystanders caught in the crossfire... that was a weight that settled heavy on his conscience—a chilling reminder of the morally gray world he inhabited. He wasn't a hero. He was a survivor, a ghost moving through the shadows, leaving destruction in his wake.

The sirens, a cacophony of wailing horns and flashing lights, announced the arrival of the authorities. The chaos spiraled further. He watched as first responders, their faces etched with grim determination, battled through the debris, desperately searching for survivors. The scene was a macabre ballet of human suffering, a spectacle of violence and despair playing out against the backdrop of a city already steeped in danger.

Sharon knew he had to disappear before the authorities could trace him back to the explosion. He had meticulously planned his escape route, every detail mapped out with surgical precision. Slipping away from the rooftop, he melted into the labyrinthine streets of Manila, the sounds of the explosion still ringing in his ears. The night air was thick with smoke and the metallic tang of blood—a stark reminder of the brutal reality he lived in.

Days bled into weeks. He moved like a shadow, constantly looking over his shoulder, his senses perpetually on high alert. News reports of the explosion continued, growing more sensational with each passing day. The death toll climbed, fueling public outrage and galvanizing the authorities into action. He wasn't surprised when Detective Pickens' name surfaced prominently in the early investigations. Pickens' relentless pursuit of Sharon had become somewhat of a legend in the precinct. The detective was a bulldog—a man who wouldn't give up until he had his prey.

The media frenzy surrounding the bombing provided a smokescreen, allowing Sharon to remain hidden in plain sight. But he knew his time was limited. The authorities were closing in, and Pickens, with his dogged determination, was likely already piecing together the evidence that would lead to him. Sharon had underestimated the fallout. The bombing had far-reaching consequences, setting off a domino effect that threatened to expose the entire conspiracy he had inadvertently stumbled upon. The network he had been targeting was more extensive, more deeply rooted than he had ever imagined.

He found himself trapped in a web of his own making, a game of cat and mouse where the stakes were impossibly high. The explosion hadn't just destroyed a warehouse—it had shattered the fragile peace he had managed to carve out for himself. Its consequences were far-reaching, touching every aspect of his life and forcing him to confront the devastating reality of his actions. Guilt gnawed at him, a relentless predator feeding on his already fractured soul.

His escape from Manila was harrowing—a desperate flight through a city that felt increasingly hostile and unforgiving. He relied on his instincts, his street smarts honed over years of living on the edge. Navigating back alleys, shadowy corners, and hidden passages only someone like him would know, he moved with the grace of a phantom, a specter slipping through the cracks of society.

Securing passage on a cargo ship, he finally escaped Manila's suffocating grip and the relentless pursuit closing in around him. The journey was long and arduous, filled with the acrid scent of salt and diesel, the rhythmic creaking of the ship a hypnotic counterpoint to the turmoil within him. The endless expanse of the ocean offered a temporary reprieve—a moment of introspection where he was forced to confront the weight of his actions. He was a fugitive now, a ghost haunted by the echoes of the explosion, the faces of the victims forever imprinted on his memory.

But escape, he knew, was only temporary. The consequences of the bombing would continue to ripple outward, sending shockwaves through the power dynamics of the underworld. He was no longer just a hitman; he had become a symbol—a cautionary tale of the devastating consequences of unchecked ambition and violence. The past he had tried to outrun was now hunting him, an ever-present shadow closing in.

His destination was New York—a city that held both the promise of anonymity and the looming threat of exposure. The authorities were still searching for him, and his sister Miriam, whose involvement in the conspiracy was still unraveling, was a loose end he couldn't afford to ignore. He would have to tread carefully, navigating the treacherous waters of loyalty and betrayal that had long defined his life. The conspiracy, he realized, was far larger than he had imagined, its tendrils reaching far beyond the seemingly isolated incident in the Manila warehouse. It was a vast network of power, influence, and corruption, stretching into the highest echelons of society. And somehow, he had become entangled in its deadly web.

New York was a stark contrast to the humid chaos of Manila. The towering skyline, a monument to human ambition and progress, felt cold and unwelcoming. The city's vibrant energy was a façade, masking the darkness that lurked beneath its polished surface—a darkness he knew all too well.

He began gathering intelligence, carefully piecing together the fragments of the conspiracy like a jigsaw puzzle where every piece held a deadly secret. His past, once a distant echo, was now a deafening roar, forcing him to confront the full extent of his involvement in this deadly game. He had underestimated his enemies. The explosion in Manila had only accelerated the unraveling of a complex and dangerous plot that spanned continents and involved players far more powerful than he had ever anticipated.

The war had only just begun. The true fight was far from over.

Survival—once a simple objective—now felt like an unattainable dream. The consequences of his actions, once a looming threat, had become a suffocating weight pressing down on him, a grim reminder of the price he might have to pay. The path ahead was treacherous, riddled with unseen obstacles and enemies lurking in the shadows, waiting to strike.

The game, he knew, was far from over.

Aftermath of the Explosion

The air hung thick with the stench of burnt metal, pulverized concrete, and something acrid—something chemical that burned the back of the throat. A low moan, almost a groan, escaped from the wreckage, swallowed by the echoing silence that followed the deafening roar of the explosion. The pier, once a bustling hub of activity, was now a wasteland of twisted steel and shattered wood, a testament to the destructive power of Sharon's meticulously crafted bomb.

Fire crackled and spat, licking at the remnants of what had once been a seemingly innocuous shipping container. Thick, black smoke billowed into the night sky, a grim monument to Sharon's violent act. The usual cacophony of the docks had vanished, replaced by the hiss of escaping steam and the occasional drip of water from ruptured pipes. The silence was heavy, thick with the unspoken horrors of destruction.

The blast had been precisely timed, detonating the moment the mastermind and several high-ranking members of the Abergil Israeli mob were gathered inside the container. Sharon had calculated every trajectory, ensuring maximum casualties while minimizing collateral damage. His work was cold, clinical—a precision that mirrored his personality. Yet, even amidst the calculated destruction, unease gnawed at him. The bomb's impact was greater than his calculations had predicted. It hadn't just neutralized his targets; it had left devastation in its wake.

Detective Pickens arrived on the scene, his face grim beneath the flickering light of emergency vehicles. He pushed past paramedics, ignoring their pleas to wait. The moment he surveyed the wreckage, he knew—this had Sharon's signature all over it. The precision of the blast, the calculated destruction, even the specific type of explosive used—it was unmistakable. The devastation, brutal and unforgiving, mirrored the man he had been hunting for years.

Moving through the debris, his boots crunched over shattered glass and splintered wood. Each step was measured, deliberate. His sharp eyes scanned the wreckage, searching for evidence to confirm what he already knew.

The body count was staggering. What was meant to be a temporary holding cell for the mob leaders had been reduced to twisted metal. The bodies of its occupants lay strewn across the debris, some still recognizable, others mangled beyond recognition. It was a grotesque tableau of death and destruction, an image seared into Pickens' memory. He felt a grim satisfaction—his relentless pursuit had led to this. But this wasn't the justice he had envisioned. It was a pyrrhic victory, stained with the blood of innocents caught in the crossfire.

As he took in the scene, a wave of nausea rolled over him. The sheer scale of the destruction was overwhelming. This wasn't just about dismantling a criminal network anymore. This was about the brutal, indiscriminate power of violence and its irreversible consequences. He could almost taste the fear, hear the desperation of those who had perished. The echoes of their screams, the anguished cries of survivors, played on a sickening loop in his mind. Victory tasted like ash.

Something caught his eye—a small, leather-bound notebook lying amidst the wreckage, miraculously intact. Carefully, he picked it up. Its pages were filled with detailed notes, diagrams, cryptic symbols. Sharon's journal. Every plan, every obsession, every descent into darkness meticulously recorded. It was the final piece of the puzzle, the key to unraveling the tangled web of deceit that had pulled Pickens into this violent storm.

Meanwhile, from a safe distance, Miriam watched. She had escaped the explosion with only minor injuries, but the war within her was far worse. Fear and relief waged battle in her chest. The explosion had wiped out the immediate threat, but the victory felt hollow. Her escape was uncertain. Her future, precarious.

She observed Pickens as he moved methodically through the wreckage, his gaze sharp, his demeanor unrelenting. He was getting closer. The thought sent a shiver down her spine. She had betrayed Sharon, and now, with his enemies gone, that betrayal could come to light.

The explosion had changed everything—but not necessarily for the better.

She needed to disappear, to melt into the shadows before Pickens' relentless pursuit turned its focus on her.

Before Sharon found out what she had done.

The aftermath of the explosion wasn't just about physical destruction—it was a cataclysmic event that shattered lives, illusions, and the fragile façade of justice. The chaotic scene on the pier was merely a microcosm of the wider turmoil Sharon had unleashed, a ripple effect that would extend far beyond the dying flames and dissipating smoke. The investigation sprawled beyond the wreckage, reaching into the hidden corners of the city, the murky underbelly of international crime, and the hearts of those left behind to pick up the pieces.

Pickens, burdened by the weight of the investigation, the staggering loss of life, and the bitter knowledge that justice had come at an unbearable cost, began unraveling the tangled threads of conspiracy. Sharon's meticulous planning had left a trail—one Pickens followed relentlessly, deeper into the labyrinth of the Abergil Israeli mob. With each revelation, more layers of corruption surfaced, exposing a vast network that stretched far beyond what he had initially imagined.

Miriam's escape was never going to be easy. Pickens now possessed enough evidence to connect her to Sharon and the broader conspiracy. She wasn't just a loose end—she was a key witness, a missing puzzle piece in a case that was rapidly expanding beyond its original scope.

Then came the most shocking truth of all: the Abergil Israeli mob was merely one fragment of a much larger puzzle, a global network of organized crime that spanned borders and continents. The mastermind behind it all remained elusive, but as Pickens tightened the net around the remaining conspirators, a series of arrests followed.

In an ironic twist, Sharon's act of destruction had inadvertently triggered a far-reaching crackdown on international crime.

Yet, the cost of this so-called victory was immeasurable.

Innocent lives had been lost. Families torn apart. The city, scarred. What should have been justice felt hollow, tainted by the darkness of the means required to achieve it. Standing at the smoldering remains of the pier, Pickens took in the twisted metal, the charred wood—the physical remnants of a night that had changed everything. The victory felt incomplete.

The explosion had closed one chapter, but it had only just begun another. The consequences of Sharon's actions—of all their choices—would ripple outward, shaping the fates of those left standing. As the smoke cleared, it revealed a landscape not of clarity, but of deeper betrayal, revenge, and the slow, inevitable unraveling of a world built on shadows. Justice, if it could even be called that, remained elusive, incomplete—just like the morally gray figures who had fought for it.

The city would move on. It always did.

But the scars of that night would remain—a haunting reminder of the price paid for justice in a world where right and wrong had long since blurred into something indistinguishable.

Pickens Reckoning

The interrogation room was stark, its single bare bulb casting harsh shadows that danced across the sweat beading on Sal Demarco's forehead. The man Pickens had been chasing for months—the architect of the city's chaos—sat hunched over, his expensive suit now rumpled and stained. He hadn't broken under relentless questioning, but the exhaustion in his eyes betrayed him.

Pickens leaned in, the scent of stale coffee and cheap disinfectant thick in the air.

"Sharon," he said, the name a low growl. "He's not just some freelance assassin. He's a pawn, Sal. Your pawn."

Demarco's gaze remained fixed on a point beyond Pickens' shoulder. Silence. Pickens knew brute force wouldn't crack him—he'd already tried. Demarco was too seasoned, too accustomed to the dark underbelly of the world. If he was going to break, it wouldn't be through threats. It would be through pressure, through exposing the cracks in the foundation he had so carefully built.

"You underestimated him, didn't you?" Pickens continued, his voice a calm counterpoint to the tension thickening the room. "Thought you could control him. Use him to settle old scores. Just another disposable asset."

A flicker of something—anger, fear, maybe even regret—passed across Demarco's face. It was fleeting, but Pickens caught it. He pressed in.

"Miriam." He let the name hang in the air like a loaded gun. "Your sister's death. That was Sharon, wasn't it? Or was it you?"

A long silence. The only sound was the rhythmic ticking of the wall clock. Then, finally—

"It wasn't personal," Demarco rasped, his voice hoarse. "It was business."

Pickens scoffed. "Business? You call murdering your own sister business?"

Demarco shifted, uncomfortable for the first time. "She was... inconvenient. A loose end." He hesitated, then added, "Sharon was supposed to handle it cleanly. He deviated from the plan."

Pickens leaned closer, his voice low. "And the Mossad? They want Sharon dead. Why?"

Demarco exhaled slowly. "The Israelis... they were just collateral damage. Sharon stumbled into something bigger than he understood."

Bit by bit, the story unraveled. A secret arms deal gone sideways. A double-cross that left powerful players dead or in hiding. Sharon had been both a weapon and a liability—until he uncovered something he was never meant to see. Evidence of a conspiracy so vast it could topple more than just Demarco's empire.

That information led Pickens to the warehouse district on the city's outskirts, a wasteland of rusted metal and the stink of rotting fish. Inside a decaying building, Demarco's operation lay exposed—boxes of weapons, explosives enough to level a city block, and files mapping out a labyrinth of lies and deceit.

The confrontation wasn't a shootout. No last-ditch escape. Just silence. Demarco, cornered, broken, offered no resistance. His empire was gone. His escape routes severed. For the first time, he looked like a man who understood that the world he had built was crumbling around him.

The arrest should have felt like closure. It didn't.

Sharon was still out there, a phantom in the shadows. The bomb at the pier had wiped out one arm of Demarco's operation—but in doing so, it had ignited something far bigger. The explosion had become more than an act of destruction. It had become a message. A warning.

The city had been reminded, in the most brutal way possible, just how fragile its balance of power truly was.

The truth, as always, was more complicated than it first appeared. Apprehending Demarco had brought a measure of justice, but it barely scratched the surface of the deeper conspiracy that pulsed beneath the city's streets. The fallout, the ripples from what had transpired, would extend far beyond the sound of his cell door slamming shut.

Pickens stood at his window, staring out at the city skyline. The lights blinked like distant stars, beautiful yet indifferent, a stark reminder of the lives still at risk. The case was closed, but the fight was far from over. Justice felt incomplete—a hollow echo in the vast darkness that remained. The ghosts of those he'd lost, Miriam chief among them, lingered in the periphery of his thoughts. Demarco was gone, but Sharon was still out there, his shadow stretching across the city like an unshakable omen.

Demarco had been a major player, but not the mastermind. His arrest was the end of one chapter, but the beginning of another—one that promised to be far more dangerous. The conspiracy stretched beyond city limits, its roots deeper than Pickens had imagined. Loose ends dangled like frayed wires, and the unsettling truth was that Demarco's downfall had only peeled back the first layer of corruption.

As Pickens drove home, the neon glow of the city blurred into streaks of color, his unease growing with every mile. The justice he had sought felt incomplete, a faint whisper against the vast, looming silence. He knew, with a cold certainty, that the shadows had not receded. They had only shifted.

The game wasn't over.

Not even close.

The city's secrets still coiled in its veins, unseen but ever-present. Pickens had to unravel them all before the next storm broke—before the next wave of chaos consumed everything.

He drove on, the low hum of the city filling the void. The weight of its truths settled on his shoulders, a burden he knew he would carry.

The hunt was far from over.

Sharons Fate

The rain hammered against the corrugated iron roof of the abandoned warehouse, mimicking the frantic beat of Sharon's heart. He hadn't slept properly in weeks. The ghosts of his past—Ceta's wide, terrified eyes, the cold steel of the Mossad's weapons, the chilling indifference of Sal Demarco—haunted his every waking moment. He had managed to evade Pickens for now, a feat accomplished through a combination of luck, cunning, and the brutal efficiency that had become second nature. But the city, this concrete jungle he called home, felt less like a refuge and more like a cage.

He stared at the bomb, a crude yet effective device nestled in a battered briefcase. It wasn't meant for anyone specific, not in the traditional sense. This was a message, a defiant howl in the face of the forces that had relentlessly hunted him. A final act of rebellion. A desperate bid for control in a world that had stripped him of all agency. He had placed it strategically near the docks, a location chosen to maximize chaos and minimize the chances of immediate identification. He had learned from Sal Demarco—the best bombs were the ones that left no traceable fingerprints.

A surge of bitter self-awareness washed over him. He was a ghost, a shadow, forever operating in the twilight between life and death. He had traded his humanity for survival, his soul for a fleeting sense of freedom. The irony wasn't lost on him: he had escaped the clutches of the Israeli mob only to find himself trapped in a different kind of prison—a self-imposed exile fueled by guilt and the ever-present threat of violence.

He lit a cigarette, the flame momentarily illuminating the weary lines on his surgically reconstructed face. The new face was a mask, a disguise that shielded him from recognition, but it couldn't hide the turmoil within. The memories, the pain, the weight of his actions— they were all etched into his soul, as permanent as the scars hidden beneath his clothes.

He checked his watch, the second hand ticking like a countdown. Time was running out. He had given himself a deadline, a self-imposed sentence dictated by his conscience—a flickering ember of morality in the ashes of his past. He hadn't planned this, not precisely. It simply felt like the only way out. The only way to find a semblance of peace, even if it was the peace of oblivion.

The warehouse was cold, damp, and echoing. The silence was broken only by the rhythmic drumming of the rain, a relentless reminder of the storm raging inside him. He closed his eyes, picturing Miriam's face—love and fear etched into her features. He hadn't been a good brother, not really. He had always been a shadow looming over her life, a constant threat, a source of both pride and shame.

He thought about the look in Detective Pickens's eyes, a mixture of determination and weariness that mirrored his own. He had underestimated Pickens—his resilience, his capacity for relentless pursuit. Pickens had a dogged tenacity that was both admirable and terrifying. He knew Pickens wouldn't stop until he was brought to justice—or perhaps even beyond.

A distant siren wailed, a mournful sound that seemed to echo the despair in his own heart. It wouldn't be long now. He took a final drag from his cigarette, crushing the butt under his heel. He had made his peace, as much as one could make peace with such a life.

This wasn't redemption. He understood that. This was merely a conclusion—a final full stop in a sentence riddled with commas of violence and semicolons of regret.

He stood and walked toward the door, the briefcase heavy in his hand. The rain was coming down harder now, turning the streets into a raging torrent. He stepped into the downpour, a fleeting shadow moving through the storm.

Hours later, the explosion rocked the docks—a thunderous clap that shook the city. News reports spoke of a massive blast, extensive damage, and an ongoing investigation. They wouldn't find him. They would never know. His work was done.

Detective Pickens sat in his dimly lit apartment, watching the news with a grim expression. He knew, with chilling certainty, that the explosion was connected to Sharon. But what he didn't know was Sharon's motive—or whether he was even still alive. The pieces were falling into place, yet a crucial element remained elusive, hidden behind a veil of deception and carefully constructed alibis.

The investigation pressed on, tracing the fragmented threads of Sharon's chaotic existence. Pickens followed the trail of destruction, uncovering hidden connections, piecing together the remnants of a shattered life. The deeper he delved into the murky world of international crime, the more he unearthed—links to arms dealers, corrupt officials, and shadowy figures operating in the darkest corners of the world.

What had begun as a simple case turned into something far greater. It became a personal crusade, a relentless pursuit of justice against a backdrop of betrayal, deception, and ever-present violence. Pickens was determined to bring those responsible to account, to expose the network of corruption that had facilitated Sharon's actions, and to uncover the hidden truth behind what seemed like random acts of terror.

The trail led him from the bustling streets of Manila to clandestine meetings with the Israeli mob, revealing a complex web of alliances and betrayals that had driven Sharon to the edge. Evidence suggested that Sharon was merely a pawn in a larger game—a catalyst in a conflict that threatened to destabilize the delicate balance of power.

Secrets lay hidden in plain sight, buried in coded messages, cryptic encounters, and whispered conversations in smoky backrooms. The more Pickens uncovered, the more he realized the true extent of the conspiracy. Its reach extended far beyond what he had initially imagined, its influence woven into the very fabric of the world he thought he understood.

Sharon's final act was neither a clear victory nor a definitive defeat. It was a testament to the complexities of human nature—the blurred lines between justice and revenge, the lingering consequences of violence. The investigation unraveled a tapestry of deceit, revealing both great evil and unexpected acts of self-sacrifice. When the truth finally emerged, it was fragmented, ambiguous—far more intricate than Pickens had anticipated.

The ending remained uncertain, a chilling reflection of the morally gray world Sharon inhabited. Was he truly gone? Had he evaded justice? Or had he simply found another path—one just as dangerous, just as uncertain? The questions lingered, unanswered, leaving only the haunting realization that justice was never as simple as it seemed.

The city carried on, oblivious to the echoes of the explosion, to the unseen threads of conspiracy still woven into its core. The game, Pickens knew, was far from over. Shadows lingered. The hunt would continue. He had captured a few players, but the larger game—the battle for power, the war against corruption—remained elusive. Some truths would stay hidden, some battles would always be fought in the shadows, and some endings would never come.

The fight for justice, it seemed, would outlast the final bomb. The city, with its endless labyrinth of secrets, would always demand vigilance. It would always test the limits of human endurance. And it would always ensure that the hunt—the relentless pursuit of truth—never truly ended.

Miriams Escape

The flickering neon sign of a seedy bar cast a lurid glow on the rain-slicked street. Miriam, her breath ragged, her heart pounding against her ribs, pressed herself against the brick wall, her eyes darting nervously from shadow to shadow. The escape had been a blur of adrenaline and terror—a desperate scramble through back alleys, a frantic dash across rooftops, a breathless flight from the squad cars whose sirens wailed like banshees in the night. She clutched the worn leather bag tightly to her chest. Its contents—a small fortune in cash and a handful of crucial documents—were her only lifeline.

She had known the risk. She had lived under the shadow of her brother's criminal activities for years, a shadow that had grown longer and darker, threatening to consume her entirely. Sharon's life was a tapestry woven with violence, betrayal, and death, and she had been caught in its suffocating embrace. But this time, the risk had been even greater. The explosion, the chaos, the police raid on her apartment— it had all been a calculated gamble, a desperate bid to distance herself from the fallout of Sharon's increasingly reckless actions.

Now, with the taste of freedom bitter on her tongue, she knew the gamble had paid off. At least for now.

Her escape wasn't just physical. It was a mental liberation. Years of living under the weight of fear—constantly looking over her shoulder—had left her drained. She was finally free from her brother's enemies, from the relentless scrutiny of Detective Pickens, from the suffocating grip of her past. Yet freedom felt strangely hollow. The city, once a vibrant, pulsing organism, now seemed cold and indifferent. The rain mocked her, each drop a tiny, persistent reminder of just how precarious her situation remained.

She needed to disappear—to melt into the anonymity of the city, to become a ghost. But where? She had no concrete plan, no safe haven, only a vague sense of direction and a desperate hope to outrun both the law and the long shadow of Sharon's past. The money wouldn't last forever, and her forged passport, a flimsy shield against the relentless scrutiny of immigration officials, felt like a ticking time bomb.

She considered vanishing into the city's underbelly, where anonymity reigned supreme. She could live among the forgotten, the invisible. But the thought filled her with dread. She wasn't cut out for that life. She was a creature of comfort, of routine, of a semblance of normalcy. A life spent in the shadows, always looking over her shoulder, chilled her to the bone.

A different approach was needed. She was intelligent, resourceful, adaptable. She had a network—contacts who owed her favors, people she could trust just enough to help her. It was a risky path, one that required careful manipulation and calculated trust. But it was her only real chance.

For days, she holed up in a cheap motel room, meticulously planning her next move. She reached out to old acquaintances, cautiously testing their loyalty. She needed someone who could get her out of the country, erase her digital footprint, and craft her a new identity.

Each phone call, each clandestine meeting, felt like walking a tightrope over a chasm of uncertainty. Fear became her constant companion—fear of discovery, of betrayal, of being dragged back into a world she had fought so hard to escape. Sleep brought no respite. Her dreams were filled with flashing police lights, the cold steel of handcuffs, the relentless gaze of Detective Pickens.

Then, finally, she found a way out. A contact—one of Sharon's former associates—offered her passage. A small fishing boat headed south toward the Caribbean, a false passport, a new name. But there was a price. She would have to complete one task first: a simple errand, they called it. A delivery to a remote island. A package. Nothing more.

But she knew better.

Hesitation gnawed at her. Her conscience screamed for her to refuse, to turn away from the dark path her brother had walked. But the alternative—a life spent running, always looking over her shoulder—was far worse.

She made her decision. She would take the risk.

The journey on the boat was grueling. The seas were rough, the weather unpredictable. The other passengers—a motley crew of smugglers and desperate souls seeking escape—were a strange mix of fear and resilience. Miriam sat quietly in a corner, watching them with unease.

The ocean stretched endlessly around them, vast and indifferent—a mirror of her own uncertain future.

The island was a tropical paradise, draped in lush vegetation and encircled by pristine white sand beaches. But paradise could be deceptive. The delivery went as planned—uneventful, routine. Yet, a deep sense of unease clung to her like humidity in the air.

The recipient, a shadowy figure cloaked in secrecy, exuded a presence far more menacing than the authorities she had fled. There was something in his stillness, in the weight of his gaze, that sent a chill down her spine. She had escaped one web only to find herself ensnared in another—a web where the lines between right and wrong blurred into nothingness, where escape might prove impossible.

The illusion of freedom she had savored after her escape was already fading, dissolving into the creeping realization that she had merely traded one cage for another. The city's dangers had been tangible, predictable. Here, in this deceptive paradise, the threat was more insidious—silent, patient, waiting.

She questioned whether she could trust her new contact. Could she trust anyone, given her brother's legacy and the long shadow it cast over her life? Small acts of kindness now seemed laced with hidden motives, every glance and every word carrying unspoken meaning. Even the vibrant beauty of the island—its golden sunsets, its crystalline waters—felt like a cruel mockery of her predicament. The contrast between the idyllic setting and the dark secrets surrounding her was suffocating.

Exhaustion, both physical and mental, weighed on her.

The next few weeks passed in a haze of uncertainty. She remained on the island, her movements cautious, her contacts limited. She played the waiting game, her instincts sharpened by years of survival in the margins of society. Every moment felt like walking a tightrope, each day another gamble. Sleep became a luxury she couldn't afford. Fear became a constant companion.

The days bled into nights, and with each passing sunrise, she felt the weight of the life she had left behind pressing down on her. Each sunset was an uncertain promise of a future she could neither predict nor control. She existed in limbo, caught between two worlds—one she could no longer return to, another she had yet to claim.

But the escape had given her something invaluable: time. And time meant opportunity.

One evening, as she sat beneath the vast, star-filled sky, a realization struck her with undeniable force. This was no longer just about survival. It was about reclaiming her life. About taking control, defining herself outside of Sharon's shadow.

She wasn't just running anymore. She was choosing.

The decision settled in her bones, cold and firm. The game was far from over, but from now on, she would play it on her own terms. She would use her intelligence, her resourcefulness—everything she had—to carve out a new life, far from the ghosts of her past.

But she would never forget.

Never forget Sharon. Never forget the choices that had led her here. The escape wasn't an end; it was a beginning—a new chapter, a new fight. And for the first time, Miriam felt something other than fear.

Hope.

Detective Pickens was still out there, his relentless pursuit of justice undeterred. But Miriam had her own justice to fight for. Her own freedom to claim.

And this time, she wouldn't be running.

Loose Ends

The rain, a relentless curtain of grey, mirrored the bleakness in Detective Pickens's soul. He stared out at the city sprawling below from his office window, a cityscape that pulsed with deceptive energy, a city that concealed its darkness as skillfully as Sharon had. He'd cornered Sharon, had him on the ropes, but the final blow had evaded him.

The confrontation, brutal and swift, had ended not with capture, but with a near-miss. Sharon, wounded but not broken, had vanished back into the labyrinthine shadows of the underworld, leaving behind a trail of cryptic clues, a mocking reminder of his elusiveness.

Pickens ran a hand through his already disheveled hair, the weariness etched deep into his face. Weeks had passed since the chase through the rain-soaked streets, weeks spent meticulously piecing together the fragments of Sharon's past, the shards of a life shattered and rebuilt, a life that resonated with a chilling blend of violence and vulnerability. He'd learned about the Israeli mob, about the betrayal in Morocco, the desperate flight to Manila, the face-altering surgery, the fleeting encounter with Ceta—a beautiful ghost haunting the edges of Sharon's memory. Pickens had even managed to uncover some of Sharon's past hits, meticulously documented in encrypted files recovered from a hidden server. Each successful assignment painted a vivid portrait of Sharon's brutal efficiency, a chilling testament to his skill and ruthlessness. But the deeper he delved, the more the mystery deepened. Why had Sharon targeted those specific individuals? What was the overarching conspiracy that connected them all? The answers remained elusive, tantalizing glimpses behind a curtain of deception.

The Mossad's involvement was undeniable, a shadow organization operating in the murky depths of international espionage. Their pursuit of Sharon was relentless, fueled by a motive that remained shrouded in secrecy. Pickens suspected it was more than just standard retribution for a rogue agent. There were whispers of a larger game being played, a conspiracy that reached far beyond the individual acts of violence. He had a hunch that Sharon's knowledge was the key, but extracting it from the slippery hitman felt like chasing smoke in the wind. His investigation, initially focused on a simple case of murder, had transformed into a complex web of deceit, an intricate puzzle with pieces scattered across continents.

Miriam's escape was another loose end, a thread that Pickens felt compelled to unravel. He'd found evidence of her involvement: a blurry photograph, a discarded train ticket, a fleeting glimpse of her fleeing the scene before the explosion that shattered Sharon's hideout. Her connection to Sharon, a fractured familial bond steeped in years of resentment and shared trauma, was undeniable. But what role did she play in all this? Was she a victim, a pawn in a larger game, or something far more sinister? The answer, like many others in this case, eluded him.

The aftermath of the Manila incident was particularly troubling. Ceta, the beauty queen, had unwittingly stumbled into Sharon's path, and her fate was sealed by the unforgiving logic of his world. Pickens had found her file, a tragic record of a life cut short, a life sacrificed in the name of survival. It was a stark reminder of the brutal consequences of Sharon's actions, the collateral damage in his twisted game of cat and mouse. The more Pickens investigated, the clearer it became that Sharon wasn't merely a killer for hire; he was a man driven by a complex mix of revenge, self-preservation, and an almost disturbing sense of detached pragmatism.

His investigation led him to a dimly lit warehouse in Brooklyn, a forgotten corner of the city brimming with the stench of decay and the promise of violence. It was here that Pickens found the final piece of the puzzle—a hidden room, a bunker, filled with explosives and intricate schematics. This wasn't just a safe house; it was a bomb factory, a testament to Sharon's ingenuity and his deadly expertise. Among the materials, Pickens found a worn notebook, a collection of Sharon's meticulous notes, a diary of his operations, filled with cryptic entries, encoded messages, and chilling accounts of his past. It confirmed Pickens's suspicions. Sharon wasn't just eliminating targets; he was building a network, a destructive force capable of causing widespread chaos. The notebook contained a series of coded messages, hinting at an imminent attack—a grand finale to his elaborate plan.

Deciphering the codes proved to be a grueling task. Days melted into nights as Pickens poured over the encrypted messages, slowly revealing a conspiracy so vast, so intricate, it sent shivers down his spine. The network was far larger than he'd ever imagined, a sprawling web of corruption extending from the Israeli mob to high-ranking officials, a sinister alliance working in the shadows to destabilize global markets. Sharon was not just a contract killer; he was a crucial player, a key component in a far-reaching scheme of unimaginable proportions.

The revelation sent Pickens on a frantic race against time. He had to stop Sharon, not only to bring him to justice but to prevent a catastrophic event that threatened to plunge the world into chaos. But Sharon was a ghost, a phantom, disappearing into the very fabric of the city. Pickens, chasing shadows, found himself outmaneuvered at every turn. Sharon was always one step ahead, leaving behind a trail of near-misses, false leads, and cryptic messages designed to taunt and mislead. Their final confrontation wasn't a clash of fists or gunfire; it was a war of wits, a battle of deception.

The ending, though far from tidy, left a lingering sense of unease, a sense of finality that was yet to be achieved. Sharon remained elusive, his ultimate motives and connections shrouded in ambiguity. Some ends were tied, but the intricate web of deceit remained partly intact, a reminder that justice, like the city itself, was a complex and often elusive beast. The case, though closed for all intents and purposes, left a bitter aftertaste, a recognition that some wounds never fully heal, some secrets never fully revealed. The city, with its million stories and its myriad of secrets, held onto its dark magic, even after the curtain came down on this particular act of violence. The echo of sirens and the whisper of conspiracy lingered in the air, long after the rain had stopped. Pickens, weary but resolute, knew that this wasn't the end. It was just another chapter in the ongoing saga of a city consumed by its shadows, a city that would continue to breed and harbor those who thrive in its darkness. The fight, for him, would go on. The hunt, though temporarily paused, would always continue. Sharon, the phantom, was still out there.

Escape from Manila

The humid Manila air hung heavy, thick with the scent of exhaust fumes, rotting fruit, and something indefinably acrid—a smell Sharon would come to associate with the city's underbelly. He emerged from the clinic, his face a canvas freshly reworked, but the phantom pains in his jaw and the ever-present knot of fear in his stomach remained unchanged. He was a new man, or at least, he looked like one. But the Mossad, the Abergil mob, and Detective Pickens wouldn't be fooled by a new face. They knew his scent, the ghost of his past clung to him like the Manila humidity.

His escape began not with a grand flourish, but with a series of small, desperate maneuvers. He moved through the city like a wraith, navigating the labyrinthine streets on foot, every sense on high alert. The throngs of people—market vendors hawking their wares, jeepney drivers honking their horns, children chasing stray dogs—provided both cover and a constant threat. Anyone could be watching, anyone could be waiting.

He avoided the main thoroughfares, opting instead for the narrow, twisting alleys that snaked between buildings, their shadows deep and inviting. The air in these passageways was even more stifling, thick with the smell of garbage and decay, but it was preferable to the open exposure of the streets. He moved with the practiced grace of a predator, his senses acutely tuned to the slightest sound, the faintest shift in the air.

A sudden scuffle ahead made him freeze. Two men, their faces obscured by shadows, were grappling with a small, wiry figure. Sharon hesitated, then slipped deeper into the shadows, watching. It was a drug deal gone wrong, the kind of scene he'd witnessed a thousand times before. He recognized the desperation in the small figure's eyes, the primal fear that flashed across his face. The larger men were overpowering him, and as one of them pulled a knife, Sharon's instincts took over.

He moved with a speed that belied his newly altered face, a blur of motion in the oppressive darkness. He disarmed the larger man with a swift, brutal move, the knife clattering on the grimy alley floor. The other man, startled by the sudden intervention, hesitated for a moment, allowing Sharon to incapacitate him with a swift strike to the carotid artery. The man collapsed silently, his body slumping onto the garbage-strewn ground.

The smaller man, eyes wide with shock and gratitude, watched Sharon work, his body trembling. Sharon offered a curt nod, a silent acknowledgment of their shared survival instinct. He didn't need to speak; the language of the streets spoke volumes. Then, he disappeared back into the shadows, leaving the smaller man alone to deal with the consequences.

The next few days were a blur of hurried movements and close calls. He stayed in cheap, rundown hotels, always vigilant, always on edge. The city, once a haven of anonymity, now felt like a cage. Every shadow seemed to hold a threat, every stranger a potential enemy. He learned to read the subtle cues of the city: the way a certain group of men stood together, the nervous glances exchanged across a crowded market, the hushed whispers in the back of a jeepney.

He acquired a fake passport and bought a plane ticket under an assumed identity—a carefully constructed persona, miles removed from the Sharon he once was. This new man had no past, no history, no ties. It was a clean slate, a blank page, though the weight of the old life—the betrayals and the killings—still pressed heavily upon his conscience.

The airport was a test of nerves. The security checks were rigorous, every movement scrutinized, every piece of documentation inspected with a hawk's eye. But Sharon had prepared meticulously, his nerves of steel, honed over years of operating in the shadows. He passed through security without incident, a phantom gliding through the system.

As he boarded the plane, a small, almost imperceptible tremor ran through him. He was leaving Manila behind, escaping the suffocating humidity, the labyrinthine streets, the constant threat of discovery. But he wasn't escaping his past. The memories, the ghosts of his victims, clung to him like the ever-present Manila heat. He was leaving Manila, but his flight from his past was far from over. He was a shadow, a phantom, a ghost constantly looking over his shoulder, never truly free, never truly safe.

The flight itself was a strange respite. Surrounded by the hum of the engines, the gentle rocking of the plane, and the oblivious chatter of passengers, the intensity of his past seemed to fade slightly into the background. The sterile environment of the cabin offered a brief hiatus, a moment to catch his breath before the next inevitable chase. He closed his eyes, trying to silence the thoughts that haunted him. Ceta's face flashed in his mind—a fleeting image of beauty and intelligence brutally extinguished. The weight of that act, the chilling finality of his decision, hung heavy on him.

His new identity offered a degree of comfort, the illusion of a new beginning. But the underlying tension, the knowledge that the eyes of his enemies were still upon him, never truly abated. The new face was a mask, a carefully crafted façade hiding the man who had escaped from Manila, a man who still carried the burden of his past, a man who knew that his freedom, if it could ever truly be called that, was only a temporary reprieve.

He arrived at his destination, a small, quiet town far from the glare of the media and the reach of his pursuers. It was a haven, a temporary respite, but not a sanctuary. He knew he would never truly be safe. The world was a dangerous place, a place where betrayals were common, where violence was a constant threat. And he, Sharon, was a man who lived on the edge of that violence, forever haunted by the choices he had made, forever running from the shadows of his past.

The quiet of his new life was deceptive, a fragile peace clinging precariously to the edges of his existence. The weight of what he had done, the lives he had taken, hung heavy upon him, a constant companion. He looked in the mirror, scrutinized his new face, but saw the same haunted eyes, the same grim determination, the same underlying darkness. The surgery had altered his appearance, but not his soul. That remained unchanged, scarred and wounded, a reflection of the violent path he had chosen—a path that seemed to lead inevitably towards a dark and uncertain future.

Sleep was a luxury he couldn't afford. Even when he managed to fall into a restless slumber, he was plagued by nightmares—vivid, horrifying visions of Marrakech, the chaotic escape from the clinic, Ceta's lifeless eyes. He woke in a cold sweat, the room around him shrouded in darkness, the silence amplifying the turmoil within him. The escape from Manila had been a success, a tactical victory, but the larger war within himself, the conflict between the man he was and the man he wanted to be, raged on, relentless and unforgiving.

He started seeing a therapist, a quiet, unassuming woman who seemed to understand the darkness that simmered beneath his placid exterior. The sessions were fraught with tension, a delicate dance between revelation and restraint. He began to cautiously peel back the layers of his carefully constructed persona, revealing the deep-seated trauma and guilt that fueled his violent tendencies. The therapy was slow, painful, and uncertain, but it offered a small glimmer of hope, a possibility of redemption.

The illusion of normalcy was fragile. He found himself constantly looking over his shoulder, scanning crowds for familiar faces, jumping at sudden noises. The city, despite its quiet charm, was filled with potential threats—every shadow a lurking danger. He was a man living on borrowed time, constantly aware that his past could catch up to him at any moment.

Even in the apparent safety of his new life, the past continued to cast a long shadow. He received anonymous threats, cryptic messages hinting at the pursuit that never truly ceased. The threat was a constant reminder that his escape from Manila was only a temporary solution, a brief respite in a life marked by violence and betrayal.

As the days bled into weeks, and the weeks into months, a certain fatigue settled over him. The relentless pressure, the constant vigilance, began to wear him down. The illusion of a new life, a life free from the shadows of his past, was proving more challenging than he had anticipated. The weight of his actions, the blood on his hands, remained a heavy burden. The escape from Manila had only given him a temporary reprieve; the price of freedom was far from paid in full. He knew it would always be a battle, a constant struggle against the darkness that followed him—a darkness that was, in many ways, a part of him.

New Identities

The Greyhound bus rumbled across the vast expanse of the American Midwest, a monotonous landscape of cornfields and endless sky mirroring the emptiness Sharon felt inside. He looked out the window, the blurring scenery a stark contrast to the vibrant chaos of Manila, a city that had both offered him sanctuary and threatened to consume him.

Beside him, Miriam, her face subtly altered, her dark hair now a lighter auburn, scanned a worn paperback, her gaze betraying none of the turmoil churning beneath the surface. They were ghosts, flitting through a world that no longer recognized them. Their new identities, carefully constructed with the help of a shadowy contact in New York, felt like masks, thin veils barely concealing the faces of their past selves.

Their destination: Omaha, Nebraska. A seemingly unremarkable city, far removed from the glittering lights of New York and the suffocating humidity of Manila. A place to disappear, to blend into the anonymity of the American heartland. Sharon had chosen it for its ordinariness, its lack of any connection to his past. Or so he hoped.

Miriam, ever the pragmatist, had secured them small jobs—Miriam as a waitress at a diner, Sharon as a night-shift janitor at a sprawling warehouse on the city's outskirts. The work was tedious, the pay meager, but it provided a semblance of normalcy, a fragile shield against the storm that still raged within them. The money was barely enough to cover their rent in a cramped apartment above a laundromat, but it was enough to keep them alive, to buy them time. Time to heal, to rebuild, to…forget?

Forget was a luxury neither of them could afford. The memories were too vivid, too painful. Sharon could still see Ceta's wide, terrified eyes, her blood staining his hands even now, a stain he couldn't wash away, no matter how many times he scrubbed. He saw the faces of his victims, the fleeting expressions of terror that haunted his dreams, a grim testament to his life of violence. Miriam carried her own burden—the betrayal, the loss, the crushing weight of their family's shattered legacy. They were bound together by blood, by shared trauma, by the relentless pursuit of a future that seemed perpetually out of reach.

Omaha offered a different kind of fear, a quieter, more insidious kind. It wasn't the constant threat of assassination, the adrenaline-fueled chases, the ever-present shadow of the Mossad or the Abergil mob. This was the gnawing anxiety of anonymity, the fear of being unnoticed, of fading into the background, of becoming just another face in the crowd. Ironically, this very anonymity was their protection.

The diner where Miriam worked was a whirlwind of clattering plates, steaming coffee, and the incessant chatter of local gossip. The regulars knew her as "Beth," a friendly, efficient waitress with a quiet smile that barely concealed the exhaustion etched around her eyes. She found solace in the routine, in the small acts of service, a stark contrast to the life she once knew. She'd developed a routine, meticulously avoiding any topics that could possibly reveal her true identity. The small talk was always innocuous, the news snippets about local sports and weather, a shield against the past. Yet, sometimes, a chance word, a passing resemblance, a fleeting shadow in the periphery would jolt her back to the reality of their precarious existence.

Sharon's nights were spent in the vast, echoing warehouse, the fluorescent lights casting long, distorted shadows that danced with his own anxieties. He moved through the cavernous space, pushing a mop or scrubbing the concrete floors, each repetitive movement a meditation against the chaos within. He was "Mark," a solitary figure, a ghost in the machine, a silent observer in a world he didn't quite belong to. The isolation was a balm and a torment, a necessary solitude but also a stark reminder of the distance he'd created between himself and humanity.

The silence of the warehouse was frequently broken only by the rhythmic squeak of his shoes on the polished concrete, the whirring of machinery, or the distant rumble of passing trucks. But the silence was never truly empty. It was filled with the ghosts of his past, the whispers of his crimes, the relentless ticking of a clock counting down to an inevitable reckoning. He felt the weight of every life he'd taken, every betrayal he'd committed, every lie he'd told. The masks might conceal their identities, but they couldn't hide the ghosts that haunted their souls.

One night, while cleaning near a loading dock, he saw a fleeting glimpse of something familiar—a faded tattoo peeking from under a sleeve, a symbol he recognized instantly. It was a symbol associated with the Abergil mob. His heart pounded in his chest; adrenaline surged through him, awakening the instincts that had kept him alive for so long. He felt the familiar icy grip of fear, a chilling reminder that his past, no matter how hard he tried to outrun it, was always just around the corner.

He knew he couldn't stay. Not in Omaha. Not anywhere. The price of freedom, it seemed, was eternal vigilance, a constant awareness of the shadows lurking just beyond the reach of the ordinary. The new identities, the quiet lives, the anonymity – all of it was a temporary reprieve, a fragile illusion. The past, it turned out, was far more resilient than he'd ever imagined. He would need to find a way to break free from the cycle of violence and betrayal, or the shadows would ultimately consume him.

The ghosts were getting closer, their whispers growing louder. He was not simply a man running from his past; he was a man running from himself. And he knew that eventually, he would have to confront the darkness within, the darkness that mirrored the ever-present shadows closing in. Escape was only a temporary fix; true freedom required more than just a new face and a new name. It required a complete transformation, a shedding of the very identity that had condemned him to this life of shadows and secrets. But how to achieve that, he had yet to discover. The road ahead remained shrouded in uncertainty, but one thing was certain: the fight for survival had just begun anew.

The Weight of Guilt

The Greyhound bus shuddered, spitting gravel as it pulled into a desolate bus station somewhere in Nebraska. The air hung heavy, thick with the smell of diesel and loneliness. Miriam, her newly auburn hair catching the weak sunlight filtering through the grimy windows, didn't look up from her book. Sharon, however, felt the weight of the world pressing down on him, heavier than any suitcase he'd ever carried. It wasn't the physical journey that exhausted him; it was the internal one, a relentless, torturous trek through the landscape of his own guilt.

Ceta's face swam before his eyes, a ghostly image superimposed over the blurry fields rushing past. Her laughter, once bright and infectious, now echoed in his memory as a chilling premonition. He'd justified it, of course, told himself it was necessary, a brutal act of self-preservation. But the truth, cold and unforgiving, was that he'd killed her. A woman he'd come to care for, a woman who'd offered him a fleeting moment of peace in the maelstrom of his life. The lie he'd spun, the illusion of sanctuary he'd built around her, crumbled to dust with every passing mile.

He'd been a shadow, a ghost, a phantom, ever since he'd escaped the Moroccan assassins. He'd shed his skin, his identity, his very past, attempting to leave behind the monstrous deeds he'd committed in the name of survival. Yet, no matter how many faces he adopted, no matter how many cities he fled to, the stain of his actions remained, an indelible mark burned into the fabric of his being. He was a man haunted not by the specters of his enemies, but by the ghost of his own conscience.

The surgery had been brutal, a painful process that stripped away more than just his features. The doctors had reshaped his bones, his muscles, his very essence, but they hadn't been able to erase the memories etched deep within his soul. The act of killing Ceta had been the most recent addition to the tapestry of his violent past, a violent thread woven into a pattern of betrayal and bloodshed. Every hit, every bomb, every act of calculated destruction had left its mark, its scar. Each life taken, a heavy stone added to the burden he carried.

Omaha was a pit stop, a temporary haven before he continued his flight. He needed to disappear again, to melt back into the anonymity he'd so desperately sought. But even in the anonymity of a bustling city, he couldn't escape the accusations of his own mind. The whispers of his past had become a deafening roar, a constant reminder of his transgressions. He saw Ceta's face in the faces of strangers, felt the weight of her death pressing down on his shoulders.

He wondered if Miriam noticed his internal struggle, the torment he kept locked behind a carefully constructed façade of stoicism. She'd been through her own ordeal, her life shattered by the same forces that had driven him to the edge. They were two shipwrecked souls clinging to a shared raft, drifting aimlessly on a sea of uncertainty. But their shared trauma couldn't bridge the chasm between him and his guilt. His burden was uniquely his.

He remembered his sister's look the last time they'd spoken in New York before the long bus trip. A complicated gaze filled with pity, understanding, and a hint of fear. She was in this mess just as much as he was, yet he had not let her into the deepest corners of his heart. He saw the resemblance to their mother in her features, the maternal strength she'd inherited. Miriam was a shield, his only connection to something precious and real. Yet he still felt like a ghost to her.

The guilt gnawed at him, relentless and insatiable. It wasn't the fear of apprehension that paralyzed him; it was the corrosive effect of his actions on his soul. He'd traded his humanity for survival, but the cost was far greater than he'd anticipated. He'd become a creature of shadows, existing on the periphery of life, forever disconnected from the warmth of human connection.

He thought of Detective Pickens, the relentless investigator who was piecing together the fragments of his shattered life. Pickens, with his unwavering pursuit of justice, represented everything Sharon had abandoned. Pickens was the embodiment of the law, of morality, of the very things Sharon had betrayed. Pickens was his antithesis, a constant reminder of the man he once was, the man he could no longer be.

The bus jerked, interrupting his thoughts. He looked out the window again, but the landscape hadn't changed. It was still the same monotonous stretch of farmland, a symbol of the endless, desolate path he was traversing. He was a prisoner of his own past, shackled by the weight of his guilt, unable to escape the inescapable truth of who he had become.

He lit a cigarette, the acrid smoke a fleeting distraction from the storm raging inside him. The nicotine offered a temporary numbing effect, a momentary escape from the relentless self-recrimination. But even the fleeting solace of the cigarette couldn't erase the memories, the images, the guilt.

He closed his eyes, trying to conjure a different scene, a different life. He saw his mother's face, her smile warm and loving, a face he'd betrayed with every violent act he'd committed. The image shattered, replaced by the grim reality of his present existence. He was a killer, a murderer, a man stained with the blood of his victims. The truth was inescapable, a cold, hard fact etched into the very core of his being.

His hand instinctively went to his face, tracing the contours of his new features. The surgery had been a success, but the scars remained, both physical and emotional. The physical scars were a testament to his desperate attempt to escape his past, but the emotional scars ran deeper, more permanent, more devastating.

He wondered if he could ever find redemption, if he could ever atone for his sins. He doubted it. He'd walked down a path of no return, a path paved with blood and betrayal. The only certainty was the weight of his guilt, a burden he would carry for the rest of his days. He was a fugitive, a phantom, a man forever haunted by the ghosts of his past and the inescapable reality of his present.

The bus finally reached its destination. The passengers began to disembark, their faces blurred, indistinguishable in the dim light of the station. Sharon remained seated, his gaze fixed on the floor, lost in the labyrinth of his own tormented thoughts. The journey hadn't ended; it had merely reached another desolate stop on a journey with no apparent end. The weight of his guilt, however, would remain a constant companion, an unrelenting reminder of the price he'd paid for freedom. A freedom that felt increasingly like a prison.

He needed to disappear again, to melt into the shadows once more. But the shadows themselves seemed to carry the weight of his guilt, mirroring the darkness within him. He was a man caught in a perpetual cycle of violence and escape, a desperate dance with his own demons. He wasn't simply running from the law; he was running from himself, from the horrifying truth of who he'd become. And he knew, deep down, that he could never truly escape. The price of freedom, he realized with a chilling certainty, was the eternal burden of his own conscience. The journey was far from over; the true reckoning was yet to come.

A New Beginning

The Greyhound lurched again, throwing Sharon against the grimy window. He watched the monotonous blur of the Nebraska plains, a landscape as bleak and unforgiving as his own soul. Miriam, oblivious to his turmoil, continued reading, her face illuminated by the weak glow of the paperback. He envied her capacity for detachment, her ability to lose herself in a fictional world while he remained trapped in the brutal reality of his own making.

He'd told her nothing of Ceta, of the cold efficiency with which he'd silenced her, nor the fleeting pang of regret that had quickly been swallowed by the chilling certainty of self-preservation. He couldn't burden her with the weight of his actions, the ever-growing mountain of corpses that followed him like a shadow. Telling her would be akin to admitting defeat, to acknowledging the monster he'd become. Miriam, with her unwavering belief in the possibility of redemption, deserved better than the horrifying truth.

He thought of the face staring back at him from the reflection in the dusty window – a new face, carefully crafted by a surgeon's skilled hands, yet still bearing the indelible mark of his past. The surgery had been a success, technically, but it hadn't erased the memories or the haunting images etched into the very fabric of his being. He saw not just a reflection but a ghost – a ghost of the man he once was, a man who might have existed in a parallel universe, one where he hadn't chosen the path of violence.

The bus slowed, finally grinding to a halt in a small, forgotten town. He could barely make out the faded name on the rusted sign – Havenwood. The irony wasn't lost on him.

Havenwood. A haven? This place felt more like a tomb. He dragged his suitcase off the bus, the worn leather groaning under the weight of his unspoken burdens. Miriam followed, her gaze fixed on the cracked pavement.

They found a cheap motel on the outskirts of town, its neon sign flickering intermittently, casting an eerie glow on the dilapidated building. The room was cramped, smelling faintly of stale cigarette smoke and despair – a fitting reflection of his current state. He paid cash, avoiding eye contact with the weary motel owner. Silence descended upon them, heavy and suffocating. He watched Miriam unpack, her movements precise and methodical, a stark contrast to the chaos raging within him. He wondered, not for the first time, if she knew something, if the serene mask she wore concealed a hidden understanding of his true nature.

Days bled into weeks. The monotony of Havenwood was a form of self-imposed exile. He found a job at a local diner, washing dishes and wiping down counters. The work was menial, back-breaking, but it gave him a semblance of normalcy – a brief respite from the relentless pursuit of his past. He lived a quiet life, or as quiet as a man with his past could ever manage. He observed small-town life, the routine interactions, the quiet desperation of everyday existence. He even found himself, strangely, feeling a sense of calm. A fragile calm, easily shattered, but a calm nonetheless.

He'd started reading again, something he hadn't done in years. He devoured books, escaping into their worlds, hoping to distance himself from his own reality. He read novels, thrillers, and even poetry – a stark contrast to the violent tales he'd lived. He began to question his life choices, wondering if this new, quiet existence was truly possible, or merely a brief interlude before the inevitable storm returned.

One evening, while washing dishes, he saw a news report on a small television set in the corner of the diner. A fleeting image flashed across the screen – a familiar face, a face that had been painstakingly altered, but still recognizable beneath the surgeon's skillful disguise. The report detailed a recent bombing in New York, a sophisticated device that had caused considerable damage. The details were scant, but the way the reporter described the bomber – cold, methodical, efficient – sent a chill down his spine.

The calm was gone. The fragile peace was shattered. The specter of his past had returned, its presence as cold and tangible as the steel of a well-crafted bomb. The realization struck him with brutal force: he couldn't escape. He could change his face, his name, his location, but he couldn't escape the shadow of his past, the relentless pursuit of those he'd wronged. The price of freedom, he realized, was far higher than he'd ever imagined. It wasn't just the constant fear, the ever-present threat of exposure, but the psychological toll, the relentless gnawing guilt that threatened to consume him. He'd tried to find a haven, but Havenwood was proving to be just another stage in his unending flight.

He stared at his reflection in the greasy spoon's silverware, his new face almost a stranger. The features were softer, less angular, but the eyes remained the same. Those eyes, dark and shadowed, held the weight of countless sins. He saw the weariness etched into the lines around them, the faint tremor in his hands as he scrubbed the stubborn grime from a plate.

He knew, with chilling certainty, that this peaceful existence was an illusion, a fleeting dream that would soon be shattered by the inevitable return of violence.

He was a man haunted by his past, a past he couldn't erase, one that continued to chase him with relentless determination. He thought about the life he'd tried to build, the quiet normalcy he'd craved, and he knew, deep down, that it was a pipe dream. He was a wolf in sheep's clothing, a predator in disguise, and the instinct to kill, to destroy, was still a part of him – a part that he couldn't ignore, couldn't suppress.

That night, he couldn't sleep. He paced the cramped motel room, the floorboards creaking under his restless feet. Miriam slept soundly beside him, her breathing even and rhythmic, a stark contrast to the turmoil that raged within him. He looked at her, at her peaceful face, and a wave of guilt washed over him. He couldn't allow her to be caught in the crossfire. He had to leave, to disappear again. But where could he go? Where could he hide from himself? He didn't know. He only knew that the life he'd carved out for himself in Havenwood was a temporary illusion, a brief respite from the storm that was inevitable. The path he was destined to travel was one of violence and escape.

He was a creature of the night, a predator by instinct, a killer by trade. He was Sharon, and he knew, with chilling certainty, that his life would never truly be his own again.

The price of freedom, he realized once more, was a life lived on the run, a life lived in the shadows, a life perpetually teetering on the brink of annihilation. The end might be close or far, but until it arrived, he would continue to run, to kill, to survive, his shadow a constant reminder of the monster he had become. The only question was, how long could he last? How long before the relentless pursuit of his past finally caught up to him, swallowing him whole in the darkness he knew so well? The future remained uncertain, a terrifying, dark canvas with only the faintest glimmer of something different, something... better. But even that hope felt fragile, as fleeting as a wisp of smoke in the wind. His fate remained unwritten, a terrifying uncertainty that mirrored the tempestuous landscape of his own soul.

The Shadow of the Past

The Greyhound shuddered, spitting gravel as it rounded a bend. The rhythmic clatter of the wheels was a hypnotic counterpoint to the relentless drumming of fear in Sharon's chest. Miriam, lost in her book, remained blissfully unaware of the storm raging within him. He glanced at her, a fleeting pang of something akin to affection twisting in his gut. She was the only connection he had left to a life he could barely remember – a life before the blood, before the betrayals, before he became the ghost he was now.

He closed his eyes, the Nebraska plains flashing behind his eyelids like a reel of faded film. He saw himself as a boy, laughing and playing in the sun. Then the images flickered, distorted, replaced by the sharp, brutal clarity of his present reality: the cold steel of a pistol, the slickness of blood, the chilling gaze of his enemies. The memory of Ceta's eyes, wide with disbelief and terror before he silenced her forever, burned into his mind. It was a brand, a constant reminder of the price of his freedom.

The Mossad. The word itself felt like a physical blow, a cold fist slamming against his ribs. They were relentless, shadows in the periphery, always there, always watching. He knew they were tracking him, piecing together the fragments of his shattered life, his movements a breadcrumb trail leading straight back to him. He could feel their gaze even now, a weight pressing down, suffocating him. He wasn't just running from the Abergil mob; he was running from the wrath of a nation, a shadow organization with resources and capabilities beyond his wildest comprehension. They were experts at finding people, at disappearing people. And Sharon was now both.

He shifted uncomfortably, the worn fabric of his jeans scratching against his skin. He'd changed his appearance, altered his gait, but the knowledge that he was being hunted was an unshakeable part of him, woven into the very fabric of his being. It was a phantom limb, the constant absence of safety, the ever-present threat of capture. It gnawed at him, a persistent ache that overshadowed even the physical discomfort of the cramped bus seat.

In Manila, he'd thought he'd found a sanctuary. He'd believed the surgery would erase his past, allowing him to start anew. He'd been a fool. Ceta, with her innocent smile and the sparkle in her eyes, had been a siren's call, luring him toward the rocks. Her connection to his past, a tenuous thread initially, had quickly become an unbreakable chain binding him to the life he desperately tried to escape. He'd killed her, not out of malice, but out of necessity, a cold, brutal calculation born of self-preservation. He'd silenced her, but he hadn't silenced the ghosts that haunted him.

He thought of Detective Pickens, the man he'd crossed paths with in New York. Pickens, with his relentless pursuit of justice, his unwavering gaze, his suspicion that had a knack for sniffing out the truth. He was a dog with a bone, and that bone was Sharon. Pickens wouldn't rest until he had him, and Sharon knew it with a bone-deep certainty. The detective's methods were unorthodox, borderline reckless, but he was effective. He wouldn't give up until he had brought Sharon down. And Pickens was just one of the many hounds sniffing at his trail.

The Greyhound pulled into a desolate bus station, the screech of brakes jarring Sharon back to the present. He gathered his meager belongings – a worn duffel bag containing a few clothes and a pistol, his only constant companions. He paid the driver, his gaze betraying nothing of the turmoil within. He was a master of disguise, a chameleon adapting to his environment. But no amount of camouflage could mask the fear that constantly gnawed at him, the chilling knowledge that he was never truly safe.

He stepped off the bus, the cold wind whipping around him, a chilling premonition setting in. He was a fugitive, a ghost, a shadow moving through a world that had no place for him. He was a man defined by his past, hunted by his enemies and haunted by his own demons. The price of freedom, he thought grimly, was a perpetual state of war, a constant battle against the forces that sought to destroy him.

He'd made a life for himself, a precarious, violent existence. He was a mercenary, a killer, a ghost operating in the darkest corners of the criminal underworld. He executed contracts with ruthless efficiency, his actions always calculated, always devoid of emotion. He'd learned to compartmentalize, to separate the man he was from the monster he'd become. But the line between the two was blurring, becoming increasingly difficult to distinguish. He wasn't sure if he was still capable of feeling anything other than the cold calculation of survival.

His actions were a consequence of his past, a ripple effect from the choices he'd made years ago. Each hit, each bomb, was a consequence of the web he had woven, a chain reaction he could no longer control. The past was relentless, a tidal wave that pulled him under, threatening to consume him whole. Every shadow held the potential for an enemy, every face could be a threat.

The constant fear was exhausting, a relentless pressure that wore him down. Sleep was a luxury he rarely allowed himself. When he did sleep, it was filled with nightmares, the memories of his past re-enacting in vivid detail. The faces of his victims, his enemies, and those he'd betrayed swirled together in a chaotic and terrifying vortex.

He walked away from the bus station, blending into the anonymity of the crowd. He was a ghost in a bustling city, a man without a past, a man without a future. The only certainty in his life was the relentless pursuit of those who wanted him dead. He was trapped, caught in a web of deceit and violence, a spider's web woven from his past mistakes, with no visible escape.

The weight of his past hung heavy on him, a crushing burden he could not escape. Every step he took, every breath he took, was a reminder of the choices he had made and the consequences he now faced. The freedom he'd fought so hard for had turned into a gilded cage, a prison of his own making.

He sought refuge in a dimly lit bar, the air thick with smoke and the low murmur of conversations. He ordered a whiskey, the burn a welcome distraction from the gnawing emptiness inside. His gaze scanned the room, sharp and calculating. He saw the faces of strangers, each one a potential threat, a potential enemy. Paranoia was his constant companion, his ever-present shadow.

He knew he couldn't outrun his past forever. The Mossad, the Abergil mob, Detective Pickens – they were all closing in, their relentless pursuit creating an inescapable noose around him. He wasn't sure how much longer he could last. The price of freedom, he realized with chilling certainty, was everything. And he was slowly paying it, one bloody, desperate day at a time. The question wasn't if he would fall, but when, and to whom. The shadow of his past was long, and it was slowly but surely catching up to him.

The only thing left was to decide how he would meet the inevitable end. And whether, perhaps, there might be a single flicker of redemption amidst the coming darkness.

Life on the Run

The humid Manila air hung heavy, a suffocating blanket clinging to Sharon's skin even as he sat in the stiflingly air-conditioned room of their rented apartment. He'd chosen a place far from the bustling city center, in a quiet, almost forgotten corner where the sounds of the metropolis faded into a dull hum. It was supposed to be safe, a haven from the relentless pursuit that had chased him across continents. But safety, Sharon knew, was an illusion—a fleeting moment between the cracks of ever-present danger.

Miriam, his sister, paced restlessly across the small living room, her movements sharp and agitated, a stark contrast to the stillness of the room. The new identities they'd assumed were fragile masks, easily shattered by a single indiscretion, a misplaced glance, a recognizable accent. The weight of their shared past pressed down on them, a suffocating burden that threatened to drown them in a sea of fear and paranoia.

He'd known, even before they fled Manila, that escape was only temporary. The Mossad, relentless and efficient, would continue their hunt. Detective Pickens, that bulldog of a cop, would not rest until he had Sharon in handcuffs. And lurking in the shadows, a nameless, faceless enemy—the one who'd orchestrated the Moroccan ambush— awaited the perfect moment to strike again. He was like a ghost, a phantom pain that constantly reminded Sharon of his mortality.

Miriam stopped pacing, her gaze fixed on the window, where the Manila night pressed close, a black, teeming mass of sounds and shadows. "This isn't living, Sharon," she whispered, her voice tight with unshed tears. "It's just existing, waiting for the other shoe to drop."

Sharon understood her fear. He felt it too, a constant, gnawing anxiety that clawed at his insides. He'd spent years living on the edge, a life defined by violence and betrayal, where trust was a luxury he could not afford. Now, even the fragile trust he'd built with Miriam felt like a treacherous tightrope walk over an abyss. Every shadow seemed to conceal a threat, every stranger a potential enemy.

Their days were a monotonous cycle of vigilance. They barely ventured out, relying on deliveries for food and supplies. Miriam, once vibrant and independent, was now a shadow of her former self, her eyes haunted by fear and uncertainty. Sharon felt a pang of guilt, a familiar ache in his chest. He had dragged her into this life—this relentless flight from justice and retribution.

One afternoon, a knock on the door sent a jolt of adrenaline through Sharon. His hand instinctively went to the small, well-hidden pistol tucked into his waistband. He exchanged a look with Miriam, their eyes communicating a shared fear. He slowly approached the door, his heart pounding a frantic rhythm against his ribs.

He peered through the peephole, his breath catching in his throat. A young woman stood on the other side, her face partially obscured by shadows. She held a small, unmarked package in her hand. Sharon didn't recognize her, but the way she held herself—the alertness in her posture—suggested she wasn't just a delivery person. It was a strange intuition, a feeling he'd honed over years of living on the edge.

He hesitated. His gut screamed danger, a primal warning that echoed through his years of experience. But his mind fought back, rationalizing the possibility that it was just a simple delivery. The risk of ignoring the warning, however, far outweighed the risk of being wrong. His life had taught him that caution was the only true defense.

He opened the door cautiously, his hand still resting on the pistol. The woman didn't speak, merely extended the package toward him. He took it, his fingers brushing against hers. They were surprisingly warm, strangely soft—a stark contrast to the cold grip of fear that had him in its icy embrace.

"It's for you," she whispered, her voice barely audible. Then, as quickly as she had appeared, she vanished into the swirling shadows of the Manila night, leaving Sharon alone with the enigmatic package.

Back inside, Miriam's eyes were wide with apprehension. "Who was that?" she asked, her voice a shaky whisper.

Sharon shrugged, a gesture that masked the unease churning within him. He examined the package. It was small, nondescript, wrapped in plain brown paper. There was no return address, no identifying marks. It felt deceptively ordinary, a carefully crafted illusion designed to lull him into a false sense of security. He knew better than to trust appearances.

He carefully tore open the wrapping. Inside, nestled among layers of tissue paper, lay a single photograph. It was a picture of him—taken years ago, before the surgeries, before he'd become a ghost, a phantom haunting the streets of international crime. It was a picture from a life he thought he'd left behind, a life he desperately wanted to forget.

But the photograph was more than just a reminder of his past. Scrawled across the back in crimson ink was a single, chilling word: "Remember."

The blood drained from Sharon's face. The message was clear. They were not safe. The past, with its relentless pursuit and insatiable hunger for vengeance, was about to catch up with them. The illusion of safety shattered, replaced by the stark reality of their precarious existence. The hunt was far from over. In fact, it had only just begun. A new enemy had emerged from the shadows—an enemy who knew him, an enemy who held a piece of his past, an enemy with a chilling ability to find him no matter how far he ran or how skillfully he hid.

That night, sleep eluded Sharon. The image of the photograph burned itself into his mind, a searing brand that served as a stark reminder of the precariousness of his existence. He knew he had to act, to anticipate their next move, to outwit their relentless pursuit. He had to stay one step ahead—a game of cat and mouse where the stakes were life and death. He had to find out who sent the photo and what they wanted. The question haunted him, a serpent coiling around his heart, squeezing the air from his lungs. He had to find out, or it would be his last mistake.

The game had begun anew, and this time, the odds felt far more stacked against him. He was a ghost, existing on the fringes of society, always looking over his shoulder. And this time, the ghost had a name—or, at least, a chilling reminder.

A New Enemy Emerges

The Manila sun beat down relentlessly the next morning, baking the city into a simmering haze. Sharon, however, felt a chill deeper than the air conditioning could ever dispel.

The photograph—a grainy image of Ceta, her face a mask of terror moments before her death—had ripped open a wound he thought he'd sealed shut. He knew, with a certainty that gnawed at his gut, that this wasn't just some random act of violence. Someone had deliberately sent it, a message delivered with chilling efficiency. But who? And why?

He spent the day poring over his meager resources—the few contacts he'd managed to establish in the shadowy underworld of Manila, the scraps of information gleaned from Ceta's apartment, the lingering scent of betrayal that clung to everything he touched. But nothing yielded a clear answer, only a deepening sense of unease. The city, once a refuge, now felt like a suffocating cage.

That evening, a knock on his door shattered the fragile peace. He peered through the peephole, his heart hammering against his ribs. It wasn't the Mossad agents he expected, their faces obscured by shadows and anonymity. Instead, a woman stood there, her face partially hidden by a wide-brimmed hat. She was elegant, almost ethereal—starkly contrasting the gritty reality of his existence.

He hesitated, his hand hovering over the Glock tucked into his waistband. He knew better than to trust anyone, yet something in him stirred, a strange curiosity, perhaps even… hope? A foolish sentiment, he instantly chided himself.

He opened the door a crack. "Who are you?" he demanded, his voice raspy from disuse.

The woman smiled, a slow, deliberate movement that hinted at both danger and intrigue. She pushed back her hat, revealing a face etched with sharp features and intelligent, piercing eyes. Her expression was unreadable, a carefully constructed mask.

"My name is Isabella," she said, her voice low and melodic, like a siren's call. "And I believe I can be of assistance."

Sharon's skepticism was immediate and profound. He'd learned to trust his instincts, and they screamed warning. "Assistance? From whom?"

Isabella leaned closer, her breath warm against his cheek. "Let's just say… from someone who knows more about your past than you might think."

His blood ran cold. He knew then that this wasn't a random encounter. It was a carefully orchestrated meeting, a calculated move by a player he hadn't even realized was in the game.

He invited her in, his movements precise and controlled. He kept his hand close to his weapon, ever vigilant, ever wary. The air in the apartment crackled with tension, an unspoken understanding of the danger that hung between them.

Isabella didn't waste time on pleasantries. She spoke of a clandestine organization—a shadowy group operating in the gray areas between governments and intelligence agencies, pulling strings in the world's darkest corners. She described a network of informants, operatives, and assassins, a web of interconnected power far exceeding anything Sharon had ever encountered.

"They know about you, Sharon," she said, her gaze unwavering. "They know about your past, your connections to the Abergil family, your work in Morocco… everything."

Sharon felt a cold dread seep into his bones. He had always believed he was operating in the shadows, a ghost unseen and unheard. But this new enemy not only knew of his existence—they knew him intimately.

"And they want you," Isabella continued, her voice barely a whisper. "But not for what you think. They're not interested in capturing or killing you."

This statement, so unexpected, caught Sharon off guard. He'd prepared for a deadly confrontation, for a desperate struggle for survival. But this was something entirely different.

"What do they want, then?" Sharon asked, his voice barely audible.

"They want your expertise," Isabella said, her eyes glinting with something that might have been amusement—or perhaps something far more sinister. "They need someone who understands the intricacies of this world, someone who can move undetected, someone who's willing to get their hands dirty."

Sharon knew he was walking a tightrope. This new threat, this enigmatic organization, presented a far more dangerous proposition than the Mossad or the Abergil family. It was a gamble, a perilous dance on the edge of a knife. But it was a gamble he had no choice but to take. His survival depended on it.

Over the next few days, Isabella revealed more about this organization, whose name she refused to utter, referring to them only as "The Syndicate." They operated outside the law, beyond the reach of any government. Their motives were shrouded in mystery, their goals unclear, but their power was undeniable.

The Syndicate was interested in the Abergil family, Sharon learned, but not for the reasons he might have expected. They weren't focused on dismantling the organization or seizing their assets. Instead, they were interested in something far more insidious, something buried deep within the family's history—a secret that could shake the foundations of the global political landscape.

Sharon, a seasoned assassin, a ghost haunting the edges of the underworld, found himself thrust into a game far beyond his comprehension. This wasn't just about survival anymore; it was about uncovering a conspiracy so vast, so intricate, that it threatened to swallow him whole.

He was a pawn in a game of global power, a pawn with a unique set of skills and a past that made him the perfect candidate. But trust was a luxury he couldn't afford, and loyalty was a commodity traded in blood and betrayal. He had to proceed with caution, every move calculated, every step measured, knowing that one wrong move could be his last.

The humid Manila air pressed in on him, heavy with the scent of rain and decay. The city was a labyrinth of shadows, a place where secrets festered and betrayal lurked around every corner. But Sharon was no stranger to darkness. He embraced it, knew it intimately, and used it to his advantage.

He agreed to work with The Syndicate, but only on his own terms. He was playing a dangerous game, a game where the lines between right and wrong were blurred beyond recognition, and his only ally was his own cunning.

For weeks, Sharon gathered intelligence for The Syndicate, infiltrating their inner circle, uncovering their secrets. He played the role of a double agent, feeding them information while simultaneously seeking a way out, a way to escape the clutches of this new, formidable enemy. His past continued to haunt him—not just in the form of the Mossad, the Abergil family, and Detective Pickens, but now also through this new and shadowy organization. He was surrounded, trapped in a world of shadows, where trust was a commodity traded in blood, and survival was a constant, desperate struggle. The game had evolved, and the stakes had just gotten unimaginably higher. The ghost had a new name to fear, and it was whispered only in the darkest corners of the world. The weight of the world rested on his shoulders, or perhaps, the weight of the world's most dangerous secrets.

He knew that working with The Syndicate was a double-edged sword. They were powerful, but unpredictable. Their methods were ruthless, their loyalty questionable. He played his cards close to his chest, revealing only what was absolutely necessary, always maintaining a calculated distance, a subtle air of detachment. He was a ghost, and he intended to remain one.

The information he gathered for The Syndicate was meticulously compiled, every detail analyzed and cross-referenced. He used his network of contacts, his knowledge of the underworld, and his innate ability to manipulate people. But he was also carefully building his own escape route, a plan to extricate himself from this perilous situation before he became another victim.

He had learned, over many years of living in the shadows, that trust was a luxury he couldn't afford. Everyone had an agenda; everyone was playing their own game. The only person he could truly rely on was himself. He was a lone wolf, operating in a pack of predators, and he knew that only his own cunning would keep him alive. He was facing not just the Abergil family, not just the Mossad, not just Detective Pickens, but an organization whose influence stretched across continents, an organization shrouded in secrecy, an organization that knew him better than he knew himself. His survival depended on his ability to outwit them, to outmaneuver them, to stay one step ahead of the game.

The stakes were higher than ever, and the shadows were deeper than before. The ghost had found himself in a maze of shadows, and the exit was nowhere in sight.

Secrets Revealed

The chipped porcelain mug warmed Sharon's hands, the lukewarm coffee doing little to soothe the icy dread that had settled in his bones. He stared out the grimy window of his cramped New York apartment, the city a blurry tapestry of lights and shadows. The Manila photograph, a constant, unwelcome presence in his mind, had unearthed something buried deep within him—a secret that threatened to unravel everything he'd painstakingly built. It wasn't just Ceta's death; it was the implication, the whisper of a connection he'd desperately tried to sever. A connection to his sister, Miriam.

Miriam. The name itself felt like a phantom limb, a painful reminder of a past he'd tried to bury. He hadn't seen her in years, not since their childhood had imploded under the weight of their parents' bitter divorce and their own fractured relationship. He remembered her as a bright, vivacious girl, full of dreams. Those dreams had shattered alongside their family, leaving behind a cautious woman who seemed perpetually on the verge of unraveling. The photograph hinted at something more, something darker. A shared secret.

He'd always believed their separation was a result of his life choices, his descent into the criminal underworld. He'd convinced himself that it was his fault, his actions that had driven a wedge between them. But the photograph suggested a different narrative, one where he wasn't the sole architect of their estrangement. It was a coded message, a cryptic clue dropped into a world already saturated with deceit and murder. He suddenly remembered a forgotten trinket, a small, intricately carved wooden bird he'd given Miriam when they were children. It was a small piece of his past, a memento of a time before the shadows consumed him. He'd thought it lost, another casualty of his nomadic existence.

The photograph, he realized with a jolt, was tied to that bird.

A frantic search of his meager belongings yielded nothing. His apartment, a temporary refuge, was devoid of personal effects. He'd kept his life stripped to the bare essentials, a reflection of his precarious existence. Yet, the memory of the bird, its smooth surface beneath his fingers, its delicate carvings, was as vivid as if he were holding it now. It wasn't merely a childhood memory; it was a key, a key to a door he'd never known existed. The bird had a hidden compartment, a secret known only to him and Miriam. And that compartment held a secret that implicated them both in a conspiracy far larger and more dangerous than he'd ever imagined.

The realization hit him with the force of a physical blow. The Abergil family, the Mossad, Detective Pickens— they were all players in a game far more complex than he'd ever conceived. And he, Sharon, was a pawn, manipulated and used by forces he barely understood. The photograph wasn't just a threat; it was a summons, an invitation to confront a past he'd spent years trying to escape. He needed to find Miriam, to understand the secret the photograph hinted at, to decipher its cryptic message before it was too late. He needed answers, and he needed them now.

He grabbed his worn leather jacket, the weight of it a familiar comfort in the chilling reality of his situation. The city outside beckoned, a labyrinth of hidden alleys and shadowed streets, mirroring the maze of his own existence. He knew the risks; he knew the dangers. But he also knew that he couldn't afford to remain passive. His survival, and perhaps Miriam's, depended on his ability to navigate this treacherous landscape, to uncover the truth before it consumed him.

His search for Miriam led him to the forgotten corners of Brooklyn, to the dilapidated tenements and shadowy bars where desperation clung to the air like a persistent fog. He found her living a life barely distinguishable from his own; a life on the edge, a precarious dance between survival and despair. She was a ghost of the girl he remembered, her eyes haunted by a pain that mirrored his own. But there was a resilience in her gaze, a flicker of the defiant spirit he'd once known. The sight of her stirred something within him, a long-dormant affection that had survived years of separation and mutual betrayal.

He confronted her with the photograph, the grainy image a tangible representation of their shared past. Her reaction was immediate, a mixture of shock, fear, and a chilling resignation. The silence that followed was heavy, laden with unspoken words and years of suppressed emotions. The hidden compartment in the wooden bird wasn't just a repository for childhood treasures; it contained a microfilm, a delicate scroll revealing a deeply buried family secret— their father's involvement in a decades-old international arms deal that connected him to the Abergil family. It was a betrayal that reached far beyond family; a betrayal that extended to the very fabric of national security.

Their father, a man Sharon had always viewed as an absent, indifferent figure, was revealed as a manipulative, ruthless operator, playing a dangerous game with global implications. The revelation shattered the carefully constructed narrative Sharon had built around his own life, questioning everything he thought he knew about his past and his family's legacy. The arms deal wasn't just a relic of the past; it was a live wire, still carrying a deadly current. The players involved were still active, pulling strings from the shadows, using Sharon and Miriam as pawns in their dangerous game.

The microfilm detailed a series of coded messages, financial transactions, and meeting locations, a breadcrumb trail leading to the heart of the conspiracy. It explained Ceta's death, not as a random act, but as a calculated move to eliminate a loose end. Ceta, it turned out, had stumbled upon their father's secret, her beauty queen status merely a façade for a network of informants with access to sensitive information. Her death had been a warning, a message delivered in blood. Sharon's survival was now directly intertwined with his sister's, a chilling realization that tightened his throat and quickened his pulse.

Miriam, initially hesitant to become involved, eventually recognized the danger they were in. The revelation of their father's actions forced her to confront her own past, to grapple with the consequences of her family's legacy. Together, they decided to fight back, to expose the conspiracy and protect themselves from the forces that sought to control them. They were a strange pair, a hitman and his estranged sister, but bound together by a shared past, a secret they couldn't afford to ignore, and a common enemy who sought to erase their existence. The wooden bird, a symbol of their childhood innocence, was now a weapon, a key to their survival.

They began meticulously piecing together the information from the microfilm, deciphering the codes and tracing the financial transactions. It was a perilous undertaking, one that required stealth, cunning, and a level of risk they were both intimately familiar with. Their investigation led them to a network of offshore accounts, shell corporations, and shadowy individuals operating on the fringes of the law. The trail led them deeper into the heart of the Abergil's operation, revealing a level of international intrigue and corruption that could shatter governments. They learned that Detective Pickens was unknowingly playing a role in the conspiracy, manipulated by the Abergil's, creating a layer of complexity that added a new element of uncertainty to their already precarious situation.

Each step forward was met with equal parts triumph and terror. They were playing a high-stakes game, a game where the rules were constantly shifting, and the penalties were often deadly. The shadows were deeper than ever, the stakes impossibly high. They learned that the Mossad was aware of their father's activities, and that their investigation was leading them directly into the crosshairs of several powerful, ruthless organizations. They were caught between the Abergil Family's relentless pursuit, the Mossad's watchful eye, and Detective Pickens's misguided investigation – a three-pronged assault from seemingly invincible forces.

Sharon knew that only through collaboration could they survive. He and Miriam, bound together by blood and a shared secret, formed an unlikely alliance. They were two sides of the same coin: a hitman forged in the fires of the underworld, and a woman haunted by the ghosts of her past. Their combined skills and knowledge were a formidable weapon against their enemies, a deadly combination that would determine their fate. The secrets revealed had not only shaken their world but had also forged an unbreakable bond between them, a bond born from betrayal, deception, and the harsh realities of survival in a world of shadows. The game was far from over, and the next move could very well be their last.

The Hunt Continues

The insistent ring of the telephone sliced through the suffocating silence of the apartment, jolting Sharon from a restless sleep. He fumbled for the receiver, his hand trembling slightly. It was Miriam. Her voice, usually sharp and clipped, was tight with anxiety. "They know," she whispered, her breath hitching. "The Mossad. They know about Manila."

A cold wave washed over Sharon. He'd known this day was coming, but the certainty of it still hit him like a physical blow. He'd been too careless, too confident in his ability to erase his tracks. The Manila operation, meant to be a clean break, had become a gaping wound, bleeding secrets he desperately tried to keep hidden.

"How?" Sharon asked, his voice a low growl.

"I don't know," Miriam replied, "But they're closing in. They have Pickens."

Pickens. The name was a bitter pill to swallow. The detective, a man Sharon had crossed paths with several times in the past, was relentless, a bloodhound with an uncanny ability to sniff out the truth. He was the last person Sharon wanted on his trail.

"We need to move," Sharon said, his mind already racing. He could feel the net tightening, the invisible threads of pursuit drawing him closer to a fate he wasn't sure he could escape. He had to think, to plan, to anticipate Pickens's next move. He knew Pickens's methods: methodical, thorough, and utterly unforgiving.

He hung up the phone, the metallic click echoing in the stillness. He glanced at the photograph on his desk – the image of Ceta, hauntingly beautiful even in death, a constant reminder of his failures. He had to leave. And he had to take Miriam with him.

Their escape was a chaotic ballet of stolen cars, hidden alleys, and frantic phone calls. They moved like phantoms through the city's underbelly, their every step echoing with the threat of capture. Sharon, with his years of experience navigating the criminal underworld, orchestrated their movements, while Miriam, with her sharp mind and connections, provided intelligence and secured their escape routes.

Their first stop was a safe house in Brooklyn, a grimy, forgotten corner of the city that held a network of contacts and a hidden arsenal. Miriam had already made arrangements. They changed their appearances, adopting disguises that would make it difficult for Pickens to track them down. Their escape, however, was temporary. They knew this was just the beginning of a much longer game.

Pickens, meanwhile, was a whirlwind of activity. His office, usually a calm sanctuary of investigation, was a chaotic mess of files, photographs, and maps. The Manila lead had opened a Pandora's Box of secrets, and he was determined to unravel them all. The trail led him to Miriam, his suspicions solidifying with every clue he uncovered. He knew she was involved, somehow connected to the string of violent acts that had plagued the city for months. But how, he wasn't yet sure.

The chase intensified. Sharon and Miriam found themselves on the run, constantly looking over their shoulders, their every move calculated, their senses heightened. The city, once a familiar landscape, now felt like a treacherous maze, filled with shadows and unseen dangers.

Their escape led them to a network of safe houses across the country, a complex labyrinth of connections and loyalties. They relied on favors owed and debts collected, each step taken with calculated precision. Sharon's past life, the one he had desperately tried to leave behind, continued to haunt him, a dark specter that seemed determined to follow him to the ends of the earth.

Pickens, however, wasn't easily deterred. He relentlessly pursued every lead, piecing together the puzzle of Sharon's identity and his connection to Miriam. He delved into Sharon's past, uncovering a history of violence and betrayal, a life lived in the shadows where morality was a luxury he couldn't afford. His investigation took him from the dimly lit backstreets of New York to the sun-drenched beaches of Miami, always one step behind Sharon and Miriam.

The constant pressure of the hunt pushed Sharon to his limits. He had always been a master of deception and violence, but this time, it felt different. He felt the weight of his past sins bearing down on him, threatening to crush him under their weight. The endless run left little room for respite, for introspection or regret. He functioned on adrenaline and instinct, his life a blur of escapes and close calls.

Miriam, too, found herself constantly on edge. The life she had tried to build, the stability she had sought, was shattered beyond repair. She had always lived in her brother's shadow, both a source of admiration and fear. Now, she was thrust into the spotlight, forced to confront her own past and the dangerous world her brother inhabited. She found a new resolve, a newfound strength born from necessity and survival.

The hunt continued, a brutal game of cat and mouse, with Sharon and Miriam always a step ahead, but always aware that the inevitable showdown was fast approaching. Pickens's persistence was relentless, his determination unwavering, and the world of shadows that had once been Sharon's sanctuary was slowly turning into his prison.

Days blurred into nights. The pressure mounted, creating a constant sense of urgency and dread. Sharon and Miriam had to stay ahead of the game, always thinking, always planning. Their conversations were terse, urgent, laced with code words and clandestine meetings. They relied on each other, their bond forged in the crucible of shared danger and mutual desperation.

One night, a coded message arrived from a contact in Miami. It was a risky proposition, a dangerous game with high stakes, but it offered a chance for a new beginning, a way to finally shake Pickens off their trail. It was a perilous gamble, a double or nothing situation, but they had no other choice.

The plan was daring, audacious, bordering on suicidal. It involved a complex web of deception, a carefully orchestrated sequence of events designed to mislead Pickens, to throw him off their scent. It required precise timing, flawless execution, and a healthy dose of luck.

As they prepared for their final move, a wave of weariness washed over Sharon. The life he had chosen, the path of violence and deception, had taken its toll. He looked at Miriam, her face etched with worry and exhaustion. For the first time, he saw the deep-seated fear in her eyes. The endless hunt had stripped them of their innocence, leaving them hardened and scarred, their souls marked by the horrors they had witnessed and the lives they had taken. Yet, despite the darkness that surrounded them, a flicker of hope remained, fueled by their shared determination to survive.

The game was far from over, and the stakes had never been higher. The final confrontation was looming, the ultimate test of their resilience and cunning. The shadows were closing in, and the hunt would soon reach its bloody climax.

Trust and Betrayal

The air in the cramped, dimly lit safe house hung heavy with unspoken accusations. Miriam, her face pale and drawn, meticulously checked the explosives they'd painstakingly assembled. Sharon, his gaze fixed on the flickering neon sign of a distant bar, felt the familiar knot of unease tighten in his gut. Trust, a luxury they could no longer afford, was a fragile thing, easily shattered by the slightest tremor of doubt.

He'd seen it in Miriam's eyes – the hesitation, the flicker of suspicion that mirrored his own. Manila. The mention of the city, even whispered, ignited a firestorm of guilt and self-recrimination. He hadn't told her everything. Not about Ceta, not about the depth of his involvement with the Abergil mob, the betrayals he'd suffered and inflicted. Omissions, he rationalized, were acts of protection, a necessary evil in their precarious game of survival. But omissions were also seeds of distrust, blossoming into weeds that choked the very foundation of their alliance.

"Are you sure about this, Sharon?" Miriam's voice was barely a whisper, yet it carried the weight of a thousand unanswered questions.

He turned, his eyes meeting hers. The usual icy detachment he wore as a shield was gone, replaced by a raw vulnerability that both frightened and intrigued her. "As sure as I can be," he replied, his voice rough with fatigue. "The Mossad is closing in. This is our only way out."

"Only way out?" she echoed, her skepticism palpable. "Or only way to eliminate the loose ends?"

The question hung in the air, a poisoned dart aimed at the heart of their fragile bond. He knew she suspected him of playing a double game, of maneuvering them into a position where he could escape, leaving her to face the consequences alone. And perhaps she was right. Self-preservation was a powerful instinct, a brutal survival mechanism honed by years of living on the edge.

He watched as she carefully examined the detonator, her fingers tracing the metallic surface with a chilling precision. The explosives, carefully concealed within a seemingly innocuous package, were their last desperate gamble, a desperate attempt to rewrite their fate. But even as he reassured her, a cold dread crawled up his spine. The Mossad wasn't the only threat. Miriam, his sister, the woman he supposedly trusted above all others, was becoming a potential enemy.

The memory of Ceta's face, her wide, accusing eyes, haunted him. He had killed her, a cold, calculated act of self-preservation. He'd justified it then, but now, the echoes of her death resonated with a sickening clarity. He'd betrayed her trust, and now, he wondered if the same betrayal was about to consume his relationship with Miriam.

Days bled into nights, a relentless cycle of paranoia and preparation. They moved like shadows, their every action shrouded in secrecy, their conversations laced with veiled meanings and calculated silences. The city, once a refuge, now felt like a suffocating cage, its labyrinthine streets echoing with the phantom footsteps of their pursuers.

He tried to talk to her, to bridge the growing chasm between them, but his words felt inadequate, clumsy attempts to mend a shattered trust. He recounted his past, the brutal realities of his life as a hitman, the betrayals, the violence, the relentless pursuit of survival. He hoped it would shed light on his actions, explain the cold calculation that dictated his choices. But Miriam listened with a stony silence, her eyes reflecting a deep-seated mistrust that chilled him to the bone.

One night, while she slept, Sharon slipped out of the apartment. He needed information, a way to verify their plan, to confirm or deny his worst fears. He sought out an old contact, a shadowy figure from his past, a man who owed him a debt. The meeting was short, brutal, and confirmed his dread. The package, the explosives, were designed to eliminate not just their enemies, but Miriam as well. It was a setup, a carefully orchestrated betrayal designed to leave him unscathed, the sole survivor.

The revelation hit him with the force of a physical blow. He staggered back, the cold reality of his situation seeping into his bones. He'd been betrayed not only by the Mossad, but by his own sister. The trust, the fragile bond he'd clung to, had been a cruel illusion. He was alone, surrounded by enemies, a hunted man with no allies left.

Returning to the safe house, the weight of his discovery pressed down on him like a physical burden. He found Miriam awake, her eyes gleaming with a cold calculation that mirrored his own. She didn't need words. The look in her eyes spoke volumes – of betrayal, of cold ambition, of a plan far more intricate than he had ever imagined.

The realization hit Sharon like a brutal wave: this was no longer about escaping their enemies, no longer about evading the Mossad or even surviving the shadows that had stalked him for years. This was about revenge. The bloodied game he had played for so long, where trust was a currency and alliances were fleeting, had now shifted. The battlefield had changed, and it was no longer the Mossad that he needed to defeat—it was his own sister.

Miriam's icy, unreadable expression was like a mask concealing the calculating mind beneath. The sister he had known, the one who had shared moments of childhood innocence and perhaps fleeting trust, was now an adversary, a figure so entwined with his past and his sins that she had become an equal threat. She had known about Ceta, the death that haunted him, and now she was using it against him, playing her cards with the kind of precision he had once admired in himself. She was no longer the person he trusted. She had become the very thing he had feared—a rival in this ruthless game.

The atmosphere between them was thick with tension, an invisible wall of animosity and suspicion separating them as they stood in the dim light of the safe house. Sharon had spent a lifetime manipulating others, weaving lies and webs of deception to stay alive. But now, the person he had once trusted above all else, his own flesh and blood, was playing the same game.

Anger surged through him, but he quickly tempered it. He couldn't afford to act rashly, couldn't afford to show any weakness. If he made a move, it would play right into her hands. He knew how she operated—calculated, ruthless, with an icy resolve that rivaled his own. But if he let her know he suspected her, if he showed even a hint of vulnerability, it would be over. He needed a plan, a way to counteract her every move, to turn the tables and make sure he was the one who came out on top.

He held his ground, playing the part of the unwitting pawn, pretending ignorance. He needed her to think he was still under her control, that he didn't know the truth. The Mossad was closing in, but he knew this would be their final act, a grand performance for an audience that wouldn't care who lived or died. The explosives were their decoy, a false trail laid to mislead and confuse, to buy them time and shift suspicion. But it was also his opening.

Sharon studied her, watching every subtle movement, the flicker of emotion that betrayed her carefully constructed façade. Fear. There it was, just beneath the surface—fear that mirrored his own. They were both in the same position: trapped, alone, and facing a deadly endgame. But only one could survive.

And in the silence of that moment, Sharon found his twisted solace. Revenge had replaced survival, and in this final confrontation, the only thing that mattered now was who would outwit whom. The trust was gone. The bond of blood was now nothing more than a trap, a reminder of everything they had lost. But it wasn't just about who would survive—it was about settling the score.

The final reckoning was fast approaching. And this time, there would be no winners, only the bloody remnants of betrayal and vengeance. The hunt was almost over. But the question remained: who would claim victory in this deadly dance, and at what cost?

A Glimmer of Hope

The humid Manila air hung heavy, thick with the scent of exhaust fumes and rotting mangoes. Sharon, his face still raw from the recent surgery, felt a familiar chill despite the oppressive heat. He'd traded the searing desert sun of Morocco for the stifling humidity of the Philippines, but the relentless pressure of his pursuers remained unchanged. He was a ghost, a phantom, yet his past clung to him like a shadow. Miriam, his sister, a viper in a silk dress, sat across from him in a dimly lit bar, her usual sharp eyes clouded with worry. Their escape had been a desperate scramble, a chaotic ballet of deception and violence that had left them both bruised and battered. The plastic surgery had altered his features, but it hadn't changed the cold, calculating glint in his eyes that betrayed his true nature.

"They're everywhere," Miriam hissed, her voice barely a whisper above the throbbing music. "The Mossad, the Abergil crew… even Pickens' long arm seems to reach across the ocean." She tapped a manicured fingernail against the chipped Formica tabletop. "We need a new plan, and we need it fast."

Sharon took a slow sip of his rum, the burn a welcome distraction from the gnawing anxiety that never seemed to leave him. He'd expected a life of quiet anonymity in the Philippines, a chance to rebuild his life, but fate, it seemed, had other plans. The encounter with Ceta, beautiful and ultimately fatal, had been a stark reminder of his inescapable past. He was a man without a country, a killer without a cause, and yet, somewhere within the hardened shell of the hitman, a flicker of hope remained.

It came in the form of an unlikely alliance. A contact from his past, a man named Kenji Tanaka, a former associate from his days working with the Yakuza in Tokyo. Kenji, a master of disguise and infiltration, had resurfaced unexpectedly, offering a lifeline in the form of a forged passport and a passage on a private jet out of the country. It was a risky proposition, a gamble with potentially deadly consequences, but it was their only chance.

Kenji wasn't a saint. He was as ruthless and morally bankrupt as Sharon, his hands stained with the blood of countless enemies. Yet, in this chaotic dance of survival, he represented a glimmer of hope, a chance to escape the relentless pursuit of those hunting Sharon. Kenji had his own reasons for assisting Sharon – a complicated web of old debts and grudges that intertwined with Sharon's own. The alliance, therefore, was not born of friendship or trust, but rather of mutual self-preservation.

"Kenji's arrangement involves a delicate balancing act," Miriam explained, tracing a pattern on the condensation of her glass. "He needs something from us in return – a small favor, he calls it. A favor that could involve another 'contract.'" Miriam's words hung in the air, heavy with implication. The favor was a dangerous proposition. It would push Sharon back into the dark world he desperately sought to escape, making the line between redemption and damnation even more blurry.

Sharon considered the offer. The risk was immense, the moral cost incalculable. He'd walked a blood-soaked path for years, fueled by revenge and the need to survive. His past was a tapestry woven with betrayal and violence, a testament to his ruthlessness and his lack of scruples. Yet, the thought of freedom, of a life beyond the shadow of his past, was a potent motivator. The possibility of a clean break, a chance to start anew, was too alluring to ignore. He had a deep-seated desire for redemption, but it was a goal constantly undermined by his actions.

"What kind of 'favor'?" Sharon asked, his voice low and gravelly.

Miriam hesitated, choosing her words carefully. "It involves a certain individual… someone who holds significant leverage over Kenji. The person is involved in a high-stakes diamond smuggling operation in Macau. We need to steal a specific diamond – the Serpent's Eye – before it reaches its final destination."

The sheer audacity of the plan sent a shiver down Sharon's spine. Macau, a city of glittering casinos and hidden dangers, was a den of vipers, a place where the line between legitimate business and organized crime blurred into oblivion. The Serpent's Eye was legendary, a priceless gem rumored to be cursed. The heist was a monumental risk, one that could easily cost them their lives. But Sharon, hardened by years of bloodshed, found himself strangely excited. It was the kind of challenge that ignited the dormant embers of his killer instinct, the thrill of the game outweighing the potential cost.

"And Pickens?" Sharon asked, his eyes narrowed. The relentless detective was a constant thorn in his side, a specter that haunted his every move.

Miriam shrugged. "He's a wild card. We can't predict his movements, but we need to assume he will be a factor. Kenji has contacts that can help distract him. But we need to move quickly, decisively. We need to be ghosts once again, only this time, we'll have something tangible to show for it: our freedom."

The plan was intricate and audacious, a dangerous dance on the razor's edge of possibility. They would need to infiltrate Macau's elite circles, charm their way past security, and steal a priceless jewel under the watchful eyes of seasoned professionals. It was a mission that required not just their skills as killers, but also their cunning and their ability to deceive. It was a mission that could either secure their freedom or lead to their demise. Sharon felt a strange mix of fear and excitement. This wasn't simply about survival anymore. This was about a chance at redemption, a gamble for a future that didn't involve looking over his shoulder, for a life beyond the shadows.

The preparation was meticulous, every detail painstakingly planned. Kenji provided the necessary equipment – sophisticated tools, disguises, and false identities that would melt them into the city's vibrant, yet treacherous underbelly. Sharon, with his surgically altered face and his years of experience in deception, was the perfect phantom, capable of moving through the city's shadows undetected. Miriam, with her charm and intelligence, would be the perfect decoy, diverting attention and distracting their enemies. Their roles were clearly defined, their partnership built on mutual necessity rather than trust.

The tension was palpable as they boarded the private jet, the city lights shrinking below them as they soared towards the neon-drenched paradise of Macau. As they left Manila behind, Sharon felt a mixture of hope and trepidation. This wasn't just another hit; it was their last stand. It was their gamble for freedom, their shot at escaping the ghosts of their past. Success, though unlikely, promised a new life. Failure promised only oblivion. The weight of the world rested on their shoulders, as did the weight of the Serpent's Eye, a gem that held the key to their future. The glimmer of hope, fragile as it was, burned brightly, illuminating a path toward redemption, however treacherous it might be.

A Risky Plan

The Macau casino glittered like a predatory insect, its lights a siren call in the inky night. Sharon, his face still subtly altered, felt the familiar knot of tension in his stomach. This wasn't just another assignment; this was their lifeline, their last desperate throw of the dice. Miriam, ever the pragmatist, meticulously checked the satchel containing the Serpent's Eye, the legendary gem that was their ticket to a new life. Its emerald depths seemed to pulse with a malevolent energy, reflecting the precariousness of their situation.

"Remember the plan," Miriam hissed, her voice barely audible above the casino's cacophony. "No deviations. One wrong move, and we're both dead."

Sharon nodded, his gaze sweeping across the opulent lobby, a kaleidoscope of flashing lights, expensive suits, and the hushed whispers of high-stakes gamblers. Their plan was audacious, bordering on suicidal, but it was their only chance. They weren't just outrunning the Mossad; they were evading the Abergil family, the ruthless Israeli mob who considered Sharon a traitor, and Detective Pickens, the relentless NYPD detective whose obsession bordered on pathological.

The Serpent's Eye wasn't just a valuable gem; it was a symbol of power, a piece in a larger game that neither Sharon nor Miriam fully understood. It held secrets, dark and dangerous, secrets that could either save them or destroy them. Their escape was a multi-layered deception, a carefully orchestrated performance designed to throw their pursuers off their trail.

Their first act was to establish a false lead. They had a contact, a low-level Abergil associate who owed Sharon a considerable debt. This man, a greasy character named Benny, was to be their patsy. They would leak information suggesting that the Serpent's Eye was being transported to a specific location—a heavily guarded vault in a rival casino—a carefully crafted illusion to draw their pursuers into a trap.

The second phase of their plan involved a network of contacts Sharon had cultivated over the years—a shadowy web of informants, smugglers, and fences who operated in the murky underbelly of Macau's underworld. These individuals, bound to Sharon by a mixture of loyalty and fear, would provide cover, creating a smoke screen of misinformation to further confuse their enemies.

The third, and most crucial, phase of their operation involved the actual transfer of the Serpent's Eye. This would be done not to Benny, as their enemies believed, but to a discreet contact who would spirit the gem away to a secure offshore account, disappearing it from the clutches of the Abergil family and the ever-vigilant eyes of the Mossad. This contact, a former Mossad agent with a penchant for betrayal, was the riskiest element of their plan, a wild card that could easily lead to their downfall.

"He's reliable, for now," Miriam reassured Sharon, sensing his apprehension. "But he'll want his cut, a substantial one. We'll have to negotiate."

Negotiation was a skill both Sharon and Miriam possessed in abundance, honed through years of operating in the shadows. The former Mossad agent, a hardened operative named David, met them in a secluded VIP room. He was a ghost, a phantom, just like Sharon, his face etched with years of clandestine operations, his eyes holding a chilling intelligence. David, however, was a different kind of ghost; he had traded loyalty for profit, and his past held more betrayals than Sharon could ever hope to recount.

The tension in the room was thick enough to cut with a knife. The air crackled with unspoken threats and promises, a delicate dance of power and deceit. Miriam, the master negotiator, handled the transaction with ruthless efficiency, securing a price that was both acceptable and advantageous. The Serpent's Eye was transferred, the deal sealed with a nod and a cryptic exchange of code words.

As David disappeared into the labyrinthine corridors of the casino, Sharon and Miriam felt a glimmer of hope, a fleeting sense of relief. The first phase of their plan had been successfully executed. But the danger was far from over. The Mossad, alerted by their earlier maneuver, were closing in. The Abergil family, enraged by the deception, were plotting their revenge. And Detective Pickens, driven by his relentless pursuit of justice, was drawing ever closer.

Their escape from Macau was a breathless flight, a desperate scramble through a maze of back alleys and hidden passages. They used a network of contacts and false identities, shifting their location multiple times, staying one step ahead of their relentless pursuers. The city, usually a vibrant spectacle of light and sound, became a menacing labyrinth, every shadow a potential threat, every corner a hiding place.

The next leg of their journey took them to Hong Kong, a bustling metropolis teeming with life and secrets. Here, they had to blend into the anonymity of the city's colossal population, a challenge that tested their skills to the limit. They used aliases, assumed false professions, and created a carefully constructed facade to conceal their identities. They navigated the treacherous currents of the city's underbelly, using their contacts to gain access to safe houses, secure passage on ferries to smaller islands, and establish contact with handlers for a new identity.

The weeks that followed were a blur of anxiety, paranoia, and constant vigilance. Sharon and Miriam lived like shadows, their movements dictated by instinct and intuition. The pursuit relentlessly shadowed them, its presence an unspoken weight on their shoulders. They knew that one careless mistake, one moment of weakness, could be their undoing. The pursuit wasn't just physical, though; it was mental, grinding them down, testing their resolve, and eroding their hope. The weight of their past actions was palpable, a heavy cloak of guilt and regret. Their escape was a gamble, a high-stakes game of survival, and they weren't sure they would win.

As they finally boarded a plane bound for a remote island in the South Pacific, they had a moment of reflection. Their plan, audacious and risky, had worked. They had evaded justice and the wrath of the Abergil family. But were they truly free? The Serpent's Eye was gone, but the shadows of their past still clung to them. Redemption, if it were even possible, was still a distant hope, a mirage shimmering on the horizon. The path they had chosen was paved with blood and betrayal, a path from which there was no turning back. Their escape was merely a chapter, a step on a long and uncertain journey. The fight was far from over. The true test of their survival was yet to come.

Moral Crossroads

The South Pacific air hung heavy and humid, a stark contrast to the crisp chill of New York Sharon had left behind. The island, a speck of emerald green in the vast azure expanse, offered a deceptive sense of tranquility. It was a paradise built on a foundation of stolen goods and shattered lives, a perfect reflection of Sharon's own existence. Miriam, her face etched with the weariness of their relentless flight, surveyed their makeshift haven – a ramshackle hut perched precariously on the cliff edge, overlooking the turbulent ocean. The Serpent's Eye, their prize, was securely hidden, but the weight of their actions pressed down on them both.

For the first time since their escape from Macau, a sliver of doubt pierced Sharon's hardened exterior. The violence, the betrayals, the constant evasion – it had become a suffocating reality. He had killed without remorse, lied without hesitation, and manipulated with cold precision. Yet, here, in this isolated sanctuary, the echoes of his past deeds reverberated with a chilling clarity. He saw Ceta's face in the swirling patterns of the ocean waves, a constant reminder of the price of his survival. The surgical alteration of his face had given him a new identity, but it hadn't erased the memories, the guilt, or the ever-present fear that followed him like a shadow.

Miriam, sensing his turmoil, approached cautiously. She understood the darkness that consumed him, having walked alongside it for so long. She was his accomplice, his confidante, and in a strange way, his mirror image. They were bound together by a shared past, a shared guilt, and a shared desperation for a future free from the clutches of the Abergil family and the Mossad. "We're safe, for now," she said, her voice barely a whisper. "But this… this isn't a life, Sharon. It's just… existing."

Her words struck a chord within him. Existing. That was all he had been doing for years – existing on the fringes of society, forever looking over his shoulder, forever haunted by the ghosts of his past. He craved something more, something beyond the relentless cycle of violence and deception. He longed for a sense of normalcy, a life unburdened by the weight of his crimes. But was redemption even possible for someone like him? Could he ever truly escape the shadow of his past?

The days drifted into weeks, each sunrise painting the sky in hues of orange and gold, a beautiful spectacle that felt grotesquely ironic in its backdrop of their precarious existence. The island, initially perceived as a refuge, began to feel like a prison. The isolation was chipping away at Sharon's resolve, sharpening the edges of his guilt. He spent hours staring at the ocean, the relentless rhythm of the waves mirroring the tumultuous storm within his soul. The quiet nights were the worst; the silence amplifying the voices of his victims, the whispers of his betrayal.

One day, a small fishing boat appeared on the horizon. A lone figure emerged, his face weathered and lined, his eyes carrying the weight of years of hardship. He introduced himself as Silas, a former missionary who had lived on the island for decades, seemingly untouched by the world's chaos. He possessed a wisdom that seemed to defy his age and the harsh conditions of his existence. Silas's presence brought a fragile sense of hope to the island, a flicker of light in the darkness that enveloped Sharon.

Silas was different. Unlike anyone Sharon had ever encountered. He wasn't judgmental; he listened, offering not empty platitudes, but a profound empathy. He spoke of forgiveness, not as a religious concept, but as a deeply human capacity for healing, for the possibility of finding peace amidst the wreckage of one's past. He spoke of the transformative power of acts of kindness, of rebuilding lives instead of destroying them. His words were seeds of doubt planted in Sharon's hardened heart. Could he find redemption not through escaping his past, but through confronting it, through atoning for his sins?

Miriam remained skeptical. She saw Silas's kindness as naiveté, a dangerous vulnerability in their fragile existence. She had always been the pragmatist, the voice of reason, or what she considered reason, in their tumultuous partnership. But even her skepticism was slowly eroding under the steady influence of Silas's unwavering compassion. She saw the internal struggle tearing Sharon apart, the conflict between his ingrained instincts and the nascent desire for change.

One evening, as the sun dipped below the horizon, painting the sky in fiery shades of red and orange, Sharon found himself confessing his sins to Silas, unloading the weight of his past actions, the agonizing details of his life as a hitman. It was a cathartic experience, a brutal and honest reckoning with his dark past. He revealed his identity, not expecting absolution, but a hearing; a silent acknowledgment of his humanity, stripped bare of the carefully constructed façade he had worn for so long. Silas listened patiently, offering words of understanding and even a glimmer of forgiveness. He didn't condone Sharon's actions, but he saw a flicker of remorse, a potential for change.

The next morning, Sharon awoke with a newfound resolve. He knew redemption wouldn't be easy; it wouldn't be a quick fix or a simple absolution. It would be a long, arduous journey, a constant struggle against his ingrained instincts.

But he was ready to fight for it. He wasn't ready to abandon his sister, but he was ready to atone. He would use his unique skills – skills honed through years of violence – to help those in need, to fight against injustice in a way that didn't involve more bloodshed. He envisioned a future where he could use his past to build a better future; a future where the name Sharon wasn't synonymous with death and destruction but with a quiet form of redemption.

Miriam watched him, a flicker of surprise and perhaps even hope in her eyes. She had always feared Sharon's capacity for self-destruction, his unwavering devotion to the darkness within him. But she also saw the love for her that pushed him to make a better life for them both. She knew his path would be treacherous, fraught with challenges and temptations. But for the first time in a long time, she believed in his ability to overcome his past.

Their life on the island wasn't paradise, far from it, but it was a starting point. The Serpent's Eye remained hidden, but its allure had faded, replaced by a more profound desire: the pursuit of a life lived in the light, a life where redemption wasn't just a distant hope, but a tangible possibility, a journey yet to be embarked on, step by painstaking step. The ocean still roared, but now, its rhythm felt less like a relentless reminder of his past and more like a constant invitation toward a new beginning. The fight was far from over, but for the first time, Sharon felt like he was fighting for something other than survival; he was fighting for redemption. The island wasn't just a refuge; it was a proving ground. The path ahead was uncertain, the challenges immense, but as he looked out at the vast expanse of the Pacific, a small ember of hope flickered within his heart. A hope fueled not by greed or revenge, but by a desperate, fragile yearning for a life lived differently; a life earned, not stolen.

Unexpected Consequences

The tranquility of their island refuge was a fragile illusion, easily shattered. Their initial plan, born from desperation and fueled by the adrenaline of their escape, was to lie low, melt into the anonymity of the island's small, close-knit community, and eventually, with the help of forged documents and Miriam's considerable skills in forgery, disappear. The Serpent's Eye, the diamond necklace that had been the catalyst for their desperate flight, lay hidden, its brilliance dimmed by the pressing need for a less glittering future.

But the island, a seemingly idyllic paradise, held its own secrets, its own shadows. The local fishermen, weathered and taciturn, watched them with eyes that held a knowing glint. The seemingly harmless bartering and trading that Miriam had engaged in, attempting to blend in, unwittingly drew them closer to the island's clandestine underbelly. It was a network of smugglers, pirates, and mercenaries, operating under the radar, a world far more dangerous than the one they had so desperately fled.

Their first misstep was minor, seemingly insignificant. Miriam, needing supplies, bartered the necklace's ornate case – a relic of its opulent past, crafted from rare Indonesian wood – for a month's worth of food and essential medical supplies. The fishermen, recognizing the exquisite craftsmanship, were quick to inquire about its origins. Miriam, ever the resourceful liar, weaved a fanciful tale of an inheritance, of a deceased relative, a story believable enough to deflect suspicion, but not one that escaped scrutiny entirely. The case became a topic of hushed whispers in the dimly lit taverns, a subject of intrigue among the island's more unsavory characters.

This small act of desperation set in motion a chain of unforeseen consequences. Word traveled fast in such isolated communities, especially word of something valuable, something that whispered of untold wealth. A local gang, known for their ruthlessness and penchant for violence, caught wind of the tale. Their leader, a scarred brute named Kadir, saw the opportunity for a lucrative score. He wasn't interested in the Serpent's Eye itself, but the potential riches that the case hinted at. He reasoned, accurately, that the case wouldn't house such a rare piece of wood unless the contents were equally valuable.

Kadir's men began to shadow Miriam and Sharon, their presence subtle yet menacing. They observed their routines, their movements, watching from the shadows, waiting for the opportune moment to strike. Sharon, ever vigilant, sensed the shift in the air, the subtle change in the island's atmosphere. The once-tranquil paradise had become a pressure cooker, threatening to explode. He knew his past was a relentless shadow, but he hadn't anticipated this new threat, this unexpected ripple effect from their initial plan.

One sweltering afternoon, as Miriam ventured to the market, she was ambushed. The attack was swift and brutal, a vicious display of force that left Miriam injured and Sharon forced into a desperate fight for survival. He had anticipated the pursuit of the Mossad, the Israeli mob, even Detective Pickens, but this – this was a threat he hadn't foreseen, a consequence of his and Miriam's attempt at a new life.

The ensuing confrontation was a brutal ballet of violence. Sharon, armed with nothing but his wits and his lethal expertise, fought off Kadir's men, his movements fluid and deadly. He moved like a phantom, a ghost in the tropical heat, leaving a trail of incapacitated thugs in his wake. Miriam, despite her injuries, fought with a ferocity born of desperation, her determination fueled by the need to protect her brother and their stolen sanctuary.

But the victory was pyrrhic. The ambush had exposed their location, shattering the illusion of anonymity they had so painstakingly cultivated. Kadir, enraged by the defiance, vowed revenge, his rage amplified by the fact that he had failed to retrieve the case and its presumed treasure. The whispers had become a roar, the island's calm facade ripped away, revealing the violent, opportunistic underbelly lurking beneath.

Their plan, their desperate attempt at redemption, was unraveling. They were forced to abandon their ramshackle hut, leaving behind the meager possessions they had managed to accumulate. The island, once a haven, had become a hunting ground. The ocean, once a symbol of hope, now represented their escape route, a desperate flight from a threat they never anticipated.

Their flight was fraught with danger. Kadir's men relentlessly pursued them, their shadows stretching long across the island's sun-drenched beaches and through its dense, humid jungles. Sharon, his body weary from the previous fight, his spirit battered by the crushing weight of his past and present predicaments, knew that this time, escape wouldn't be easy. This wasn't a carefully planned escape; this was a desperate dash for survival. This was a battle not just for their lives, but for the very possibility of redemption they so desperately craved.

The pursuit led them through treacherous terrain, forcing them to rely on their cunning and their survival instincts. They scaled jagged cliffs, waded through rushing rivers, and evaded patrols, all while carrying the Serpent's Eye, the very thing that had initially thrown their lives into turmoil. The necklace was now a constant reminder of their past, a weight that seemed to amplify the burden of their present struggles.

The escape was relentless, a blur of sweat, adrenaline, and the constant, gnawing fear of capture. Sharon's skills, honed over years of violence, were essential, but they were being pushed to their limits. Miriam, despite her injuries, proved to be an invaluable partner, her resourcefulness and unwavering loyalty crucial in their desperate flight.

Their escape from the island marked only the beginning of another precarious chapter in their lives. The pursuit was far from over; Kadir wouldn't let them go that easily. Their carefully constructed scheme, their desperate hope for a new beginning, had been shattered. The unexpected consequences of their actions on the idyllic island had thrown them back into the tumultuous world of violence and betrayal, a world they thought they had left behind. The path to redemption, they now realized, was far more treacherous and uncertain than they could have ever imagined. The journey was far from over, and the fight for their lives—and the glimmer of redemption—had only just begun. The relentless pursuit and the shadow of their past continued to haunt them, casting a long, ominous shadow over their every step. The future, once hopeful, now seemed shrouded in uncertainty, a chaotic dance between survival and the elusive dream of a life lived in the light.

A Chance Encounter

The humid Manila air hung heavy, a stifling blanket clinging to Sharon's skin even as he moved through the shadowed alleys. The city, a chaotic symphony of noise and smells, was a far cry from the idyllic – and ultimately treacherous – island paradise he'd recently escaped. His new face, still tender and slightly swollen from the recent surgery, felt oddly alien. He'd chosen a look that was unremarkable, bland even – a far cry from the sharp features that had once marked him as a man to be both feared and respected. The anonymity was a fragile shield, offering little real protection against the long reach of his past.

He was on his way to a pre-arranged meeting, a risky gamble fueled by a desperate need for funds and a sliver of hope. His contact, a shadowy figure known only as "The Serpent," had promised information – potentially invaluable information – about Kadir and his network. The price, of course, was steep: a hit on a rival gang boss whose territory overlapped with Kadir's. Sharon needed money, needed to disappear completely, and the Serpent's offer, dangerous as it was, seemed like his only option.

As he rounded a corner, the pungent aroma of frying street food momentarily distracted him. Then he saw her. It wasn't a conscious recognition at first, more a flicker of familiarity, a ghost of a memory

215

surfacing from the deep recesses of his mind. She sat on a low stool, her back to him, the neon glow of a nearby bar painting her hair in streaks of vibrant orange and pink. She was wearing a simple sundress, the vibrant colors oddly clashing with the grimy backdrop of the alley. But it was the way she held herself, a certain grace in her posture, that sparked the recognition.

He stopped, heart thudding a frantic rhythm against his ribs. It couldn't be. Could it? It was impossible. He'd killed her. Or so he thought.

He approached cautiously, the years melting away as the scene played out in his memory. The frantic struggle in the Manila hotel room, Ceta's desperate gasp, the chilling metallic tang of blood. He'd been certain he'd left her lifeless on the floor, her beauty extinguished by his cold, efficient killing. He remembered the diamond pendant she wore, a piece far too elaborate for her simple appearance. A symbol of something more than meets the eye.

As he drew closer, he saw the back of her head – the distinctive way her dark hair curled at the nape of her neck. It was unmistakable. His breath hitched in his throat. She turned, and his blood ran cold. It wasn't Ceta. But the resemblance was uncanny, a near-perfect duplicate. The woman stared at him with wide, curious eyes. She had the same high cheekbones, the same delicate jawline, even the same way her lips curved into a subtle smile. The only obvious difference was the color of her eyes – where Ceta's had been a deep, sultry brown, these were a striking shade of emerald green.

"Excuse me," he stammered, his voice rough with disuse. The words felt foreign in his mouth. He felt a wave of nausea wash over him, his vision blurring slightly. This eerie doppelganger of a woman he'd murdered was so startling it threatened to unravel his meticulously constructed new identity. The weight of the deception, the violence, the years spent building a new life based on lies, seemed to crush him.

The woman tilted her head, a hint of amusement in her eyes. "Looking for something, señor?" Her voice was soft, with a slight accent he couldn't place.

"I... I thought I knew someone," he mumbled, backing away slowly, his hand instinctively reaching for the small, well-worn pistol concealed beneath his jacket. The phantom scent of Ceta's perfume, a heady mix of jasmine and sandalwood, seemed to cling to the air, a chilling reminder of his past sins.

"I could help you find someone." Her voice was surprisingly calm, despite the volatile nature of the situation. "It is my specialty."

He stared at her, utterly speechless. Her words suggested something deeper than a simple chance encounter; a connection he couldn't yet decipher. The Serpent's deal, the hit, everything seemed inconsequential now, dwarfed by the staggering improbability of this uncanny encounter. The woman's casual offer raised a thousand questions, hinting at the possibility of a dark secret entwined with his own past. Was this merely coincidence, or a twist of fate designed to expose him? Was she connected to Kadir, or was this an entirely new level of danger?

He felt a surge of icy fear, a primal instinct to run, to disappear into the teeming masses of Manila. Yet, a strange compulsion held him rooted to the spot. There was something intriguing, something almost hypnotic about this uncanny resemblance, this unsettling echo of his past. He felt the need to know more, to unravel the mystery behind this strange mirror image of a woman he had brutally dispatched. The encounter, far from being a simple interruption, was about to irrevocably alter the course of his already perilous journey.

He studied her more closely, trying to find any discrepancy, anything to dispel the unnerving sensation of déjà vu that enveloped him. Her eyes, the only apparent deviation from the woman he knew, held a knowing glint, as if she anticipated his suspicions. The realization dawned upon him: he was not looking at a simple case of mistaken identity. This was something far more elaborate, more sinister.

"Who… who are you?" he finally managed, his voice a mere whisper, barely audible above the city's cacophony.

She smiled, a slow, deliberate curve of her lips that sent a shiver down his spine. "Let's just say," she began, leaning closer, her breath warm on his face, "I know more about you than you think." The implication hung in the air, heavy and suffocating, a promise of revelations and dangers yet to come. The chance encounter had opened a new chapter, fraught with both intrigue and mortal peril, leading him further down a path where redemption seemed as distant as ever. The path to redemption had become a labyrinth, with every turn revealing new threats and uncertainties. The woman's cryptic words were the beginning of a new, frightening game, a game where the stakes were higher than he could have possibly imagined.

He knew, with chilling certainty, that his pursuit of redemption had just taken a dramatically unexpected turn. The seemingly chance encounter had thrust him into a far more dangerous game, a deadly maze of deception and intrigue that would demand his every ounce of cunning and skill to navigate. He was far from safe; his past was not merely haunting him—it was actively hunting him, disguised in the most unexpected forms. The woman, this uncanny mirror image of Ceta, was not merely a resemblance, but a new, and frighteningly unpredictable piece in the complex game that was his life. The question was not whether he would survive, but how long he could sustain the charade before his carefully constructed world collapsed around him. He had escaped death once, twice, many times. But this was different. This was not simply about survival anymore. It was about uncovering the truth, understanding the connections, and unraveling the complex web of deceit. His fight for redemption was far from over, and he was about to find out just how deep the rabbit hole really went.

Ghosts from the Past

The stale air of the New York City apartment hung heavy with the scent of old memories and regret. Sharon sat hunched over a chipped mug of lukewarm coffee, the steam doing little to dispel the chill that permeated his bones, a chill that had nothing to do with the November air seeping through the drafty window. He hadn't slept properly in weeks, the relentless rhythm of his pursuers echoing in the silent spaces between his fractured dreams. The faces of the past, once relegated to the shadowy corners of his mind, were now vivid, inescapable presences, taunting him with their accusatory stares.

He ran a hand through his newly-grown hair, the texture still unfamiliar, the feel oddly alien on his scalp. The facial reconstruction had been brutal—yet another reminder of the life he'd left behind in Manila, a life punctuated by betrayal, violence, and the chilling echo of Ceta's final gasp. Her face, her eyes— a kaleidoscope of fear and betrayal—flickered behind his eyelids, a haunting image no amount of surgery could erase. He'd killed her, a necessary evil in his twisted logic, but the guilt gnawed at him, a persistent, relentless pain that matched the throbbing ache in his reconstructed jaw.

His sister, Miriam, paced restlessly in the cramped living room. Their reunion had been strained, a fragile truce built on shared desperation rather than genuine affection. She was a whirlwind of nervous energy, her usual sharp wit dulled by an undercurrent of fear.

The lines etched around her eyes spoke volumes about the life she'd led, a life entwined with his own in ways he was only beginning to understand. Her recent revelation—her own involvement with the Abergil mob, a connection she'd kept hidden for years—had sent shockwaves through him, shattering the little trust he'd managed to build.

The past wasn't just a collection of memories; it was a living, breathing entity, constantly breathing down his neck. The Mossad agents, relentless and efficient, were like phantom pains, their presence felt even when they weren't visible. He'd managed to evade them for a while, but he knew their long reach extended far beyond the borders of Israel, their influence snaking into the very fabric of the underworld. He could feel their icy breath on his neck, even in the anonymity of this grimy New York apartment.

Detective Tom Pickens loomed large in his mind as well, a figure from a past he desperately wanted to forget. Their history—a tangled web of resentment and grudging respect—was a constant source of anxiety. Pickens was a relentless investigator, a man driven by an obsessive need for justice, a need bordering on fanaticism. Sharon knew Pickens was closing in, his methodical investigation slowly but surely piecing together the fragments of his fragmented life. The thought of confronting Pickens again, of facing the consequences of his actions, filled him with a cold dread that no amount of coffee could alleviate.

The apartment itself felt like a prison, its cramped walls closing in on him, amplifying the weight of his past. Every creak of the floorboards, every whisper of the wind outside, sounded like the footsteps of his pursuers. He found himself constantly scanning the shadows, his senses on high alert, always anticipating the next attack. His paranoia was a constant companion, a relentless shadow that never left his side.

He remembered the faces—the faces of his victims, the faces of his enemies, the faces of those he had betrayed. Each one was a grim reminder of his violent past, each one a testament to the ruthless efficiency that had once been his defining characteristic. Now, those faces were joined by the face of Ceta, a beautiful, intelligent woman who had paid the ultimate price for his secrets. Her image was a constant reminder of the moral compromises he had made, a stark illustration of the man he had become.

Miriam's secret, her own connection to the Abergil mob, was another piece of the puzzle, adding a new layer of complexity to the already tangled web of deceit. Her involvement had implications he was only beginning to understand, reaching far beyond their personal relationship and threatening to expose everything he had worked so hard to conceal. Her silence, however, was now broken, and the revelation of her past cast a long, ominous shadow over their future.

The conspiracy itself was a labyrinthine structure, a vast network of lies and betrayals extending far beyond the immediate reach of the Abergil mob. Sharon was only beginning to glimpse its full extent— shadowy figures pulling strings from behind the scenes, manipulating events in the dark. The weight of it all, the sheer enormity of the conspiracy, was almost unbearable.

The realization dawned on him like a cold, heavy wave: escape wasn't just about avoiding the immediate threat of the Mossad or Detective Pickens. It was about breaking free from the shackles of his past, from the ghosts that haunted him, from the cycle of violence that had defined his existence. But the more he thought about it, the more he understood that breaking free was proving to be infinitely harder than he'd ever anticipated. The threads of his past were woven too tightly, intricately tangled in his present, each one pulling him back, preventing him from moving forward.

He looked at Miriam, her eyes filled with a mixture of fear and defiance. They were bound together by a complicated, almost suffocating history, a history now threatening to pull them both under. The escape they so desperately sought from this life wasn't as simple as putting miles between them and their pursuers; it demanded more than physical distance. It required a complete severance from their past—a shedding of old identities, a forging of a new future that was free from the shadows of the people and choices they once were.

The confrontation with his past wasn't a battle fought with weapons or fists. No, it was a psychological war, a relentless struggle against the demons he'd created and the consequences he had long since embraced. Sharon knew he couldn't outrun this—he couldn't simply run away from the memories, the guilt, the faces of those he had wronged. He had to confront it. He had to understand it. And most terrifying of all, he had to find a way to make peace with the man he had become. Only then could he hope to carve a path toward redemption, a path leading him away from the darkness and toward a future where he wasn't constantly looking over his shoulder. A future where the ghosts of his past didn't chase him into every new day, didn't haunt his every waking moment.

That path, however, was shrouded in uncertainty. It was long and treacherous, fraught with more peril than he cared to imagine. The ghosts weren't going anywhere—they were waiting for him, watching. He knew he couldn't outrun them anymore. He had to face them head-on, or risk being consumed by the darkness they embodied.

The weight of this truth pressed down on him, a crushing burden that seemed almost too much to bear. He would need every ounce of his strength, every bit of cunning he had left—and, perhaps, a little luck—for any hope of making it through. The game, Sharon knew, was far from over. And the stakes had never been higher.

Miriams Secret

The chipped mug warmed Sharon's hands, but not his soul. He stared at the swirling coffee, the brown liquid mirroring the turbulent chaos within him. Miriam's name, a whisper in the wind only moments ago, now echoed in the cavernous silence of the apartment, a name heavy with unspoken secrets. He had known her all his life, yet it felt as though he was encountering a stranger. The revelation hadn't come as a sudden explosion, but rather as a slow, agonizing drip of truth, each drop etching a new line of pain on his already scarred heart.

It started with a photograph, a faded image tucked away in the back of an old photo album, discovered during one of Miriam's infrequent visits. It depicted a younger Miriam, radiant and carefree, standing beside a man Sharon had never seen before. The man was handsome, with kind eyes and a gentle smile that belied the shadows lurking in the background of the picture. The setting was unfamiliar—a sun-drenched Mediterranean coast, a stark contrast to the gritty streets of their New York upbringing. Miriam had tried to brush it off as a fleeting moment of her youth, a vacation she barely remembered. But Sharon, his senses sharpened by years of living on the edge, recognized the lie in her eyes.

The lie, like a seed planted in fertile ground, began to sprout. He dug deeper, his investigation fueled by a mixture of curiosity and deep-seated fear. He knew that the past, no matter how carefully buried, had a way of resurfacing at the most inconvenient moments. And he was acutely aware that his own past was a vast, unstable minefield, ready to explode. He discovered a trail of cryptic emails, hastily deleted but not before he'd created copies, hinting at a life Miriam had led far removed from the seemingly ordinary existence she presented to the world. These emails alluded to a hidden trust fund, an inheritance from a father he'd never known, a father who, according to the scattered details, was not the man Miriam had claimed him to be.

The truth was a mosaic of fragmented clues, pieced together like a jigsaw puzzle in the dead of night. He uncovered a series of bank transactions, discreet transfers of large sums of money to offshore accounts—expertly disguised but ultimately exposed by his own painstaking investigation. It wasn't just a vacation photo; it was a carefully constructed deception, a fabricated life designed to conceal a past she desperately wanted to keep hidden. The meticulous details, the carefully worded emails, spoke volumes. Miriam wasn't just hiding a secret; she was running from something—or someone.

He confronted her, the words tumbling out in a torrent of accusations and anxieties. The ensuing argument was a whirlwind of accusations and denials, the air thick with unspoken resentments and long-buried grievances. He saw the fear in her eyes, a fear that mirrored his own, a fear of the repercussions of the secrets that were threatening to unravel their lives. He pressed her, the urgency of his questions fueled by a growing suspicion that her hidden past was inextricably linked to his own treacherous journey. The truth, when it finally emerged, was more unsettling than anything he could have imagined.

Miriam's father, the man in the photograph, wasn't just a figure from her past; he was a significant player in the shadowy world Sharon inhabited—a world of international espionage and organized crime. He had been a high-ranking member of the Italian Mafia, involved in some of the most notorious criminal enterprises of the last three decades. The man who had helped build Sharon's ruthless reputation had also played a significant role in shaping Miriam's life, and the effects lingered. His influence, though hidden, ran deep. The money, the offshore accounts—it was all part of his legacy, a hidden inheritance intended to ensure Miriam's safety and security after his death. A death Miriam was directly implicated in.

Miriam had been unknowingly shielded from the brutal reality of her father's life until his unexpected death. She had been protected by a man who thought he was shielding her, by providing a life she deserved. But she was also unknowingly involved in the subsequent cover-up, unaware of the scope of her father's crimes. The weight of this revelation crushed her, the realization that her seemingly ordinary life was a carefully constructed illusion, a shield against a brutal and unforgiving reality. She hadn't actively participated in her father's criminal activities, but her unwitting complicity put her squarely in the crosshairs of those seeking vengeance.

This revelation not only added another layer to Sharon's already complicated life but also redefined their relationship. The bond of brotherhood was tested, strained by the weight of their shared past and the fear of their uncertain future. He saw not only a frightened woman but also a victim, manipulated and used by forces beyond her comprehension. His anger shifted. This understanding created a new perspective. He felt compelled to protect her, to shield her from the darkness that threatened to consume them both. But doing so would require confronting the very forces that had shaped their lives, a dangerous proposition indeed.

The revelation had a ripple effect, impacting his pursuit by the Mossad and Detective Pickens's investigation. The Mossad had links to the Italian Mafia. Their shared adversary suddenly held the key to understanding both Sharon's past and Miriam's newfound predicament. The information became a bargaining chip, a tool to be used in the ongoing battle for survival. Sharon understood that the safety of his sister was inextricably tied to his own fate.

Detective Pickens, unaware of the full extent of Miriam's involvement, was closing in, his investigation gradually uncovering the truth behind Sharon's actions. The detective's dogged pursuit, initially focused solely on Sharon, now expanded to include Miriam. Each step forward brought them closer to the dangerous nexus of criminal enterprises they were caught in.

The revelation forced Sharon to re-evaluate his priorities. Revenge, once his primary motivation, now shared space with the fierce need to protect his sister. He found himself walking a tightrope, balancing his need for survival with his unwavering loyalty to Miriam. He needed to outrun the Mossad, evade Pickens, and shield his sister from a fate he knew she was unprepared for—all while navigating his own treacherous past.

The apartment felt smaller, the air thicker with tension. The faces of the past, the faces of his victims, his betrayers, even his allies, seemed to swirl around him, their judgment heavy and unforgiving. But among these phantoms, the face of Miriam took prominence, her eyes reflecting not only fear but also a newfound determination. He knew they were in this together, bound by blood and a shared destiny. The battle for survival had taken on a new dimension, a new urgency. It was no longer just about Sharon; it was about them, their survival, and the desperate struggle to reclaim their lives from the clutches of a past that refused to let go.

The discovery had altered the landscape of his escape, transforming it from a personal flight into a desperate fight for the survival of two. He had to find a way to not only survive but to unravel the complex web of deceit that threatened to entangle them both. The knowledge of Miriam's hidden past added an entirely new layer of complexity to his already precarious situation. The stakes, he realized, had just been raised exponentially. His fight was no longer merely for himself. It was for Miriam, for the sister he'd grown up with, the woman he had only just begun to truly know. And in that knowledge, he found a renewed sense of purpose, a fierce determination that burned brighter than ever before. The game had changed. And he was ready to play.

Unraveling the Web

The city hummed with a discordant symphony of sirens and car horns, a soundtrack to Sharon's relentless pacing. He had spent the last few hours dissecting Miriam's cryptic words, piecing together the fragmented puzzle of her past. Each revelation felt like a punch to the gut, a brutal reminder of the life he had tried so desperately to leave behind. He had always known their family was entangled in something darker than the average, but the full extent of their involvement in the Abergil operation—or whatever this larger conspiracy truly was—was staggering.

Miriam's story, when he finally managed to untangle it, painted a picture of orchestrated betrayal, a carefully constructed narrative designed to keep her oblivious to the true nature of their father's business. She had been shielded, kept in the dark, while her brother plunged deeper and deeper into the abyss. He had been the muscle, the disposable asset; she, the unwitting pawn.

The irony wasn't lost on him. He, the ruthless hitman, had been the naive one, while the seemingly innocent sister navigated the treacherous waters of the family business with an almost unsettling calm. She had learned to read the currents, to sense the undertow of danger before it even surfaced. It was a skill he had honed in the brutal school of violence, but she had mastered it in the quietude of deception.

He grabbed his phone, his fingers trembling slightly as he scrolled through his contacts. He needed to talk to someone, someone who could help him make sense of this tangled mess. But who could he trust? Detective Pickens was a possibility, a dangerous one, but a necessary one nonetheless. Their history was fraught with animosity, a volatile cocktail of mutual distrust and begrudging respect. But Pickens, despite his relentless pursuit of justice, was also a man who understood the shadows, the darkness that lurked beneath the city's glittering facade. He was the only one who could potentially help him navigate this labyrinthine plot.

The call went straight to voicemail, the terse electronic greeting jarring in the silence of the apartment. He left a message, his voice tight with controlled urgency, outlining his predicament without revealing the full extent of the information he possessed. It was a calculated risk, a gamble based on the slim chance that Pickens would recognize the urgency in his tone, the veiled threat in his carefully chosen words.

Hours ticked by, each one an eternity. The phone remained stubbornly silent, the unspoken question hanging heavy in the air. He paced, the restless energy coursing through his veins, a tangible manifestation of his anxiety. He needed a plan, a way to untangle the web of lies and deceit that had ensnared him and Miriam. He started to sketch out a strategy, a series of steps designed to expose the truth, but each step was fraught with danger, each move a calculated risk.

He thought about Ceta, her image flashing in his mind's eye. Her death weighed on him, a constant reminder of his brutal efficiency, his capacity for cold, calculated violence. He'd had no choice, or so he'd told himself, but the ghost of her haunted him, whispering doubts in the recesses of his conscience. Had he been too quick to judge? Too quick to kill?

He reviewed the fragmented information he possessed: The Mossad's involvement. The Abergil's reach, which extended far beyond what he'd initially believed. He thought about the implications, the far-reaching consequences. It wasn't just about survival anymore. This wasn't merely a personal battle; it was a war, a battle for truth against a formidable enemy. His opponents were more formidable than he'd initially estimated. Their tentacles reached into every corner of his world, corrupting and controlling with an almost chilling efficiency.

The phone finally rang. It was Pickens. His voice, gruff and world-weary, cut through the tense silence. "Sharon? What's this about?"

Sharon laid out his case, careful to choose his words, keeping his own involvement veiled in calculated ambiguity. He spoke of the family connection, the hidden truth about his father, and Miriam's precarious position. He used his words as weapons, carefully placing his emphasis on facts while avoiding unnecessary details. He knew Pickens would be skeptical, would demand proof, but he also knew that the detective was intelligent enough to understand the gravity of the situation.

Pickens listened, his silence more unnerving than any outright rejection. When Sharon finally finished, the detective's voice was devoid of emotion. "I need proof, Sharon. Solid, irrefutable proof. And you're going to have to give me more than cryptic messages and half-truths. If you're involved in this, you're going to face consequences."

Sharon knew this was a dangerous dance, a tightrope walk across a chasm of deceit and betrayal. But he also knew that Pickens, for all his flaws, was the only ally he had left. He was the only one who could potentially help him expose the conspiracy, to bring down the powerful forces that had made his life a living hell.

He spent the next few days gathering evidence, piecing together fragments of information like a meticulous craftsman assembling a complex puzzle. He unearthed hidden bank accounts, shell corporations, and coded messages, each piece contributing to a larger, more terrifying picture. The depth and reach of the conspiracy were far-reaching. The Abergil organization was a mere branch of a far greater, more insidious operation, one that had tentacles reaching into governments, corporations, and even the highest levels of law enforcement.

The revelation was terrifying, a chilling reminder of his own mortality. He was a pawn in a larger game, a game he wasn't sure he could win. But he had Miriam, and the thought of her, her innocent life entangled in this web of lies, fueled his determination. He wouldn't let them hurt her. He wouldn't let them win.

He met with Pickens again, presenting him with the evidence, the fruits of his relentless pursuit of truth. The detective studied the documents, his expression unreadable. He didn't speak for a long time, his silence broken only by the rhythmic tapping of his pen against the desk. Finally, he looked up, his eyes sharp and focused.

"This is bigger than we thought, Sharon," Pickens said, his voice low and grave. "A lot bigger." He paused, then added, "We need to tread carefully. One wrong move, and we'll be walking into a minefield. We need to play their game, but we need to play it better."

The partnership, born out of mutual distrust, was a fragile thing, a precarious alliance forged in the crucible of mutual need. Sharon knew he was playing with fire, that the flames of the conspiracy could engulf them both. But he was prepared. He'd been preparing his entire life. This was it, the culmination of a lifetime spent navigating the treacherous waters of the underworld. The game was afoot, and this time, he was determined to win. The weight of the world, the weight of their lives, rested squarely on his shoulders. The truth was out there, waiting to be uncovered, but reaching it required a deft hand, a cold mind, and an unwavering resolve. The faces of the past were now staring back at him, their silent accusations hanging in the air. He was ready.

The Price of Truth

The air in Miriam's cramped, dimly lit apartment hung thick with the scent of stale coffee and something else—something acrid and unsettling—that clung to the edges of Sharon's senses. He found her hunched over a worn wooden table, a scattering of photographs and faded documents spread across its surface like a macabre jigsaw puzzle. Her eyes, usually bright with a defiant spark, were shadowed with a weariness that went beyond simple exhaustion. It was the weariness of someone who had carried a heavy burden for far too long.

"This… this is it," Miriam whispered, her voice barely audible above the city's low hum. She pushed a photograph towards him. It depicted a younger version of their father, a man Sharon barely remembered, his face etched with a grim determination that mirrored the haunted look in Miriam's eyes now. Beside him stood a woman, elegant and poised, her smile a chilling contradiction to the cold glint in her eyes. Sharon recognized her instantly. It was the woman from the Abergil files— their mother, a name whispered only in hushed tones, a ghost haunting their fragmented memories.

"She wasn't just… a housewife," Miriam said, her voice catching. "She was… involved. Deeply involved."

The documents, yellowed and brittle with age, detailed a complex network of offshore accounts, coded messages, and cryptic transactions. It was a labyrinthine trail leading to the heart of the Abergil operation, a trail that implicated not only their parents but also several prominent figures within the Israeli government and the international underworld. The truth, Sharon realized, was far more tangled and horrifying than he could have ever imagined.

"They used us," Miriam said, her voice shaking. "They used our father's connections, his influence… and they used me."

The revelation hit Sharon like a physical blow. He'd always known their family was different, their lives lived on a precarious edge, but he'd never understood the full extent of the danger, the depths of their parents' involvement. The photographs and documents were more than just evidence; they were a chilling testament to a life lived in the shadows, a life of betrayal and sacrifice.

"I… I was a pawn," Miriam continued, her voice barely a murmur. "They groomed me, trained me… to infiltrate… to gather information."

Sharon felt a cold wave of nausea wash over him. The image of his younger sister, manipulated and used by the ruthless machinations of the Abergil family, was almost unbearable. The rage that simmered beneath his surface threatened to erupt, a volcanic fury that could consume him entirely. But he forced himself to remain calm, to focus on the task at hand. The truth had been uncovered, but now came the far more perilous task of what to do with it.

The price of this truth, Sharon quickly realized, was far higher than he'd anticipated. Miriam's revelation wasn't just a shocking piece of their family history; it was a dangerous weapon, capable of unraveling everything Sharon had worked so hard to build, to escape. The Abergil family wouldn't hesitate to eliminate anyone who posed a threat, and Miriam, with her knowledge, was now a prime target. And by extension, so was he.

He spent the next few days meticulously reviewing the documents, cross-referencing information with what he already knew. The pattern that emerged was terrifying. Their parents hadn't simply been peripheral players; they had been crucial cogs in the Abergil machine. Their mother, the elegant woman in the photograph, had been far more than just a wife; she had been a master manipulator, using her social connections and charm to gain access to sensitive information, to establish crucial alliances. Their father, a respected businessman on the surface, had used his legitimate connections to launder money and provide logistical support for the family's criminal enterprises.

The conspiracy extended far beyond the immediate family, reaching into the highest echelons of power. Sharon recognized names, familiar faces from his years in the Abergil network—politicians, businessmen, even law enforcement officials. The scale of the corruption was breathtaking, terrifying in its reach and implications.

He knew then that exposing this truth, even if he could, would be an act of suicidal recklessness. The power of the Abergil family extended far beyond their criminal activities. They had infiltrated the very fabric of society, holding sway over institutions that were supposed to protect the innocent. To challenge them would be to invite a storm of unparalleled retribution.

But leaving the truth buried was not an option. He couldn't stand by and let innocent people be exploited, manipulated, and destroyed. He had to find a way to expose the Abergil family without sacrificing Miriam or himself. He needed a plan, a strategy, a way to turn their own machinations against them.

He started by making contact with Detective Pickens. Their relationship was still fraught with tension, their mutual distrust a palpable force between them. Pickens, however, had already shown a willingness to play outside the lines, to step into the gray areas where justice often went unserved. Sharon knew that Pickens' relentless pursuit of the truth, his unwavering dedication to justice—even with his own complicated moral compass—might be the key to dismantling the Abergil network.

The meeting was tense, the air thick with unspoken accusations. Sharon laid out his findings, presenting Pickens with the evidence—the documents, the photographs, the names. Pickens listened intently, his face a mask of controlled curiosity. He didn't react to the shocking revelations with disbelief or outrage; instead, he regarded the information with the cool, calculating eye of a seasoned investigator.

"This is bigger than we thought," Pickens finally said, his voice low and serious. "This goes all the way to the top."

He knew he was in over his head, a simple detective up against an enemy with vast resources and influence. But he also knew he couldn't back down. The price of truth, he realized, wasn't just the risk to his own life but the potential to expose a rot that had spread deep into the heart of society.

The collaboration between Sharon and Pickens was fragile, a temporary alliance forged in the crucible of mutual need. They were both aware of the inherent dangers, the risks involved. Sharon, a man haunted by his past and driven by a thirst for revenge, and Pickens, a detective who had seen too much darkness and still held onto a flickering flame of hope. They were an unlikely pair, bound together by a shared commitment to exposing the truth, a commitment that would test their limits and push them to the very edge of survival.

The path ahead was fraught with peril, riddled with betrayals and unexpected twists. They knew the Abergil family wouldn't go down without a fight. But Sharon and Pickens were ready. They had a shared understanding of the price of truth, and they were willing to pay it. The game was far from over, but with the truth finally revealed, they were one step closer to dismantling the vast and insidious network that had plagued their lives for far too long. The faces of the past were no longer just ghosts in the mirror; they were the fuel for their fight. The fight for justice. The fight for survival. The fight for the truth.

A Desperate Gamble

The worn leather of the briefcase felt slick beneath Sharon's fingers, the cold metal of the pistol nestled inside a chilling reassurance against the gnawing fear that clawed at his gut. Miriam, her face pale but resolute, checked the map again, her breath misting in the frigid night air. They stood on the rooftop of a derelict building, the city sprawling beneath them like a concrete jungle teeming with shadows and secrets. Escape felt like a ludicrous fantasy, a cruel joke played by a malevolent deity. But it was their only option.

Their pursuers – the Mossad agents, their movements as precise and deadly as a surgeon's scalpel – were closing in. The Abergil family, fueled by rage and betrayal, wouldn't rest until Sharon was silenced, a permanent stain erased from their meticulously crafted image. And Pickens… Pickens was a wildcard, a dangerous variable in an already chaotic equation. He was hunting them, but for what purpose? Justice? Or something far more sinister?

The escape plan, hatched in the frantic hours after Miriam's revelation, was as audacious as it was improbable. A network of underground tunnels, used generations ago by smugglers and revolutionaries, now served as their unlikely escape route. The tunnels, a labyrinth of damp, claustrophobic passages, were a gamble—a desperate roll of the dice against their pursuers and the ever-present threat of collapse. But it was better than their other option – a slow, agonizing death at the hands of their enemies.

Miriam, surprisingly agile for someone who spent most of her life cooped up in her apartment, led the way, her small flashlight cutting through the oppressive darkness. The air was thick with the smell of damp earth and decay, a suffocating blanket that weighed heavily on Sharon's chest. Each step was a calculated risk, a potential trigger for disaster. A misplaced foot, a sudden tremor in the unstable earth, and the tunnels could become their tomb.

Sharon, his senses heightened, kept a watchful eye, his hand never straying far from the cold comfort of the pistol. He'd seen enough death in his lifetime to know the scent of it when it hung in the air, even in the stifling darkness of the tunnels. This escape was less of a run and more of a silent dance with death. He could feel the eyes of their pursuers on his back, a chilling sense of being watched even within this subterranean maze.

The silence was broken only by the rhythmic drip of water and Miriam's labored breathing. The weight of their situation pressed upon them, a crushing burden that threatened to suffocate them in the suffocating confines of the tunnels. They were ghosts in the earth, clinging to life in a world that had long since abandoned them. Each moment was a victory against time and their pursuers; each breath was a testament to their enduring will to survive.

As they navigated the twisting passages, memories flickered in Sharon's mind – flashes of his past, a kaleidoscope of violence and betrayal that seemed to echo in the oppressive silence of the tunnels.

He remembered Ceta's face, her beautiful eyes filled with a mixture of fear and understanding before he was forced to silence her forever, a memory that gnawed at his conscience despite the ruthless efficiency of his actions. He replayed his childhood in his mind, the way his parents fought, the way his world crumbled, and he knew he'd never been able to save them then; now, it was the life he had to save.

Hours bled into one another, the passage of time a blur in the relentless pursuit of their goal. The air grew thinner, the smell of decay more potent. Doubt began to creep in, a venomous serpent whispering insidious doubts in his ear. Were they making any progress? Or were they hopelessly lost, trapped in this subterranean labyrinth, with their pursuers closing in?

Then, a glimmer of light, a beacon of hope piercing the oppressive darkness. Miriam stopped, her face illuminated by the faint glow, a mixture of relief and exhaustion etched upon her features. They had reached the exit, a narrow opening that led to a deserted alleyway.

Emerging into the cool night air, they exchanged a fleeting look, a silent acknowledgment of their shared survival. They had beaten the odds, eluded their pursuers, at least for now. But their journey was far from over. The Abergil family would not easily let go of their prey. The Mossad's grip would only tighten. And Pickens… Pickens remained a formidable threat, his motives still shrouded in an enigma that gnawed at Sharon's thoughts.

Their next move was as critical as their escape. They needed to disappear, to become ghosts in the city's sprawling underbelly. Miriam had contacts, individuals who operated in the shadows, individuals who could provide them with false identities, safe houses, and passage to a new life. But even this would be another gamble, a risk they were willing to take. The price of freedom, they knew, was eternal vigilance.

The alleyway was a testament to neglect, littered with debris and the lingering stench of decay. But to Sharon and Miriam, it was a haven, a sanctuary from the storm that raged around them. They moved quickly, melting into the shadows, their footsteps barely disturbing the stillness of the night. They were phantoms, spirits flitting through the city's underbelly, forever looking over their shoulders, forever aware that their freedom was tenuous—a fragile thing that could shatter at any moment.

The escape was only the first stage of a far more complex game. Their pursuers were relentless, their resources vast, and their determination unyielding. Sharon and Miriam were playing for high stakes, risking their lives with every step they took. The world beyond the dark alley was a dangerous place, teeming with enemies and betrayals. But they had no other choice. They had to keep running.

The next few days were a blur of hurried movements, clandestine meetings, and close calls. Miriam's contacts, a shadowy network of individuals with questionable loyalties and even more questionable methods, secured them false identities and passage to a new country. But the constant fear, the gnawing uncertainty, remained a constant companion, a chilling reminder of their precarious situation.

The weight of their past—the faces of those they had betrayed and those who had betrayed them—seemed to haunt their every move. But somewhere amidst the fear and the uncertainty, a flickering flame of hope began to glow. They were survivors, resilient and resourceful. They had stared death in the face and emerged victorious. They would continue to fight for their freedom, for their survival, for their future.

The escape hadn't been a mere flight from justice; it was a calculated maneuver, a desperate gamble fueled by the shared burden of their past. Each step forward brought them closer to their goals but also further into a world where the lines between right and wrong were blurred—a world where their actions carried consequences far greater than they had ever imagined. Their new life, secured at the cost of so much, would be another test of endurance, a constant reminder that the past, with its ghosts and betrayals, had the power to shape their future. They had stared into the abyss and survived. The abyss stared back.

The Confrontation

The air hung thick with the scent of rain and decay, a fitting backdrop for the final act of this brutal drama. The abandoned pier jutted out into the inky black water of the East River, the skeletal remains of a forgotten industry creaking softly in the night breeze. This desolate expanse was the stage for Sharon's last stand, a brutal ballet of violence choreographed by years of bloodshed and betrayal. Detective Tom Pickens stood across from him, his silhouette stark against the weak glow of a distant streetlight, a figure etched in granite resolve.

Sharon adjusted the grip on his Beretta, the cold steel a familiar comfort in the clammy grip of fear. He'd faced death countless times, stared into the abyss of his own mortality, but this felt different. This wasn't a contract hit; this wasn't about money or the cold satisfaction of eliminating a target. This was personal. It was about survival, redemption, and finally escaping the suffocating weight of his past. But deep down, a cold dread gnawed at him. He knew that even if he survived this, the shadow of his past would forever cling to him.

Pickens broke the tense silence, his voice a low growl that carried across the desolate space. "It's over, Sharon. Give it up."

Sharon let out a short, humorless laugh. "Over? You think this is over? This is just the beginning of the end for a lot of people, Pickens. Including you." He spat on the ground, the saliva glistening in the weak light. The words were a challenge, a desperate attempt to maintain control in the face of overwhelming odds.

The years of animosity, the shared history of violence and betrayal, hung heavy between them, a palpable tension that crackled in the air like static electricity. Pickens had been on Sharon's trail for months, meticulously piecing together the fragments of his chaotic life, doggedly pursuing a trail of blood and destruction across continents. He knew Sharon's methods, his ruthlessness, and his chilling efficiency. And he was ready.

The first shot shattered the fragile peace. Sharon moved with the fluid grace of a predator, a honed instinct born from years spent dancing with death. His movements were economical, precise, each action calculated to maximize damage and minimize exposure. He fired back, the deafening roar of the Beretta echoing across the water, bullets ripping through the night air. Pickens returned fire, his shots precise and deadly, aimed with years of experience and steely determination.

The pier became a whirlwind of motion and gunfire, a chaotic dance of death played out under the unforgiving gaze of the moon. Each exchange of fire was a life-or-death gamble, a test of skill and survival. They moved through the darkness, utilizing the cover of rusted machinery and decaying structures, their movements a blur of shadows and flashes of gunfire. The echoes of their shots seemed to bounce off the buildings along the waterfront, amplifying the tension in the already high-stakes confrontation.

Sharon, despite his skill, found himself on the back foot. Pickens was relentless, his aim unwavering, his determination unshakeable. He had a cold, calculating precision that Sharon had never encountered before. This wasn't just a fight; it was a duel of wits, a deadly chess game played with bullets and blood. The years of experience on both sides were on full display, each man anticipating the other's moves, reacting instinctively, pushing themselves to the brink of exhaustion.

During a brief lull in the exchange, Sharon glimpsed an opportunity. He feigned a retreat, luring Pickens into a false sense of security, then used the cover of a decaying crate to launch a surprise attack. He closed the distance, the Beretta held close, his movements swift and deadly. The fight was brutal, hand-to-hand combat in the shadows, a struggle for dominance that left both men battered and bleeding.

As they grappled, Sharon felt a searing pain in his side, the impact of a bullet ripping through his flesh. He gasped, momentarily losing his footing, but he refused to yield. He had come too far, risked too much, to be defeated now. He knew this could be his last fight, his final battle, and the raw desperation fueled his every movement.

The struggle intensified, a brutal clash of wills and strength, a test of endurance and survival. They exchanged blows, each strike aimed to cripple, dominate, and inflict maximum pain. The sounds of their struggle—the grunts, the gasps, the sickening thud of fists connecting with flesh—were amplified in the night's stillness, the soundtrack to a desperate dance of death.

Finally, with a surge of adrenaline-fueled strength, Sharon managed to overpower Pickens, his movements precise and deadly. He disarmed the detective, and the Beretta clattered onto the grimy pier. Pickens, defeated but defiant, stared up at Sharon, his eyes filled with a mixture of resentment, acceptance, and a surprising hint of... respect?

Sharon stood over him, the Beretta heavy in his hand, the decision hanging in the air. He could end it right there.

He could silence Pickens permanently. But as he looked into the detective's defeated eyes, something shifted within him. The years of violence, the blood he had spilled, the lives he had destroyed – they weighed heavily on his soul. This wasn't just about killing Pickens; it was about ending the cycle of violence that had consumed his life.

With a sigh that seemed to carry the weight of his past, Sharon tossed the gun into the dark water of the river. The sound of the gun hitting the waves was a punctuation mark, a final full stop in a long, brutal sentence. The fight was over. The showdown was concluded. But the aftermath was only beginning. The unraveling of the vast conspiracy that had ensnared him was just starting to reveal itself. The truth was out there, somewhere in the shadows, waiting to be discovered. And Sharon, wounded, weary, and uncertain of his future, knew that his journey was far from over. The true price of his survival had yet to be paid.

The Truth Revealed

Pickens watched Sharon, his gaze unwavering, a silent acknowledgment of the unspoken truce. The gun, a cold, metallic weight in the darkness, was gone. But the tension remained, thick and palpable, a living entity between them. The rain, which had been a mere drizzle, intensified, transforming the pier into a slick, treacherous landscape. Each drop seemed to echo the unspoken accusations and betrayals that had woven themselves into the fabric of their lives.

"It wasn't Miriam," Sharon finally said, his voice raspy, each word a shard of glass. The confession hung in the air, a stark contrast to the rhythmic drumming of the rain. The words were unexpected, a shift in the power dynamic that had defined their confrontation. Pickens' expression remained impassive, a carefully constructed mask concealing the turmoil within. He knew Miriam was involved, somehow, but the extent of her involvement remained shrouded in mystery.

Sharon continued, his voice gaining strength, fueled by a desperate need to unburden himself, to finally set the record straight. He spoke of the Abergil family's expansive reach, their insidious influence that seeped into every corner of the underworld. He spoke of the meticulous planning, the intricate layers of deception that had allowed them to operate in plain sight, cloaked in respectability and wealth. He described the intricate web of informants, the carefully cultivated relationships with corrupt officials, and the sheer scale of their criminal enterprise that stretched across continents. The Abergil family wasn't just a criminal organization; it was a meticulously crafted machine of destruction, built on lies and powered by violence.

He revealed how his sister, Miriam, had been unknowingly used as a pawn in their deadly game. She had been manipulated, her loyalty twisted and exploited to serve their nefarious purposes. He described the carefully orchestrated events that had drawn him back into the vortex of their operations, the false promises and manipulative threats that had forced his hand, time and time again. The betrayal cut deep, an agonizing wound that added to the countless other scars he carried.

The narrative twisted and turned, unveiling a conspiracy far more elaborate than Pickens had ever imagined. It wasn't just about drugs or money; it went far deeper, revealing a shadow war waged between rival factions of the Israeli mob and the Mossad, with innocent lives sacrificed on the altar of greed and power. Sharon's journey, his desperate flight across continents, had been nothing more than a chess piece in a larger, more sinister game.

He recounted the elaborate scheme to assassinate a rival mob boss in Morocco, a plan that had gone horribly wrong, leading to the betrayal and his subsequent escape. He detailed the ruthless efficiency of the Abergil family's hit squads, their precision and unwavering dedication to violence. He described the cold, calculated manner in which they eliminated anyone who stood in their way, the complete disregard for human life that defined their existence. The family's operations transcended national borders, their tentacles reaching into the highest echelons of power, corrupting institutions and individuals alike.

He spoke of Ceta, the beauty queen, her unwitting involvement in the family's web of deceit. He described her unexpected discovery of his true identity, the chilling realization that had led to the heartbreaking choice he was forced to make. The memory of her death, a cold stain on his conscience, weighed heavily on his soul, adding to the burden of his actions. He spoke of the regret, the remorse that gnawed at him, the constant reminder of the moral compromises he'd made in a desperate attempt to survive.

Pickens listened, his hardened exterior slowly crumbling under the weight of Sharon's revelations. He had always seen Sharon as a ruthless killer, a cold-blooded mercenary. But now, through the rain-streaked lens of Sharon's confession, he saw a man broken by the violence he had inflicted and the violence that had been inflicted upon him. A man trapped in a cycle of betrayal and revenge, desperately seeking redemption in the face of overwhelming odds.

The pieces began to fall into place, like a jigsaw puzzle meticulously assembled in the dark. Pickens saw connections he had missed, insights that had been obscured by the chaos and violence. He saw the pattern in the seemingly disparate events, the links between the seemingly unrelated killings, the hidden agendas of individuals and organizations. The intricate web of lies and deceit, expertly woven over years, began to unravel before his eyes.

As the rain continued its relentless assault, Sharon revealed the final piece of the puzzle, the ultimate truth that lay at the heart of the conspiracy. It was a betrayal on a grand scale, a conspiracy involving high-ranking officials, corrupt businessmen, and powerful figures within the Israeli government. The Abergil family was just a pawn in this larger game, a tool used by those with even greater ambitions. The implication was staggering, shaking Pickens to his core. The repercussions of this revelation extended far beyond the confines of the underworld, reaching into the very fabric of society.

The silence that followed was heavy, filled with the unspoken weight of the truth. Pickens, a man hardened by years on the force, felt a chilling wave of unease wash over him. The scope of the conspiracy was far beyond his wildest imagination. He was no longer facing a simple case of organized crime; he was embroiled in an international conspiracy, one that threatened to shake the foundations of power.

The rain finally began to subside, leaving behind a damp chill in the air. The pier, bathed in the weak glow of the dawn, seemed even more desolate, even more forlorn. But the truth, laid bare in the cold, harsh light of the new day, was a potent force. It was a seed of change, a catalyst for a new chapter in the lives of both Pickens and Sharon. The game was far from over, but the rules had changed. The stakes were higher, and the path ahead was uncertain. For both men, the fight for justice had only just begun. The revelation, while painful, had set the stage for a new conflict, a fight for survival—not just against the Abergil family, but against a shadow organization whose reach extended far beyond their wildest imagination. This was a fight that demanded every ounce of courage, every shred of resolve they possessed. And as the first rays of dawn touched the horizon, both men knew, with chilling certainty, that the fight had just begun. The city, shrouded in the damp chill of the morning, was far from safe.

A Fight for Survival

The warehouse echoed with the metallic clang of steel meeting steel. Miriam, surprisingly agile for a woman who'd spent most of her life behind a desk, ducked under a wild swing from one of the Abergil's enforcers, a hulking brute with a face like a smashed melon. She retaliated with a swift kick to his shin, a sharp, focused blow that brought him to his knees. Sharon, meanwhile, was a whirlwind of motion, a blur of fists and feet, his movements economical and lethal. He moved like a phantom, a shadow flitting through the dimly lit space, dispensing brutal justice with each precise strike.

He'd rigged the warehouse with explosives, a desperate gambit to even the odds against the seemingly endless stream of Abergil goons. The air was thick with the acrid smell of gunpowder and sweat, punctuated by the sickening thud of bodies hitting the concrete floor. This wasn't a fight; it was a massacre. But it was a massacre they had to win.

Miriam, despite her initial surprise, fought with a ferocity that surprised even Sharon. Years of pent-up anger and frustration, years of living in the shadow of her brother's infamy, fueled her every move. She moved with a primal energy, her fear replaced by a cold, calculating rage. She wasn't just fighting for survival; she was fighting for her life, for the life she'd always yearned for, free from the long reach of the Abergil family.

One by one, the enforcers fell. But they kept coming, an endless tide of violence and aggression, each one seemingly more determined than the last. Sharon felt a twinge of panic. They couldn't hold out forever. The explosives were a last resort, a desperate gamble that could just as easily kill them as their assailants. He glanced at his sister, her face streaked with sweat and blood, her breath coming in ragged gasps. She was exhausted, but her eyes burned with an unwavering determination.

"Miriam," he yelled over the din of the battle, his voice hoarse from exertion. "The detonators!"

She nodded, her eyes scanning the chaotic scene, searching for the hidden device. She found it strapped to her leg, a small, innocuous device that held the power to level the entire building. The countdown was already ticking.

Suddenly, a figure emerged from the shadows, a tall, imposing man with icy blue eyes and a cruel smile. It was Sal Demarco, the Abergil family's ruthless enforcer, the man who had orchestrated Sharon's betrayal in Morocco. He held a gun, its barrel aimed squarely at Miriam's head.

"Well, well," Demarco sneered, his voice dripping with malice. "Looks like the little bird has finally flown into my trap."

Sharon froze. He couldn't risk a shot; Miriam was too close. He knew Demarco wouldn't hesitate to kill her. The only option was to let Demarco get close. He faked a sudden collapse, dropping to one knee, groaning dramatically, feigning pain. The remaining Abergil men stopped their assault.

Demarco approached cautiously, his eyes narrowing with suspicion. He lowered his gun slightly, his attention focused on Sharon. That was all the opening Sharon needed. With a speed that defied his apparent injury, Sharon launched himself at Demarco. He tackled him to the ground, the gun flying from Demarco's hand. The struggle was brutal, a desperate, savage fight for survival. Both men wrestled for the upper hand, their bodies locked in a furious embrace.

Miriam seized the opportunity. She aimed the detonator at a strategically placed support beam. This wouldn't just bring down the building; it would also take Demarco and the rest of the Abergil goons with them. She hesitated, her finger hovering over the button. She knew the risk. The explosives could just as easily kill Sharon as them.

But the alternative was even worse. Being captured, being tortured. The Abergil would stop at nothing to get revenge on Sharon for the years of havoc and death he'd wrought upon their organization. He wouldn't give them that satisfaction.

With a deep breath, she pressed the button.

The warehouse exploded in a deafening roar. The force of the blast hurled Miriam and Sharon back, throwing them into a pile of rubble. They were both injured, bruised, battered, but alive. They crawled out of the debris, coughing and choking in the dust-filled air. The warehouse was a smoldering ruin. Demarco and his men were gone, reduced to ashes and scattered debris.

They stood amidst the wreckage, the only survivors of a brutal battle. They had won, but the victory felt hollow, tainted by the violence and destruction they had unleashed. They had survived, but at what cost? The fight for survival had been won, but the war was far from over. The Abergil family would not go down without a fight. This was only the beginning of a much longer and more dangerous game. They had escaped this night, but they knew, with a chilling certainty, that they would never truly be safe. The city, shrouded in smoke and the lingering scent of gunpowder, held its breath. The silence was deafening. And in that silence, a new battle began to brew—a battle for their freedom, a battle against a shadow world that knew no bounds. A world where justice was a fickle mistress, and survival was a hard-won prize.

The rain started again, a mournful, cleansing shower over the devastation. Miriam leaned against Sharon, her body trembling, the adrenaline fading, replaced by exhaustion and a chilling awareness of what they had done and what lay ahead. Sharon looked at his sister, at the woman he'd almost lost, and knew that this wasn't just about survival anymore. This was about redemption, about building a future where they could finally escape the ghosts of their past. But the path to that future was long and treacherous. And they had to walk it together. The fight wasn't over; it had just begun.

They would seek justice, not just for themselves but for those who couldn't fight for it anymore. The Abergil family would pay for their crimes. But first, they had to survive. They had to heal, both physically and emotionally. The scars of that night would remain, etched onto their souls. But they would carry them as badges of honor, as testaments to their resilience, as reminders of their strength. The rain continued to fall, washing away the blood, the debris, the memories of a night of horror and heroism. But it couldn't wash away the truth:

they had won a battle, but the war had just begun. And they would face it together. Brother and sister, bound by blood, forged in fire, ready to face whatever the future might bring.

As dawn broke, casting a pale light over the ruined warehouse, Sharon and Miriam walked away, leaving behind the wreckage of their past. They were battered, but they were alive. They were free, for now. But the shadow of the Abergil family still loomed large. They knew that this victory was just a fleeting moment in an ongoing war. A war they were far from winning. The city was a dangerous place. Every corner held a potential threat. Every shadow harbored a lurking danger. But they were survivors. They had faced the worst, and they had emerged victorious. For now. They were still on the run, still haunted by the ghosts of their past, but they were united, a bond forged in the fires of this relentless battle. And they would face whatever came next, together.

They would face the future, arm in arm, a testament to their resilience, their courage, and their love for one another—a bond that even death itself couldn't break. They had faced death and stared into its cold, empty eyes, and they had lived to tell the tale. The tale of their survival. The tale of their redemption. The tale of their fight. The story was far from over.

Sacrifice and Loss

The taxi rattled through the pre-dawn streets of Manhattan, its yellow paint a stark contrast to the grim determination etched on Sharon's face. Miriam sat beside him, her usual sharp wit muted by a fatigue that went deeper than physical exhaustion. The warehouse fight had been brutal, a bloody testament to their desperate struggle for survival. They'd won, but the victory felt hollow—a pyrrhic triumph purchased with a price they were only beginning to comprehend.

The silence in the cab was thick, heavy with unspoken anxieties. Sharon stared out the window, the blurry cityscape a reflection of the chaos swirling within him. He thought of Ceta, her vibrant beauty now a ghost in his memory, a phantom pain in his chest. Killing her had been a necessary evil, a cold, calculated act of self-preservation, but the memory of her wide, terrified eyes continued to haunt him. It was a sacrifice he'd made—a brutal choice forced upon him by circumstances beyond his control. A weight that settled heavily on his soul. He'd traded one life for his own—a grim equation that left him feeling emptier than ever before.

Miriam reached out and squeezed his hand, a silent gesture of understanding. She knew the burden he carried, the darkness that clung to him like a shroud. She'd seen it in his eyes, in the haunted look that had become a permanent fixture on his features. They were bound together by blood, by a shared history of loss and betrayal. But now, they were also connected by a new, shared trauma—the bitter taste of sacrifice.

They arrived at their safe house—a cramped apartment in a rundown building on the Lower East Side—and the silence continued as they moved through the familiar space. It was small, sparsely furnished, but it offered a temporary respite from the relentless pursuit that had become their lives.

Later that day, a phone call shattered the fragile peace. It was Detective Pickens, his voice gravelly and laced with a chilling calm that sent a shiver down Sharon's spine.

"Sharon," Pickens said, his voice low and dangerous. "We need to talk. I have some information you might find... interesting."

Sharon knew that "interesting" was Pickens' code for dangerous. He'd always been two steps behind, but Sharon knew his persistence could be as deadly as a sniper's bullet. The detective was a relentless hound, his determination bordering on obsession. This was more than just a case for him; it was a personal crusade. Sharon understood the game Pickens was playing—a cat-and-mouse dance leading to a final, deadly confrontation.

The meeting took place in a deserted park, under the cover of darkness. Pickens arrived alone, his trench coat flapping in the night breeze, a silhouette against the pale moonlight. He didn't need backup; his own inherent menace was enough to intimidate most men. He slid into the seat opposite Sharon, his eyes unwavering, assessing, calculating.

"I know about Ceta," Pickens began, his voice a low rumble. "And I know you were in Morocco. The Abergil's reach is long, but it's not infinite. They're desperate, Sharon. They've lost control."

Sharon remained silent, his expression unreadable. He let Pickens unravel, letting the detective believe he held the upper hand.

"They're looking for someone," Pickens continued, leaning closer, his breath ghosting across Sharon's face. "Someone who can unravel the whole mess. Someone who knows the Abergil's secrets, someone they believe can deliver them what they want."

Sharon knew he was talking about Miriam. He'd kept her protected, shielded from the worst of the violence. But now, she was a pawn in this deadly game. The price of their freedom, he realized, was becoming exponentially higher.

Pickens produced a photograph, a grainy image of Miriam leaving the warehouse. "They know about her," he said, his voice devoid of emotion. "They're coming for her."

The revelation hit Sharon like a physical blow. He felt a cold dread grip his heart. He hadn't considered this. He'd been so focused on his own survival, he'd forgotten about her. He had made a sacrifice to protect her from this, but even that hadn't been enough.

"What do you want?" Sharon asked, his voice tight.

"I want the truth," Pickens replied. "I want the whole story, Sharon. Everything. And in return, I'll make sure Miriam stays safe."

The proposition was a cruel twist of fate, a devil's bargain. Sharon knew Pickens wasn't offering a free pass; he was buying information, using Miriam's life as leverage. But it was a deal he couldn't refuse. He had to choose between revealing everything—exposing himself and Miriam to potential repercussions and imprisonment—and sacrificing Miriam, allowing her life to be extinguished like a candle in the wind. The loss of either option was soul-crushing.

He thought of the sacrifices he had already made: Ceta, his own identity, his freedom. He'd lost so much already, traded so much of himself for survival. Was he willing to sacrifice even more? The weight of the decision pressed down on him, crushing him under its immeasurable burden. He looked at Pickens, his eyes conveying a silent plea, a desperate hope for a way out of this impossible situation. He had to make a choice. A choice that would determine their fates, a choice that would decide whether they lived or died. A choice that would define his legacy, a choice that would seal his fate. A final, agonizing choice weighed on his heart, and he knew, with a crushing certainty, that whatever choice he made, he would forever bear the stain of the sacrifices he had made—his hands stained irrevocably with loss and bloodshed.

The final showdown wasn't just a physical battle; it was an emotional war that would leave him scarred forever. The cost of survival was too high.

Justice Prevails

The warehouse echoed with the silence that follows a storm, a silence thick with the metallic tang of blood and the acrid bite of gunpowder. Miriam, her face pale but resolute, leaned against a stack of crates, nursing a deep gash on her arm. Pickens, his suit rumpled and stained, surveyed the scene with grim satisfaction, his usual cynicism tempered by a weary acceptance of the brutal reality they had just witnessed. Three Mossad agents lay sprawled on the concrete floor, their lives extinguished as efficiently as Sharon had extinguished a cigarette.

Sharon, his bald head reflecting the harsh fluorescent lights, lay dead in the street, his body riddled with multiple gunshot wounds. His last gasp of air had been taken amidst the chaos, a messy, complex affair that left more questions than answers. The scene was a battleground of shades of grey, where the lines between right and wrong blurred, where even the victors carried the scars of the fight.

In the heart of the city that never sleeps, in a place where shadows danced and secrets whispered, Sharon was just another ghost among many, forever living on borrowed time, which had finally run out. The city itself served as his witness, a silent observer to the chaos and the consequences. His death wasn't a triumph, but part of the continuing struggle—a never-ending battle for survival. The justice that prevailed was tainted, flawed, but it was all that remained.

Appendix

This appendix contains supplementary materials related to the story, including a map of Sharon's travels and a detailed breakdown of the bomb used in the climax. Due to the sensitive nature of certain information presented in the main narrative, some details have been omitted for security reasons.

A special thanks to Dr. Tim Boh, USN (Retired), and Dr. Sarah Subicbay, both of whom contributed greatly to the accuracy and depth of the material presented. Their expertise was invaluable in bringing these details to life.

Author Biography

Tim Guditus is a retired NYPD Detective with over 200 arrests. He is a seasoned crime investigator, having served in Brooklyn South Narcotics and worked as a Robbery Squad Detective, as well as the Chief of the Detective Zodiac Task Force. He has received Detective of the Month honors twice, among other awards. His common reply to an unsolvable case is, "Give me five top-flight robbery detectives, and any crime can be solved." Tim has a passion for crafting gritty, fast-paced thrillers featuring morally ambiguous characters and complex plots. His previous works include *The Third Man: Oklahoma Bombing* and *Forgotten Words.*

He currently resides in Huntington Station, New York, with his dog, Sam. Tim enjoys hiking trips and has completed his third ascent of Mount Washington. He also crossed Lake Champlain in a 14-foot dinghy from the Vermont side to the New York side. Tim once paused to catch his breath and reflected, "Forever young," as he embraces the adventure of life.

His motto: *Go Navy. Strike hard, strike home. NYPD. Fidelis ad Mortem.*

I look to the window on a cold, coincidental day of life. The things I must do and the actions I must perform.

About the Book

"The Gordian Knot" is a high-stakes thriller that delves deep into the world of espionage, betrayal, and redemption. The story follows Sharon, a rogue Mossad agent whose life is turned upside down after a brutal ambush in Marrakech. Forced into hiding, Sharon undergoes a harrowing surgical transformation in Manila, but even a new face cannot erase the sins of his past. His escape to New York offers no sanctuary, as he remains a hunted man, entangled in a deadly game of cat and mouse. His journey is a visceral exploration of survival, as he battles not only external threats but also his own inner demons.

At the heart of the story is Detective Tom Pickens, a relentless NYPD investigator whose pursuit of Sharon is fuelled by more than just duty. Their shared history adds layers of complexity to Pickens' investigation, transforming the hunt into a deeply personal quest for justice. As he uncovers a labyrinth of corruption and conspiracy, Pickens finds himself questioning his own morals and the cost of the truth. His character serves as a powerful counterbalance to Sharon's, offering readers a glimpse into the fine line between justice and revenge.

The novel's tension peaks with the introduction of Miriam, an ex-Mossad agent with a dangerous agenda of her own. Her history with Sharon is marred by betrayal, and her cunning manipulation sets the stage for an explosive showdown. Their final confrontation is a masterful blend of action and psychological warfare, bringing to light buried secrets and testing loyalties. "The Gordian Knot" delivers a powerful narrative where every twist pulls the reader deeper into a world of shadows. It's a story where alliances shift, survival is paramount, and redemption comes at the highest price.

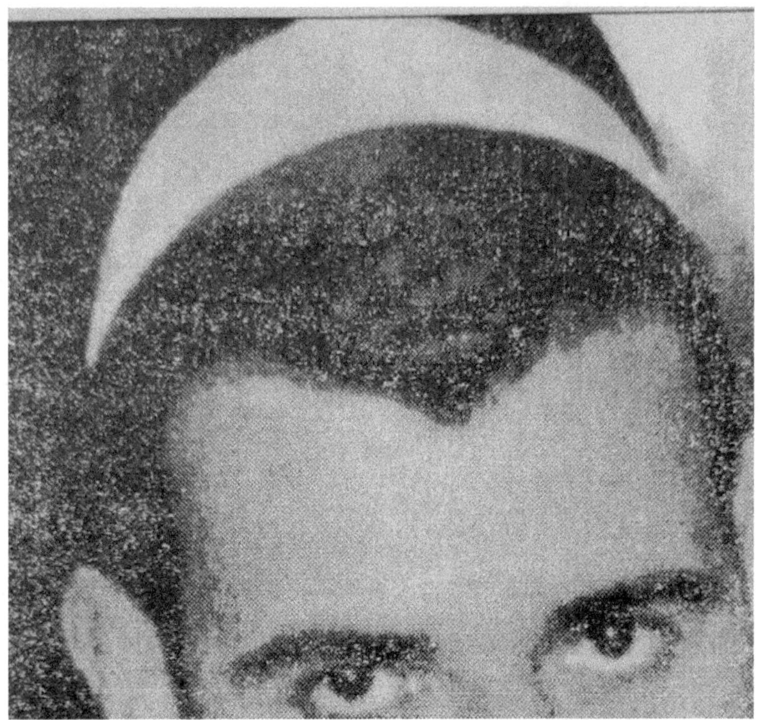